A Book Of

INTERNET PROGRAMMING - II

Semester IV : Paper - IV

For Third Year B.Sc. Computer Science
As Per Revised Syllabus
Effective from June 2015

Bhupesh Taunk
M.Sc. (Computer Science)
Lecturer, Computer Science Department
Fergusson College, Pune

Aniket Nagane
M.Sc. (Computer Science), NET
Asst. Professor Computer Science Department
MIT Group of Institutions
MAEER's Arts, Commerce and Science College
Pune

NIRALI PRAKASHAN
ADVANCEMENT OF KNOWLEDGE

N0897

INTERNET PROGRAMMING - II **ISBN 978-93-5164-912-0**

First Edition : December 2015

Published By : **Polyplate**

NIRALI PRAKASHAN

Abhyudaya Pragati, 1312, Shivaji Nagar,
Off J.M. Road, Pune – 411005
Tel - (020) 25512336/37/39, Fax - (020) 25511379
Email : niralipune@pragationline.com

➢ DISTRIBUTION CENTRES

PUNE

Nirali Prakashan : 119, Budhwar Peth, Jogeshwari Mandir Lane, Pune 411002, Maharashtra
Tel : (020) 2445 2044, 66022708, Fax : (020) 2445 1538
Email : bookorder@pragationline.com, niralilocal@pragationline.com

Nirali Prakashan : S. No. 28/27, Dhyari, Near Pari Company, Pune 411041
Tel : (020) 24690204 Fax : (020) 24690316
Email : dhyari@pragationline.com, bookorder@pragationline.com

MUMBAI

Nirali Prakashan : 385, S.V.P. Road, Rasdhara Co-op. Hsg. Society Ltd.,
Girgaum, Mumbai 400004, Maharashtra
Tel : (022) 2385 6339 / 2386 9976, Fax : (022) 2386 9976
Email : niralimumbai@pragationline.com

➢ DISTRIBUTION BRANCHES

JALGAON

Nirali Prakashan : 34, V. V. Golani Market, Navi Peth, Jalgaon 425001,
Maharashtra, Tel : (0257) 222 0395, Mob : 94234 91860

KOLHAPUR

Nirali Prakashan : New Mahadvar Road, Kedar Plaza, 1st Floor Opp. IDBI Bank
Kolhapur 416 012, Maharashtra. Mob : 9850046155

NAGPUR

Pratibha Book Distributors : Above Maratha Mandir, Shop No. 3, First Floor,
Rani Jhanshi Square, Sitabuldi, Nagpur 440012, Maharashtra
Tel : (0712) 254 7129

DELHI

Nirali Prakashan : 4593/21, Basement, Aggarwal Lane 15, Ansari Road, Daryaganj
Near Times of India Building, New Delhi 110002 Mob : 08505972553

BENGALURU

Pragati Book House : House No. 1, Sanjeevappa Lane, Avenue Road Cross,
Opp. Rice Church, Bengaluru – 560002.
Tel : (080) 64513344, 64513355,Mob : 9880582331, 9845021552
Email:bharatsavla@yahoo.com

CHENNAI

Pragati Books : 9/1, Montieth Road, Behind Taas Mahal, Egmore,
Chennai 600008 Tamil Nadu, Tel : (044) 6518 3535,
Mob : 94440 01782 / 98450 21552 / 98805 82331,
Email : bharatsavla@yahoo.com

niralipune@pragationline.com | www.pragationline.com

Also find us on f www.facebook.com/niralibooks

Preface ...

We take an opportunity to present this book entitled as **"Internet Programming - II"** to the students of T.Y.B.Sc. Computer Science as per the revised syllabus, June 2015.

The book covers theory of Web Techniques, Handling E-mail with PHP, PHP Framework, XML, JavaScript, DHTML, AJAX etc.

A special word of thanks to Shri. Dineshbhai Furia, Mr. Jignesh Furia for showing full faith in us to write this book. We also thank to Mr. Amar Salunkhe, Mr. Akbar Shaikh, Ms Chaitali Takle of M/s Nirali Prakashan for their excellent co-operation.

Although every care has been taken to check mistakes and misprints, any errors, omission and suggestions from teachers and students for the improvement of this text shall be most welcome.

Our efforts shall be more than rewarded if this book proves beneficial to the students.

Authors

Syllabus ...

1. **Web Techniques** **[10]**
   - 1.1 Variables
   - 1.2 Server information
   - 1.3 Processing forms
   - 1.4 Setting response headers
   - 1.5 Maintaining state
   - 1.6 SSL
2. **Handling Email with PHP** **[8]**
   - 2.1 Email background
   - 2.2 Internet mail protocol
   - 2.3 Structure of an email message
   - 2.4 Sending email with php
   - 2.5 Email attachments.
   - 2.6 Email id validation and verification
   - 2.7 PHP error handling.
3. **PHP Framework** **[4]**
   - 3.1 Introduction to PHP framework.
   - 3.2 Features, Applications.
   - 3.3 One example like JOOMLA, DRUPAL.
4. **XML** **[8]**
   - 4.1 What is XML?
   - 4.2 XML document Structure
   - 4.3 PHP and XML
   - 4.4 XML parser
   - 4.5 The document object model
   - 4.6 The simple XML extension
   - 4.7 Changing a value with simple XML
5. **Web Designing Technologies (JavaScript-DHTML)** **[10]**
   - 5.1 Overview of JavaScript, DHTML
   - 5.2 Object Orientation and JavaScript
   - 5.3 Basic Syntax (JS datatypes, JS variables)
   - 5.4 Primitives, Operations and Expressions
   - 5.5 Screen Output and keyboard input (Verification and Validation)
   - 5.6 JS Control statements
   - 5.7 JS Functions
   - 5.8 JavaScript HTML DOM Events (onmouseup, onmousedown, onclick, onload, onmouseover, onmouseout).
   - 5.9 JS Strings.
   - 5.10 JS String methods
   - 5.11 JS popup boxes (alert, confirm, prompt).
   - 5.12 Changing property value of different tags using DHTML (ex. adding innerhtml for DIV tag, changing source of image etc.).
6. **AJAX** **[8]**
   - 6.1 Introduction of AJAX
   - 6.2 AJAX web application model
   - 6.3 AJAX –PHP framework
   - 6.4 Performing AJAX validation
   - 6.5 Handling XML data using php and AJAX
   - 6.6 Connecting database using php and AJAX

Contents ...

CHAPTER 1

Web Techniques

Contents ...

Objectives...

- To Understand Variables Concepts
- To Study Server Information
- To Learn Forms and Processing of Form
- To Setting Response Headers and Maintaining State
- To Understand SSL

1.0 INTRODUCTION

- Nowadays, PHP is becoming a standard in the world of web programming with its simplicity, performance, reliability, flexibility and speed.
- PHP was designed/developed as a web scripting language and although it is possible to use it in purely command-line and GUI scripts, the Web accounts for the vast majority of PHP uses.
- A dynamic web site may have forms, sessions, and sometimes redirection. This chapter explains how to implement those things in PHP.
- The web runs on the HyperText Transfer Protocol (HTTP) and this protocol governs how web browsers request files from web servers and how the servers send the files back.

1.1 VARIABLES

- Every time you click a link or submit a form, you send a great deal of data about your system and your browser to the web server, and each time the web server responds, it sends you a great deal of data about itself. PHP has the capability to capture that data.
- For instance, if you go to a PHP driven website and log in, it's likely that a predefined variable $_POST is filled (on server) with your username and password, another predefined variable named $_SERVER contains information about the current web server environment.
- PHP automatically have some variables called predefined variables available anywhere in your program. They are array variables. These variables are: $_ENV, $_GET, $_POST, $_COOKIE, and $_SERVER, referred to as EGPCS.
- There is a setting in your configuration file (php.ini) called register_globals. The default value is off, and it restricts how you can access some predefined variables.
- register_globals determine whether or not to register the EGPCS variables as global variables.
- Regardless of the setting of the option register_globals, PHP creates six global arrays that contain the EGPCS information as given below:
  1. **$_COOKIE**: This global array contains any cookie values passed as part of the request, where the keys of the array are the names of the cookies.
  2. **$_GET**: This global array contains any parameters that are part of a GET request, where the keys of the array are the names of the form parameters.
  3. **$_POST**: This global array contains any parameters that are part of a POST request, where the keys of the array are the names of the form parameters.
  4. **$_FILES**: This global array contains information about any uploaded files.

5. **$_SERVER**: This global array contains useful information about the web server, as described in the next section.
6. **$_ENV**: This global array contains the values of any environment variables, where the keys of the array are the names of the environment variables.

- Above variables are not only global, but also visible from within function definitions, unlike their longer counterparts.
- The $_REQUEST array is also created by PHP if the register_globals option is on. The $_REQUEST array contains the elements of the $_GET, $_POST, and $_COOKIE arrays.
- PHP also creates a variable called $PHP_SELF, which holds the name of the current script, relative to the document root.
- Several predefined variables in PHP are "superglobals", which means that they are always accessible, regardless of scope - and you can access them from any function, class or file without having to do anything special.
- The PHP superglobal variables are $GLOBALS, $_SERVER, $_REQUEST, $_POST, $_GET, $_FILES, $_ENV, $_COOKIE, and $_SESSION.

1.2 SERVER INFORMATION

- The $_SERVER is an associative array contains a lot of information from the web server.
- The following table lists the most important elements that can go inside $_SERVER:

Sr. No.	Element/Code	Description
1.	$_SERVER['PHP_SELF']	Returns the filename of the currently executing script.
2.	$_SERVER['GATEWAY_INTERFACE']	Returns the version of the Common Gateway Interface (CGI) the server is using.
3.	$_SERVER['SERVER_ADDR']	Returns the IP address of the host server.
4.	$_SERVER['SERVER_NAME']	Returns the name of the host server (such as www.nirali.com).
5.	$_SERVER['SERVER_SOFTWARE']	Returns the server identification string (such as Apache/2.2.24).
6.	$_SERVER['SERVER_PROTOCOL']	Returns the name and revision of the information protocol (such as HTTP/1.1).

contd. ...

7.	$_SERVER['REQUEST_METHOD']	Returns the request method used to access the page (such as POST).
8.	$_SERVER['REQUEST_TIME']	Returns the timestamp of the start of the request (such as 1377687496).
9.	$_SERVER['QUERY_STRING']	Returns the query string if the page is accessed via a query string.
10.	$_SERVER['HTTP_ACCEPT']	Returns the Accept header from the current request.
11.	$_SERVER['HTTP_ACCEPT_CHARSET']	Returns the Accept_Charset header from the current request (such as utf-8,ISO-8859-1).
12.	$_SERVER['HTTP_HOST']	Returns the Host header from the current request.
13.	$_SERVER['HTTP_REFERER']	Returns the complete URL of the current page (not reliable because not all user-agents support it).
14.	$_SERVER['HTTPS']	Is the script queried through a secure HTTP protocol.
15.	$_SERVER['REMOTE_ADDR']	Returns the IP address from where the user is viewing the current page.
16.	$_SERVER['REMOTE_HOST']	Returns the Host name from where the user is viewing the current page.
17.	$_SERVER['REMOTE_PORT']	Returns the port being used on the user's machine to communicate with the web server.
18.	$_SERVER['SCRIPT_FILENAME']	Returns the absolute pathname of the currently executing script.
19.	$_SERVER['SERVER_ADMIN']	Returns the value given to the SERVER_ADMIN directive in the web server configuration file (if your script runs on a virtual host, it will be the value defined for that virtual host) (such as someone@w3schools.com).

contd. ...

20.	$_SERVER['SERVER_PORT']	Returns the port on the server machine being used by the web server for communication (such as 80).
21.	$_SERVER['SERVER_SIGNATURE']	Returns the server version and virtual host name which are added to server-generated pages.
22.	$_SERVER['PATH_TRANSLATED']	Returns the file system based path to the current script.
23.	$_SERVER['SCRIPT_NAME']	Returns the path of the current script.
24.	$_SERVER['SCRIPT_URI']	Returns the URI of the current page.

1.3 PROCESSING FORMS

- Forms are essential parts in web development. Forms are used to communicate between users and the server.
- Form is a way to get information of the user to the server and let the server do something in response to the user's input.
- We use form to register in a website, to login, to send feedback, to place order online, to book ticket online etc.
- After submitting the form, the form is processed by PHP on the server. In PHP the form parameters are available in the $_GET and $_POST arrays.
- When user submits a form then the form parameter is send to the server. Before sending the information, browser encodes it using a scheme called URL encoding. In this scheme, name/value pairs are joined with equal signs (=) and different pairs are separated by the ampersand (&).

```
name1=value1&name2=value2&name3=value3
```

- Spaces are removed and replaced with the + character and any other non alphanumeric characters are replaced with a hexadecimal values. After the information is encoded it is sent to the server.
- There are two HTTP methods that a client can use to pass form data to the server i.e., GET and POST. The method is specified with the method attribute to the form tag.

1.3.1 GET Method (Oct. 14)

- The GET method sends the encoded user information appended to the page request (to the URL).
- The page and the encoded information are separated by the? character.

```
http://www.test.com/index.htm?name1=value1&name2=value2
```

- The GET method produces a long string that appears in your server logs, in the browser's Location: box.
- The GET method is restricted to send up to 1024 characters only.
- Never use GET method if you have password or other sensitive information to be sent to the server.
- GET cannot be used to send binary data, like images or word documents, to the server.
- The data sent by GET method can be accessed using QUERY_STRING environment variable.
- The PHP provides $_GET associative array to access all the sent information using GET method.
- Try out following example by putting the source code in test.php script.

```
<?php
  if( isset($_GET["s1"]) )
  {
    echo "Welcome ". $_GET['name']. "<br />";
    echo "You are ". $_GET['age']. " years old.";
  }
?>
<html>
<body>
  <form action="<?php $_PHP_SELF?>" method="GET">
  Name: <input type="text" name="name" /><br>
  Age: <input type="text" name="age" /><br>
  <input type="submit" name="s1" value="Ok"/>
  </form>
</body>
</html>
```

- The above program having two parts HTML and PHP. After executing the program in the browser, HTML part will be displayed first as follows as shown below:

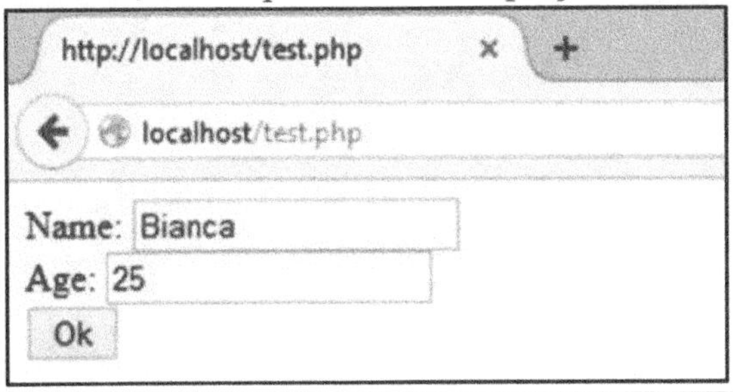

- Enter name and age and submit the form. Now PHP will process the form and you will get the following output.

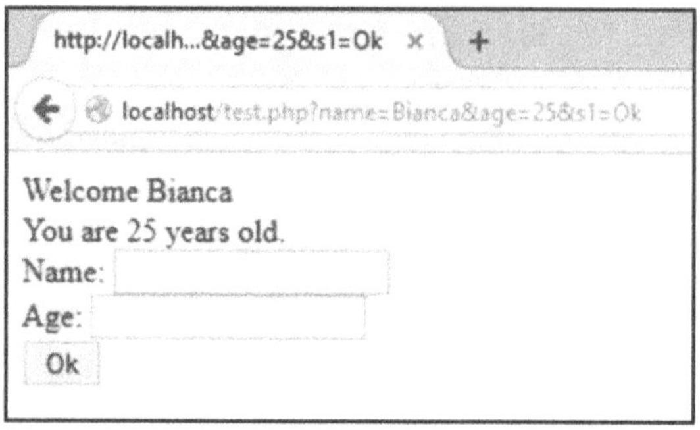

- After submitting the form the URL in the address bar is as follows:

```
http://localhost/test.php?name=Bianca&age=25&s1=Ok
```

  It shows all the three form parameter's name/value pairs.

- In the program, the isset() method is used to check whether the "Ok" submit button is pressed or not. After entering name and age submitting the form will store the entered value of the text field into the $_GET array, and that can be displayed.

1.3.2 POST Method

- The POST method transfers information via HTTP headers, not through the URL.
- The information is encoded as described in case of GET method and put into a header called QUERY_STRING.
- The POST method does not have any restriction on data size to be sent.
- The POST method can be used to send ASCII as well as binary data.
- The data sent by POST method goes through HTTP header so security depends on HTTP protocol. By using Secure HTTP you can make sure that your information is secure.
- The PHP provides $_POST associative array to access all the sent information using POST method.
- Try out following example by putting the source code in test.php script.

```
<?php
  if( isset($_POST["s1"]) )
  {
    echo "Welcome ". $_POST['name']. "<br />";
    echo "You are ". $_POST['age']. " years old.";
  }
?>
```

```
<html>
<body>
  <form action="<?php $_PHP_SELF?>" method="POST">
  Name: <input type="text" name="name" /><br>
  Age: <input type="text" name="age" /><br>
  <input type="submit" name="s1" value="Ok"/>
  </form>
</body>
</html>
```

Output:

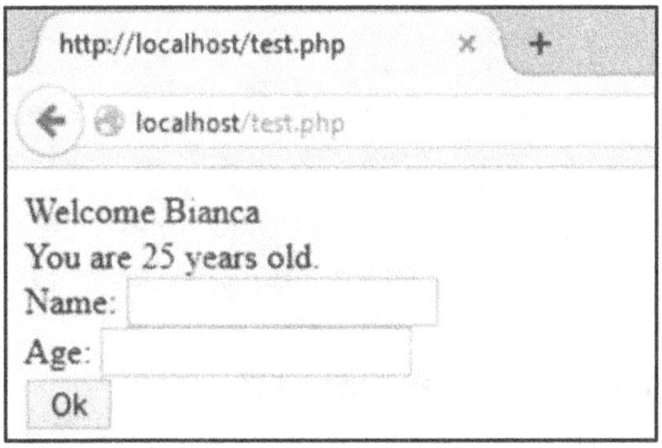

- The output of the above program is same, except URL, the URL in the address bar will not get changed after submitting the form.

GET vs. POST Methods: **(April 13, 15)**

- Both GET and POST create an array (For example, array(key => value, key2 => value2, key3 => value3, ...)). This array holds key/value pairs, where keys are the names of the form controls and values are the input data from the user.
- Both GET and POST are treated as $_GET and $_POST. These are superglobals, which means that they are always accessible, regardless of scope - and you can access them from any function, class or file without having to do anything special.
- The biggest difference between GET and POST requests is that, GET requests are idempotent—that is, one GET request for a particular URL, including form parameters, is the same as two or more requests for that URL. Thus, web browsers can cache the response pages for GET requests, because the response page doesn't change regardless of how many times the page is loaded. Because of idempotence, GET requests should be used only for queries such as splitting a word into smaller chunks or multiplying numbers, where the response page is never going to change.

- POST requests are not idempotent. This means that they cannot be cached, and the server is recontacted every time the page is displayed. You've probably seen your web browser prompt you with "Repost form data?" before displaying or reloading certain pages. This makes POST requests the appropriate choice for queries whose response pages may change over time—for example, displaying the contents of a shopping cart.

When to use GET?

- Information sent with the GET method is visible to everyone (all variable names and values are displayed in the URL). GET also has limits on the amount of information to send. The limitation is about 2000 characters. However, because the variables are displayed in the URL, it is possible to bookmark the page. This can be useful in some cases.
- GET may be used for sending non-sensitive data.

Note: GET should NEVER be used for sending passwords or other sensitive information!

When to use POST?

- Information sent with the POST method is **invisible to others** (all names/values are embedded within the body of the HTTP request) and has **no limits** on the amount of information to send.
- Moreover POST supports advanced functionality such as support for multi-part binary input while uploading files to server.
- However, because the variables are not displayed in the URL, it is not possible to bookmark the page.

1.3.3 Automatic Quoting of Parameters

- php.ini file is a initialization file and is used to configure the behavior of PHP.
- In php.ini file if the option magic_quotes_gpc is enabled then PHP automatically add slashes (call addslashes()) on all cookie data and GET and POST parameters.
- **For Example:** If you enter the word "O'clock" as the form parameter value then the word is converted to "O\'clock".
- If you don't want to add slashes automatically and want to work with the strings as typed by the user, you can either disable magic_quotes_gpc in php.ini or use the stripslashes() function on the values in $_GET, $_POST, and $_COOKIES.

1.3.4 Self Processing Pages

- A single PHP program can be used to both generate a form and process it, using combination of HTML and PHP. This type of PHP page is known as self processing page.

- We can write a program which can decide whether to display a form or process it depending on the one of the parameter has been supplied or not.
- **For Example:**

```
<html>
<head><title>Greet User</title></head>
<body>
<?php
if(isset($_GET['name1']))
{
    $nm = $_GET['name1'];
    echo "Hello " . $nm;
} else {
?>
    <form action="<?php echo $_SERVER['PHP_SELF']?>" method="GET">
        Enter Your Name:
        <input type="text" name="name1" /> <br />
        <input type="submit" name="Ok" />
    </form>
<?php
}
?>
</body>
</html>
```

- In this example if the value of the form parameter 'name1' is present then it gets processed, and in the absence of value only form will be displayed as shown below:

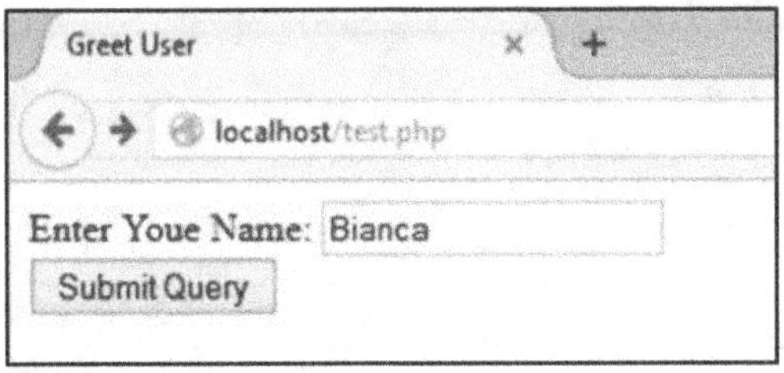

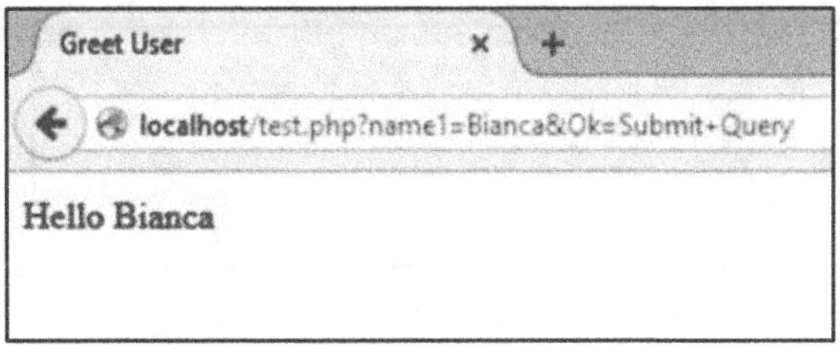

1.3.5 Sticky Forms (Oct. 14)

- Many web sites use a technique known as sticky forms. In sticky forms the values entered by user remain displayed with the form component, if we display the form after submit.

- **For example:** if you search Google (http://www.google.com) for "PHP Cookbook", the top of the results page contains another search box, which already contains "PHP Cookbook". To refine your search to "PHP Cookbook from O'Reilly", you can simply add the extra keywords.
- Consider the following Example:

```
<html>
<head><title>Greet User</title></head>
<body>
<form action="<?php echo $_SERVER['PHP_SELF']?>" method="GET">
        Enter Your Name:
        <input type="text" name="name1" /> <br />
        <input type="submit" name="Ok" />
    </form>
<?php
if(isset($_GET['name1']))
{
    $nm = $_GET['name1'];
    echo "Hello " . $nm;
}
?>
</body>
</html>
```

Output:

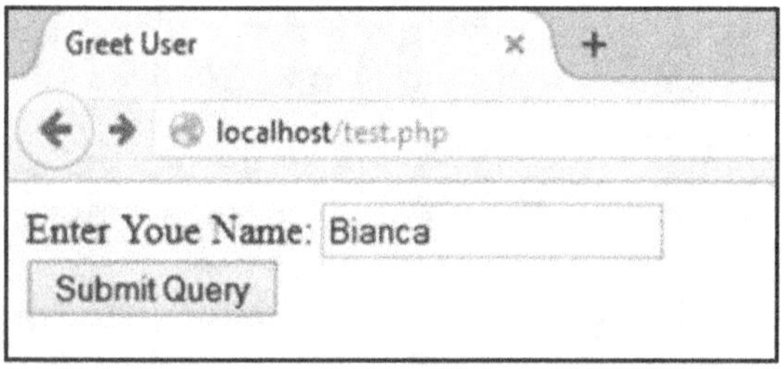

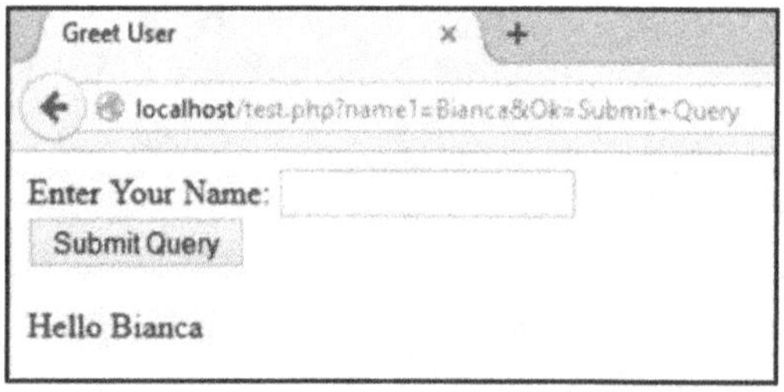

- The above form is not a sticky form, since the name entered in the text field is lost after submitting the form.
- To make form sticky we use the submitted form value as the default value when creating the HTML field. In the following program the submitted name is assigned to the value of the 'name1' parameter. So that the value remain displayed in the text field after form submission.

```
<html>
<head><title>Greet User</title></head>
<body>
<form action="<?php echo $_SERVER['PHP_SELF']?>" method="GET">
        Enter Youe Name:
        <input type="text" name="name1" value="<?php echo
                                                        $_GET['name1'];?>"/> <br />
        <input type="submit" name="Ok" />
   </form>
<?php
if(isset($_GET['name1']))
{
   $nm = $_GET['name1'];
   echo "Hello " . $nm;
}
?>
</body>
</html>
```

Output:

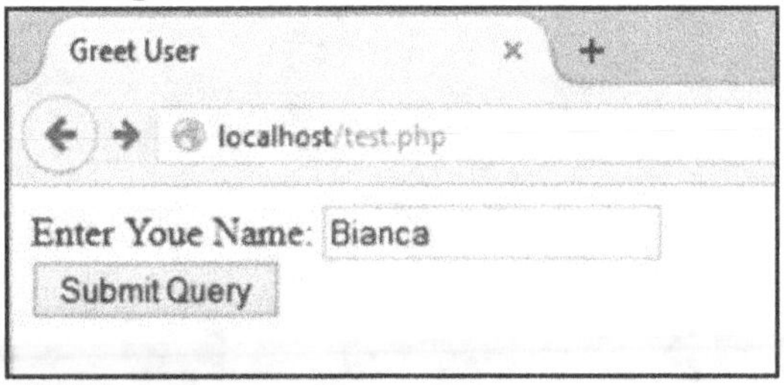

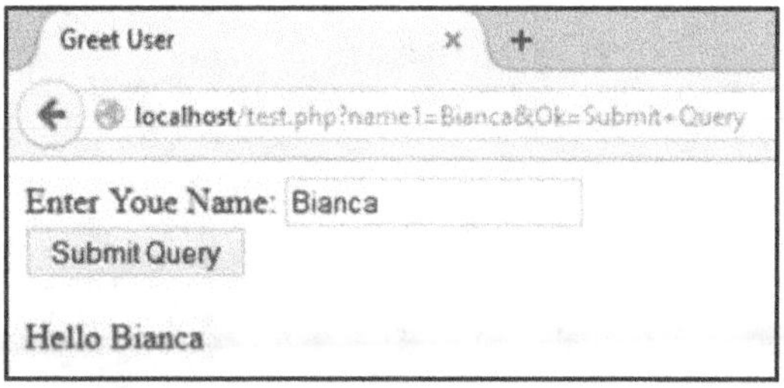

1.3.6 Multivalued Parameters

- The HTML selection lists can allow multiple selections, when name of the field in the HTML form end with [] and the 'multiple' attribute is used.
- When the user submits the form, $_GET[' languages'] contains an array instead of a simple string. This array contains the values that were selected by the user.
- Following example shows multiple selections. The form provides the user with a set of programming languages name. When the user submits the form, he gets list of the selected of programming languages.

```
<html>
<head><title>Programming Languages</title></head>
<body>
    <form action="<?php echo $_SERVER['PHP_SELF']?>" method="GET">
        Select Programming Languages:<br />
        <select name="languages[]" multiple>
            <option value="c">C</option>
            <option value="c++">C++</option>
            <option value="php">PHP</option>
            <option value="perl">Perl</option>
        </select><br>
        <input type="submit" name="s" value="Ok" />
    </form>
<?php
    if(isset($_GET['s']))
    {
        $lan = $_GET['languages'];
        echo "You selected<br>";
        foreach($lan as $k=>$v)
            echo "$v ";
    }
?>
</body>
</html>
```

Output:

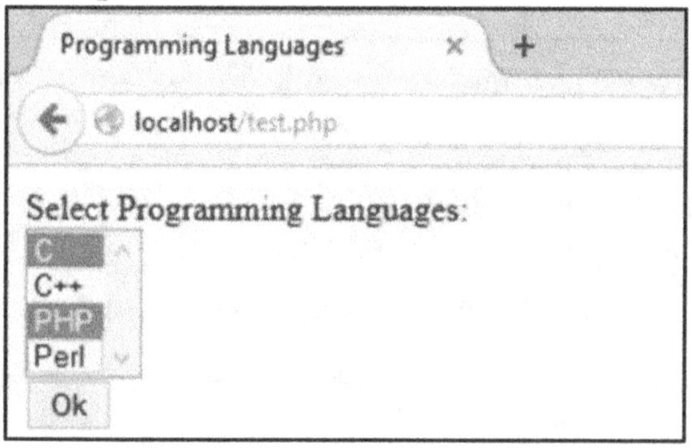

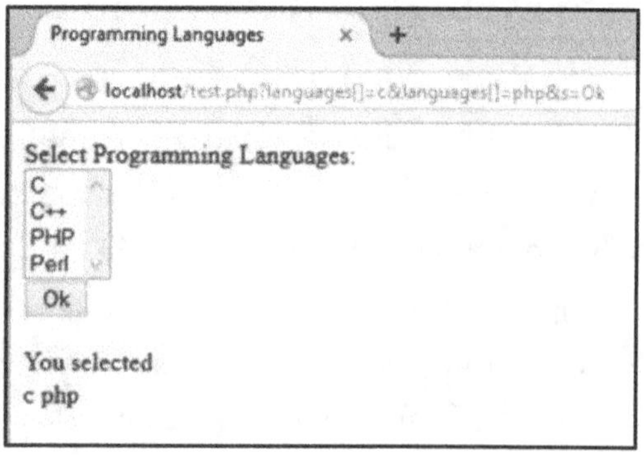

- The above program is rewritten using checkboxes in place of select box. Notice that only the HTML has changed, the code to process the form doesn't need to know whether the multiple values came from checkboxes or a select box.

```
<html>
<head><title>Programming Languages</title></head>
<body>
   <form action="<?php echo $_SERVER['PHP_SELF']?>" method="GET">
      Select Programming Languages:<br />
            <input type="checkbox" name="languages[]" value="c">C
            <input type="checkbox" name="languages[]" value="c++">C++
            <input type="checkbox" name="languages[]" value="php">PHP
            <input type="checkbox" name="languages[]" value="perl">Perl
            <br>
      <input type="submit" name="s" value="Ok" />
   </form>
<?php
   if(isset($_GET['s']))
   {
      $lan = $_GET['languages'];
      echo "You selected<br>";
      foreach($lan as $k=>$v)
         echo "$v ";
   }
?>
</body>
</html>
```

Output:

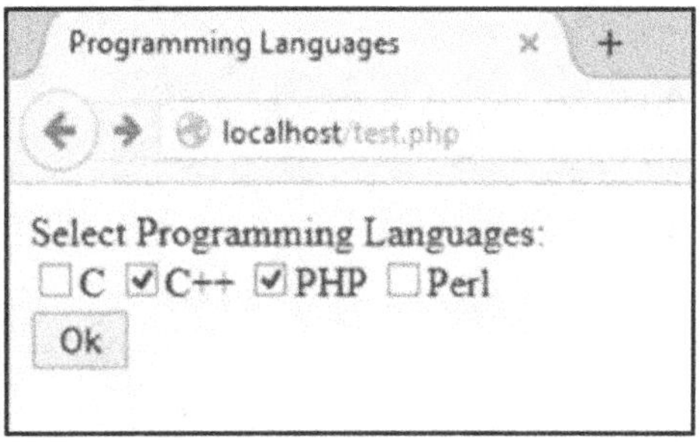

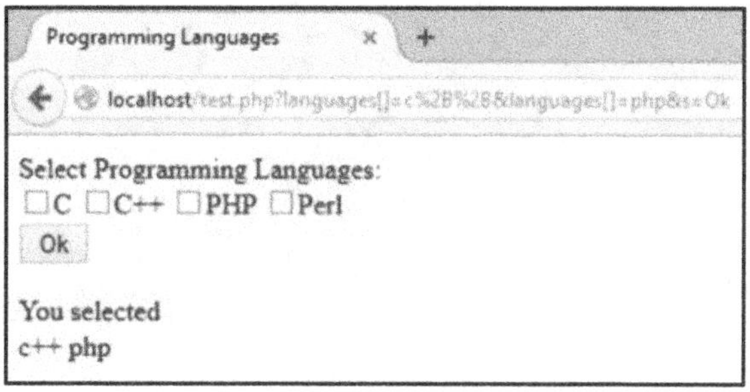

1.3.7 Sticky Multivalued Parameters

- A form can have multiple elements like text field, check boxes, radio button etc.; it is also possible to make that form sticky.
- It is also possible to make multiple selected form elements sticky. In such type of form each possible value in the form is one of the submitted values.
- In the program above the selected check boxes select (√) is lost after submitting the form.
- To make such type of form sticky so that the selected check boxes select (√) is not lost after submitting the form.
- **For Example:**

```
<html>
<head><title>Food Survey</title></head>
<body>
   <form action="<?php echo $_SERVER['PHP_SELF']?>" method="GET">
      Have you ever eaten Pizza before?
      <input type="checkbox" name="ch1" value="Pizza" <?php
   if(isset($_GET['ch1']) and isset($_GET['s'])) echo "checked";?>><br />
      Have you ever eaten Burger before?
   <input type="checkbox" name="ch2" value="Burger" <?php
   if(isset($_GET['ch2']) and isset($_GET['s'])) echo "checked";?>><br />
      Have you ever eaten Pastry before?
   <input type="checkbox" name="ch3" value="Pastry" <?php
   if(isset($_GET['ch3']) and isset($_GET['s'])) echo "checked";?>><br />
   <br>
      <input type="submit" name="s" value="Ok" />
   </form>
<?php
   if(isset($_GET['s']))
   {
      echo "You have eaten - ";
      if(isset($_GET['ch1'])) echo "$_GET[ch1] ";
      if(isset($_GET['ch2'])) echo "$_GET[ch2] ";
      if(isset($_GET['ch3'])) echo "$_GET[ch3]";
   }
?>
</body>
</html>
```

Output:

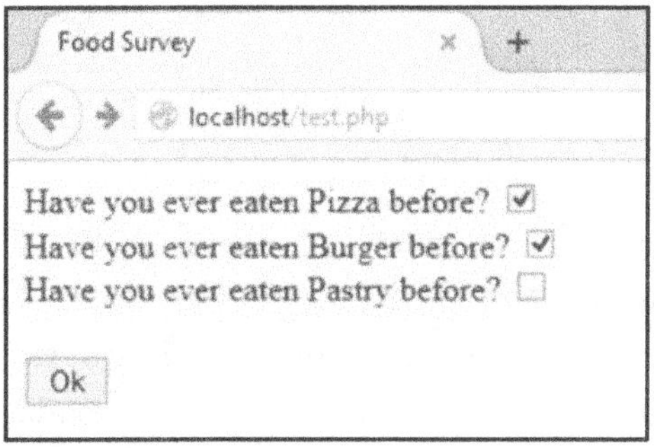

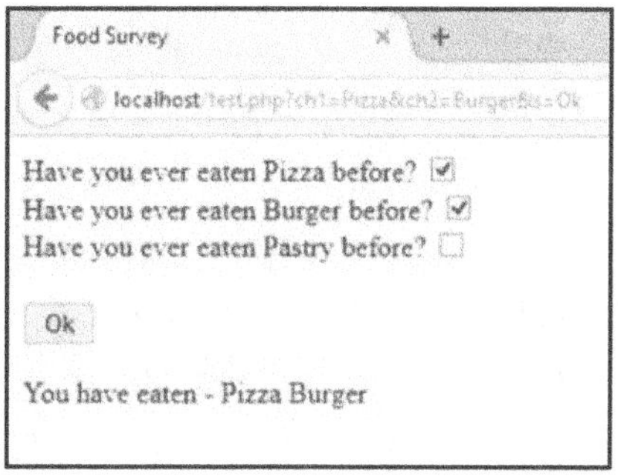

1.3.8 File Uploads (April 16)

- In PHP to handle file uploads, $_FILES array is used. The elements of the $_FILES array gives information about the uploaded file.
- The keys are:
  1. **name:** The name of the file, as supplied by the browser.
     ```
     $_FILE['filename']['name']
     ```
  2. **Type:** The type of the uploaded file. For example, image/jpeg.
     ```
     $_FILE['filename']['type']
     ```
  3. **Size:** The size of the uploaded file (in bytes). If the user attempted to upload a file that was too large, the size is reported as 0.
     ```
     $_FILE['filename']['size']
     ```
  4. **tmp_name:** The name of the temporary file on the server that holds the uploaded file. If the user attempted to upload a file that was too large, the name is reported as "none".
     ```
     $_FILE['filename']['tmp_name']
     ```
  5. **Error:** The error code resulting from the uploaded file.
     ```
     $_FILE['filename']['error']
     ```
- To test whether a file was successfully uploaded or not use the function is_uploaded_file(), as follows:
  ```
  if (is_uploaded_file($_FILES['filename']['tmp_name'])
  {
  // successfully uploaded
  }
  ```
- Files are stored in the server's default temporary files directory, which is specified in php.ini with the upload_tmp_dir option.

- We can also move the file to a permanent location using move_uploaded_file() function.

```
// move the file: move_uploaded_file() also does a check of the file's
// legitimacy, so there's no need to also call is_uploaded_file()
move_uploaded_file($_FILES['filename']['tmp_name'], '/path/to/file.txt');
```

- The value stored in tmp_name is the complete path to the file, not just the base name. Use basename( ) to chop off the leading directories if needed. Second parameter of move_uploaded_file()is the target path where the file is moved and stored permanentaly after upload.

Example:

```
upload.html file:
<html>
<head><title>File Upload</title></head>
<body>
<form action="upload.php" method="post" enctype="multipart/form-data">
    Select File:
    <input type="file" name="fileToUpload"/>
    <input type="submit" value="Upload Image" name="submit"/>
</form>
</body>
</html>
upload.php file:
<?php
$target_path = "E:/";
$target_path = $target_path.basename ( $_FILES['fileToUpload']['name']);
if (move_uploaded_file($_FILES['fileToUpload']['tmp_name'], $target_path))
{
   echo "File uploaded successfully!";
} else {
   echo "Sorry, file not uploaded, please try again!";
}
?>
```

Output:

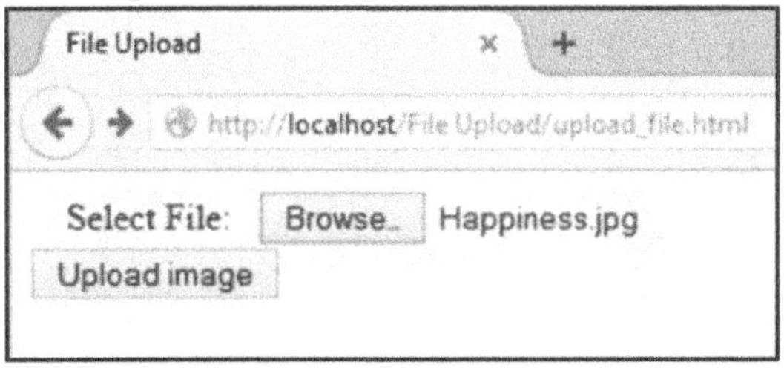

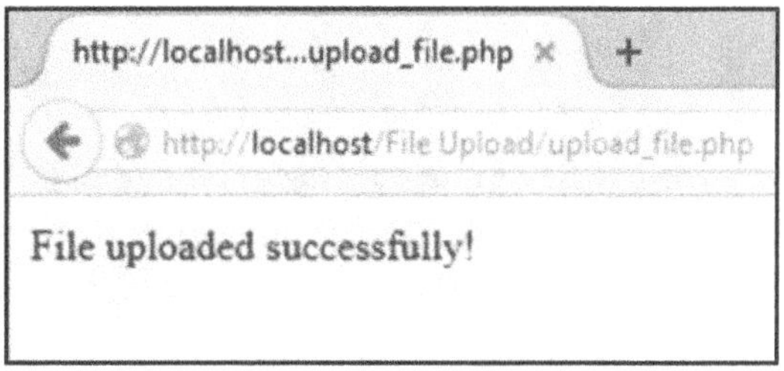

- In the above program first, you select a file using Browse button then click on 'Upload image' button, so next page will be displayed showing the message "File uploaded successfully!". The uploaded file can be seen in the E:/ directive.

1.3.9 Validating Forms

- When user input data in a form it should be validated before storing it. There are two ways to validate data i.e., client side validation and server side validation.
- For client side validation JavaScript is used, which is not secure because user can turn off JavaScript or browser may not support it.
- The more secure way is to use PHP for the validation. PHP is used for server side validation.
- **For Example:**

  form_validation.html

```
<html>
<head><title>Validated Form</title></head>
<body>
   <form name="form1" method="POST" action="form_validation.php">
      Your Name (Required):
      <input name="name" type="text">
        <br>
      Username (at least 5 characters):
        <input name="username" type="text">
        <br>
        <input name="send" type="submit" value="Submit">
   </form>
</body>
</html>
```

form_validation.php

```
<?php
    // First check if the form button has been submitted
    if(isset($_POST['send'])){
        if(!empty($_POST['name'])){ // Check if the name is empty
            echo "Name: " . $_POST['name'] . "<br />";
        }else{
            echo "Name is missing.";
            echo "<br />";
        }
        if(!empty ($_POST['username'])){// Check if the username is empty
        if(strlen($_POST['username']) < 5 ){ // Check if the username is
        at least 5 characters.
                echo "Username must be at least 5 characters long.";
                echo "<br />";
            }else{
                echo "User Name: " . $_POST['username'];
            }
        }else{
                echo "Username is missing.";
                echo "<br />";
        }
    }else{
        echo "Unauthorized access to this page.";
    }
?>
```

- In the above program there are two pages: HTML form to accept name and username from user and, second page is PHP form processing page, is used to validate user's data.
- Any user may come to this page directly. To prevent unauthorized access, we will check whether the user comes to this page clicking the form button the following condition is used:

```
if(isset($_POST['send']))
```

- If the user comes here directly the function will return false and the message "Unauthorized access to this page." is displayed.

- PHP has another function named empty() that can check whether a variable is empty. We'll check whether the name field("name") in the form is empty. If the user has entered his name that means the field is not empty and in this case the function empty() will return true, and the name prints. If the user didn't enter his name, the function will return false and the else statement will be executed. Then, the message "Name is missing." will be printed.

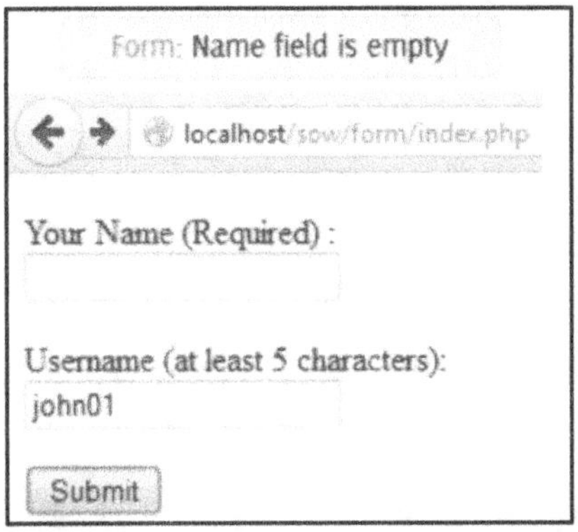

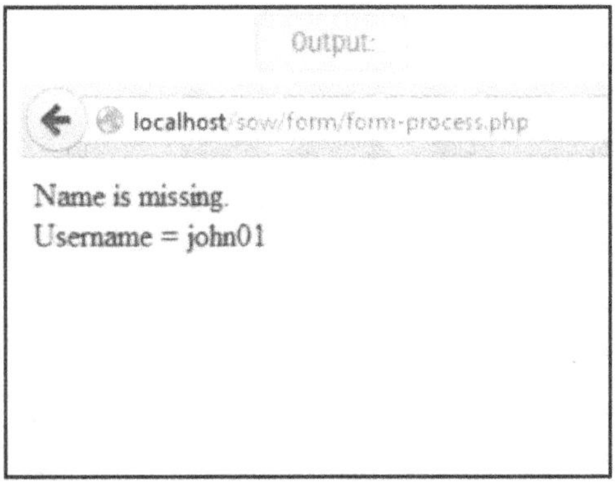

- In the same way, the username field is also checked using empty() function. The strlen() function check whether "username" is less than 5 characters. If it is, the warning "Username must be at least 5 characters long." will be displayed.

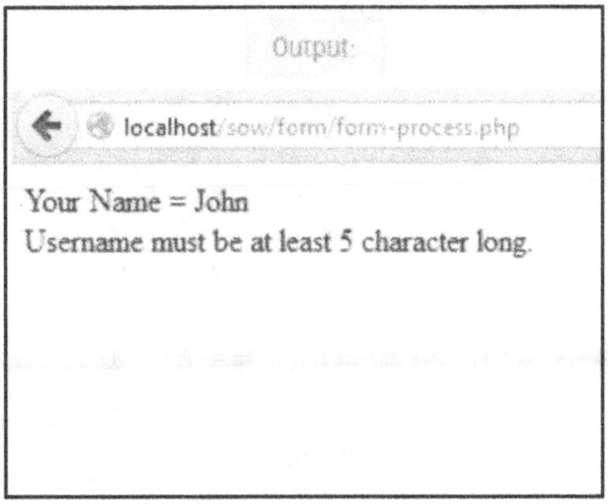

- It is easy for hackers to inject malicious code through form inputs, remove important files from server, damage your database etc. So, you need to sanitize user inputs to remove suspicious characters or to alter user inputs to usable form.
- There are few built-in php functions that help to sanitize form data. e.g. strip_tags() to remove any HTML and PHP tags from a string, htmlspecialchars(), and htmlentities() to converts all applicable characters to HTML entities etc.

- **For example:**

```
if ($_SERVER["REQUEST_METHOD"] == "POST") {
   $name = test_input($_POST["name"]);
   $email = test_input($_POST["email"]);
   $website = test_input($_POST["website"]);
   $comment = test_input($_POST["comment"]);
   $gender = test_input($_POST["gender"]);
}
function test_input($data) {
   $data = trim($data);
   $data = stripslashes($data);
   $data = htmlspecialchars($data);
   return $data;
}
<form method="post" action="<?php echo
                                 htmlspecialchars($_SERVER["PHP_SELF"]);?>">
----
</form>
```

- Regular expression can be used to validate form input data. The following example shows how to validate a form using regular expression.

```
<?php
echo "<font color=#FF0000>";
if(isset($_POST['send']))
{
   if(!empty($_POST['username']))
   {
      if(preg_match("/^[A-Za-z0-9]{3,20}$/",$_POST['username']))
      echo "Username is Valid<br>";
      else echo "Username is invalid<br>";
   }
   else  echo "Username is missing<br>";
   if(!empty($_POST['pass']))
   {
      if(preg_match("/^.*(?=.{8,})(?=.*[0-9])(?=.*[a-z])(?=.*[A-Z]).*$/",
      $_POST['pass']))
      echo "Password is Valid<br>";
```

```
        else echo "Password must be at least 8 characters and must contain at
        least one lower case letter, one upper case letter and one
        digit<br>";
    }
    else  echo "Password is missing<br>";
    if(!empty($_POST['address']))
    {
        if(preg_match("/^[a-zA-Z0-9 -.,:\"\']+$/", $_POST['address']))
        echo "Address is Valid<br>";
        else echo "Address must be only letters, numbers or one of the
        following - . ,: \" \'<br>";
    }
    else echo "Address is missing<br>";
    if(!empty($_POST['email']))
    {
        if(preg_match("/^[a-zA-Z]\w+(\.\w+)*\@\w+(\.[0-9a-zA-Z]+)*\.[a-zA-
        Z]{2,4}$/", $_POST['email']))
        echo "Email is Valid<br>";
        else echo "Email must comply with this mask:
                                    chars(.chars)@chars(.chars).chars(2-4)<br>";
    }
    else  echo "Email is missing<br>";
    if(!empty($_POST['date']))
    {
        if(preg_match("/^[0-9]{4}-[0-9]{1,2}-[0-9]{1,2}$/", $_POST['date']))
        echo "Date is Valid<br>";
        else echo "Date must comply with this mask: YYYY-MM-DD<br>";
    }
    else  echo "Date is missing<br>";
}
echo "</font>";
?>
<html>
<head><title>Validated Form</title></head>
<body>
    <form name="form1" method="POST" action="test.php">
```

```
        Username:
            <input name="username" type="text">  <br>
        Password:
              <input name="pass" type="password">  <br>
        Address:
            <input name="address" type="text">  <br>
        Email:
            <input name="email" type="text">  <br>
        Date:
            <input name="date" type="text">  <br>
             <input name="send" type="submit" value="Submit">
        </form>
    </body>
    </html>
```

Output:

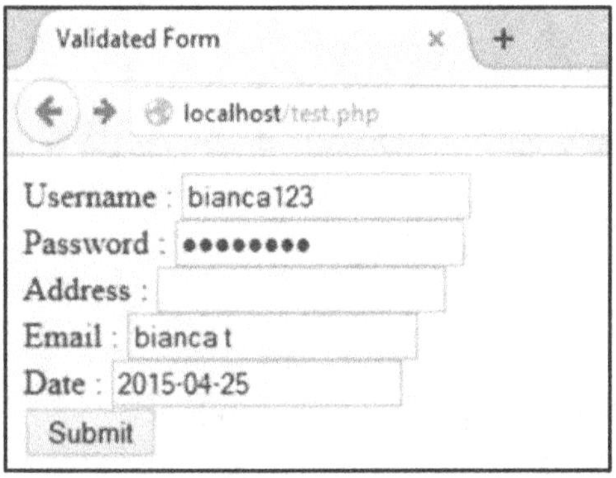

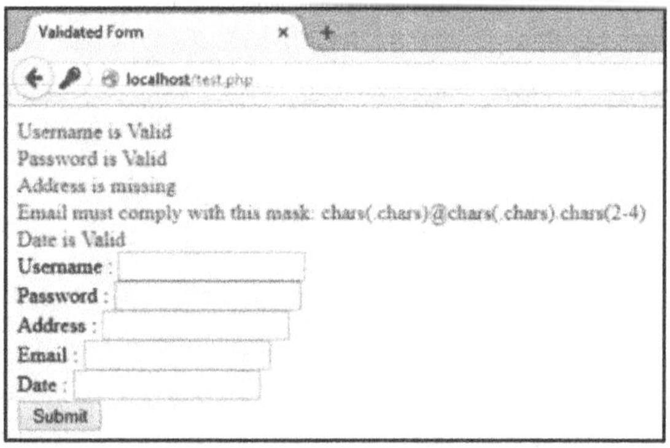

1.4 SETTING RESPONSE HEADERS

- We have already seen that when a client send a request to server for a web page, is called as HTTP request. The server sends back a response to the client is called as HTTP response. This HTTP response contains headers which include some information like, the type of content in the body of the response, how many bytes are in the body, when the response was sent, etc.
- If server sends back HTML then PHP and Apache take care of the headers, like, identifying the document as HTML, calculating the length of the HTML page, and so on.

- If you want to send back something that is not HTML, like, set the expiration time for a page, redirect the client's browser, or generate a specific HTTP error, in that case you need to use the header() function.
- The header() function sends a raw HTTP header to a client.
- **Syntax:** `header(string, replace, http_response_code)`

  `string - Specified header string to send.`

  where, replace: Optional, indicates whether the header should replace previous or add second header. Default is TRUE (will replace). FALSE allow multiple headers of same type.

  http_response_code: Optional, force the HTTP response code to the specified value.
- You must set the headers before any o the body is generated. This means that all calls to header()must happen at the very top of your file, even before the <html> tag.
- **For example:**

```
<?php
   header('Content-Type: text/plain');
?>
<html>
   . . . .
</html>
```

- Attempting to set headers after the document has started gives this warning:

```
Warning:  Cannot add header information - headers already sent
```

Different Content Types:

- Content-Type header identifies the type of document being returned. Content-type ensures that the browser displays the content correctly.
- Ordinarily this is "text/html", indicating an HTML document is about to receive by the browser.

```
header("Content-type: text/html");
```

- Other useful document type is header("Content-type: text/plain"); forces the browser to treat the page as plain text.
- Other content types are:

```
header("Content-type: image/jpeg");
```

  send a header to the web browser telling it the image type of data that it is is about to receive.

```
header("Content-type: application/pdf");
```

  will be outputting a PDF.

Redirections:

- Redirection means to send the user to a new URL. For this the Location header is used with the header function:

```
header('Location: http://www.nirali.com/books.html');
```

- When this statement executes the page containing the above statement is redirected to the page /index.html.
- If you want to pass variables to the new page, you can include them in the query string of the URL:

```
header('Location: http://www.nirali.com/books.php?id=12');
```

- The URL that you are redirecting a user to is retrieved with GET. You can't redirect someone to retrieve a URL via POST.

Expiration:

- A server can explicitly inform the browser, a specific date and time for the document to expire. The server can also inform expiration date and time to proxy cache.
- To set the expiration time of a document, use the Expires header:

```
header('Expires: Fri, 18 Jan 2014 05:30:00 GMT');
```

- Following example shows how a document expires three hours from the time the page was generated:

```
$now = time( );
$then = gmstrftime("%a, %d %b %Y %H:%M:%S GMT", $now + 60*60*3);
header("Expires: $then");
```

- The function time() returns current time and function gmstrftime() is used to generate expiration date string.

Authentication:

- HTTP authentication works through request headers and response statuses.
- A browser can send a username and password in the request headers. If the username and password aren't sent or aren't satisfactory, the server sends a "401 Unauthorized" response and identifies a string (realm) via WWW-Authenticate header. This typically pops up an "Enter username and password for ..." dialog box on the browser, and the page is then re-requested with the updated username and password in the header.
- The $_SERVER['PHP_AUTH_USER'] and $_SERVER['PHP_AUTH_PW'] global variables contain the username and password supplied by the user, if any.
- To deny access to a page, send a WWW-Authenticate header identifying the authentication realm as part of a response with status code 401:

```
header('WWW-Authenticate: Basic realm="My Website"');
header('HTTP/1.0 401 Unauthorized');
echo "You need to enter a valid username and password.";
exit;
```

- header() function is used to send a message "Authentication required" to the client browser causing it to pop up a username/password input window. Once the user has entered username and password, the same URL will be called again with the predefined variables PHP_AUTH_USER and PHP_AUTH_PW set with username and password respectively.
- **For example:**

```
<?php
if (!isset($_SERVER['PHP_AUTH_USER']))
{
header('WWW-Authenticate: Basic realm="My Website"');
header('HTTP/1.0 401 Unauthorized');
echo "You need to enter a valid username and password.";
exit;
}
else
{
        echo "Hello ". $_SERVER['PHP_AUTH_USER'] . "<br>";
        echo "You entered". $_SERVER['PHP_AUTH_PW'] . "as your password";
}
?>
```

1.5 MAINTAINING STATE

- As you provide input to some application via the user interface, you change the state of the application. State is the exact condition, movement to movement, of all the data and variables in the application.
- We know that HTTP is a stateless protocol i.e., HTTP supports only one request per connection. This means that with HTTP the client connects to the server to send one request and then disconnects.
- In other words, there is no way for a server to recognize that a sequence of requests all originate from the same client.
- When you programming for Web, you cannot keep track of a sequence of requests from a single user, because HTTP is stateless. For example, in a shopping-cart application you need to know that the same user adds items in his cart or removes items from his cart, every time when he sends request to add or remove items.

- So building an online application with PHP requires you to use some mechanism for maintaining state.
- PHP is able to bridge the gap between each request-response and provides persistence of data and prolong interactivity.
- To get around the Web's lack of state, software programmers have come up with many tricks to keep track of state information between requests which is also known as session tracking.
- Some techniques are:

1. **Hidden Fields:** One session tracking technique is to use hidden form fields to pass data from one page to another. PHP treats hidden form fields just like normal form fields, so the values are available in the $_GET or $_POST arrays. So after submitting a form, the form data can be fetched by the next page from $_GET or $_POST arrays.

   However, a more common and popular technique is to assign each user a unique identifier using a single hidden form field.

   For example, consider a form where a user selects a product from a drop-down box. You can simply place the product ID into a hidden form field.

   ```
   <form action="myform.php" method="post">
   <select name="selected_product_id">
     <option value="121">Product 121</option>
     <option value="122">Product 122</option>
   </select>
   <input type="submit" value="Select Product">
   </form>
   ```

   You could return a page to him using the following code:

   ```
   <input type="hidden" name="chosen_product_id" value="<?php echo
   $_POST[selected_product_id];?>">
   ```

   The chosen_product_id value can be fetched after submitting the form.

   While hidden form fields work in all browsers, they work only for a sequence of dynamically generated forms, so they aren't as generally useful as some other techniques.

2. **URL Rewriting:** In this technique you can add some extra information in the URL. For example, you can assign a unique ID to a user as given below, so that this ID can be passed to that page.

   ```
   http://www.nirali.com/catalog.php?userid=123
   ```

   This method is very insecure because everyone can see the values. User can also change the value of variable in the URL.

3. **Cookies:** A third technique for maintaining state with PHP is to use cookies. A cookie is a bit of information that the server can give to a client. On every subsequent request the client will give that information back to the server, thus identifying itself. Cookies are useful for retaining information through repeated visits by a browser.

- The best way to maintain state with PHP is to use the built-in session-tracking system. This system lets you create persistent variables that are accessible from different pages of your application, as well as in different visits to the site by the same user.

1.5.1 Cookies (April 13, 15, 16)

- A cookie is a small piece of data in the form of a name-value pair that is sent by a Web server and stored by the browser on the client machine.
- This information is used by the application running on the server side to customize the web page according to the past history of transactions from that client machine.
- A server can send one or more cookies to a browser in the headers of a response. Some of the cookie's fields indicate the pages for which the browser should send the cookie as part of the request.
- Servers can store any data they like there in the value field of the cookie (within limits), such as a unique code identifying the user, preferences, etc.
- PHP cookie is a small piece of information which is stored at client browser. It is used to recognize the user.
- Cookie is created at server side and saved to client browser. Each time when client sends request to the server, cookie is embedded with request. Such way, cookie can be received at the server side.

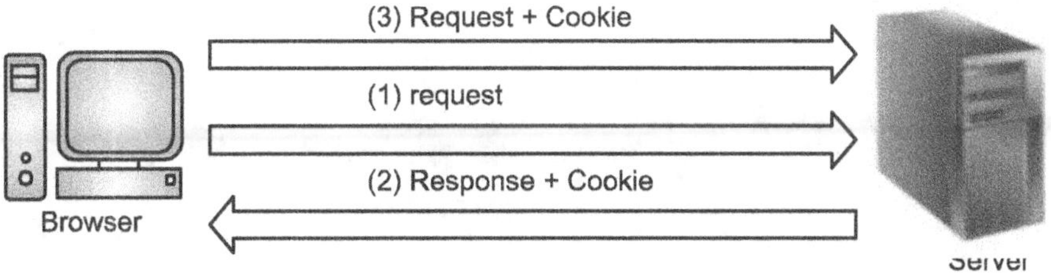

Fig. 1.1: Cookies

- In short, cookie can be created, sent and received at server end.
- Use the setcookie( ) function to send a cookie to the browser. Like header(), setcookie() must be called before any HTML is printed to the client browser because cookies are set in the HTTP headers, which must be sent before any HTML.
- The syntax is,

```
setcookie(name [, value [, expire [, path [, domain [, secure ]]]]]);
```

- Here is the detail of all the arguments in above syntax:
  - **Name:** Name of the cookie, stored in an environment variable called $_COOKIE. This variable is used while accessing cookies.
  - **Value:** Value of the named variable.
  - **Expiry:** A UNIX timestamp denoting the time at which the cookie will expire.
  - **Path:** This specifies the directories for which the cookie is valid. A single forward slash character permits the cookie to be valid for all directories.
  - **Domain:** The browser will return the cookie only for URLs within this domain. The default is the server hostname.
  - **Secure:** This can be set to 1 to specify that the cookie should only be sent by secure transmission using HTTPS otherwise set to 0 which mean cookie can be sent by regular HTTP.
- When a browser sends a cookie back to the server, you can access that cookie through the $_COOKIE array. The key is the cookie name, and the value is the cookie's value field.
- For example, to set cookie in one page:

```
<?php
    setcookie("ID", "121");
    setcookie("name", "Laptop");
?>
```

- Can be access in another page as follows:

```
<?php
  if( isset($_COOKIE["ID"]))
  {
   echo "Product ID: " . $_COOKIE["ID"] . "<br />";
       echo "Product Name: " . $_COOKIE["name"];
  }
  else
    echo "Sorry... Not recognized" . "<br />";
?>
```

Output:

```
Product ID: 121
Product Name: Laptop
```

- For instance, the following code at the top of a page keeps track of the number of times the page has been accessed by this client:

```
<?php
if(!isset($_COOKIE['accesses']))
    setcookie('accesses', 0);
else{
    $page_accesses = $_COOKIE['accesses'];
    setcookie('accesses', ++$page_accesses);
    echo "This page is accessed " . $_COOKIE['accesses'] . " times";
}
```

- Initially the cookie named "accesses" is not set, so it is set to 0. After that every time the page is accessed the program displays how many times the page is accessed.
- Following example shows an HTML page that gives a range of options for background and foreground colors.

```
<html>
<head>
<title>Example of Set Your Preferences
</title>
</head>
<body>
<form action="prefsexample.php" method="post">
Background:
<select name="background">
<option value="blue">Blue</option>
<option value="black">Black</option>
<option value="white">White</option>
<option value="red">Red</option>
</select><br />
Foreground:
<select name="foreground">
<option value="blue">Blue</option>
<option value="black">Black</option>
<option value="white">White</option>
<option value="red">Red</option>
</select><p />
<input type="submit" value="Change Preferences">
</form>
</body>
</html>
```

Output:

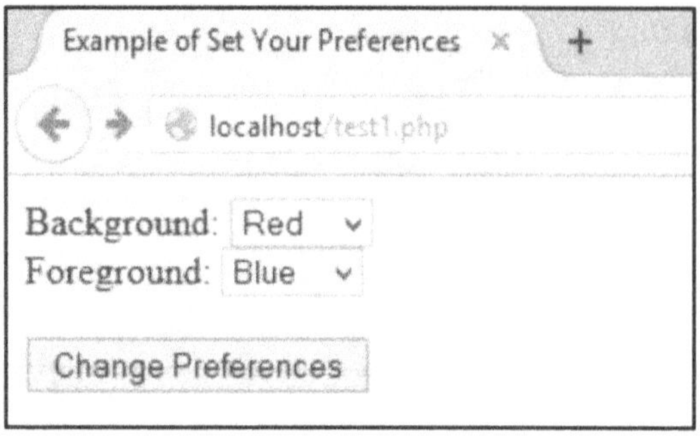

- The form in above Example submits to the PHP script prefs.php, which is shown in following Example. This script sets cookies for the color preferences specified in the form. Note that the calls to setcookie( ) are made before the HTML page is started.

```
<?php
 $colors = array('black' => '#000000',
                 'white' => '#ffffff',
                 'red'   => '#ff0000',
                 'blue'  => '#0000ff');
$bg_name = $_POST['background'];
$fg_name = $_POST['foreground'];
setcookie('bg', $colors[$bg_name]);
setcookie('fg', $colors[$fg_name]);
?>
<html>
<head><title>Example of Preferences Set</title></head>
<body>
Thank you. Your preferences have been changed to:<br />
Background: <?= $bg_name?><br />
Foreground: <?= $fg_name?><br />
Click <a href="prefs-demo.php">here</a> to see the preferences in action.
</body>
</html>
```

- The page created by above Example contains a link to another page, shown in following Example, that uses the color preferences by accessing the $_COOKIE array.

```
<html>
<head>
<title>Example of Front Door
</title>
</head>
<?php
 $bg = $_COOKIE['bg'];
 $fg = $_COOKIE['fg'];
?>
<body bgcolor="<?= $bg?>" text="<?= $fg?>">
<h1>Welcome to the Store</h1>
```

- We have many fine Services for you to view. Please feel free to browse the aisles and stop an assistant at any time. But remember, you break it you bought it!<p>
- Would you like to <a href="prefsexample.html">change your preferences?</a>

```
</body>
</html>
```

Deleting Cookie with PHP:

- Officially, to delete a cookie you should call setcookie() with the name argument only but this does not always work well, however, and should not be relied on.
- It is safest to set the cookie with a date that has already expired:

```
<?php
  setcookie( "name", "", time()- 60, "/","", 0);
  setcookie( "age", "", time()- 60, "/","", 0);
?>
<html>
<head>
<title>Deleting Cookies with PHP</title>
</head>
<body>
<?php echo "Deleted Cookies"?>
</body>
</html>
```

1.5.2 Sessions (April 13)

- A session can be defined as "a series of related interactions between a single client and the web server, which takes place over a period of time".
- Sessions allow you to store data in the web server that associated with a session ID. Once you create a session, PHP sends a cookie that contains the session ID to the web browser.
- In the subsequent requests, the web browser sends the session ID cookie back to the web server so that PHP can retrieve the data based on the session ID and make the data available in your script.
- Session provides a way to preserve certain data across subsequent accesses. This enables us to build more customized applications.
- Sessions allow you to easily create multipage forms like shopping carts, save user authentication information from page to page, and store persistent user preferences on a site.
- PHP session is used to store and pass information from one page to another temporarily (until user close the website).
- An overview of PHP session management is shown in Fig. 1.2.

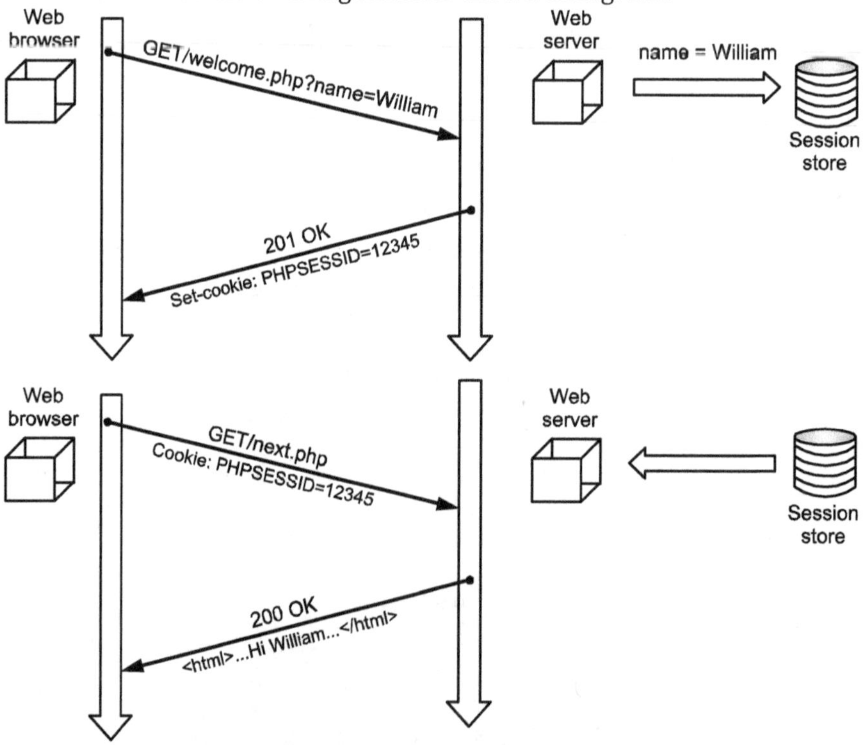

Fig. 1.2: The interaction between the browser and the server when initial requests are made to session-based application

- When user first enters the session-based application by making a request to a page that starts a session, PHP generates a session and creates a file that stores the session-related variables.
- PHP sets a cookie named PHPSESSID to hold the session ID in the response the script generates. If the user's browser does not support cookies or has cookies turned off, the session ID is added in URLs within the web site. The browser then records the cookie and includes it in subsequent requests.
- In the example shown above, the script welcome.php records session variables in the session store, and a request to next.php then has access to those variables because of the session ID.
- A session ends when the user closes the browser or after leaving the site, the server will terminate the session after a predetermined period of time.
- PHP session_start() function is used to start the session. It starts a new or resumes existing session. It returns existing session if session is created already. If session is not available, it creates and returns new session.

  Syntax: `bool session_start ( void )`
- $_SESSION is an associative array that contains all session variables. It is used to set and get session variable values.
- Session variables are stored in associative array called $_SESSION[]. These variables can be accessed during lifetime of a session.
- The following example starts a session then register a variable called counter that is incremented each time the page is visited during the session.
- Make use of isset() function to check if session variable is already set or not.
- Put this code in a test.php file and load this file many times to see the result:

```
<?php
   session_start();
   if( isset( $_SESSION['counter'] ) )
   {
      $_SESSION['counter'] += 1;
   }
   else
   {
      $_SESSION['counter'] = 1;
   }
   $msg = "You have visited this page ".  $_SESSION['counter'] . " in
this session.";
?>
```

```
<html>
<head>
<title>Setting up a PHP session</title>
</head>
<body>
<?php  echo ( $msg );?>
</body>
</html>
```

Output:

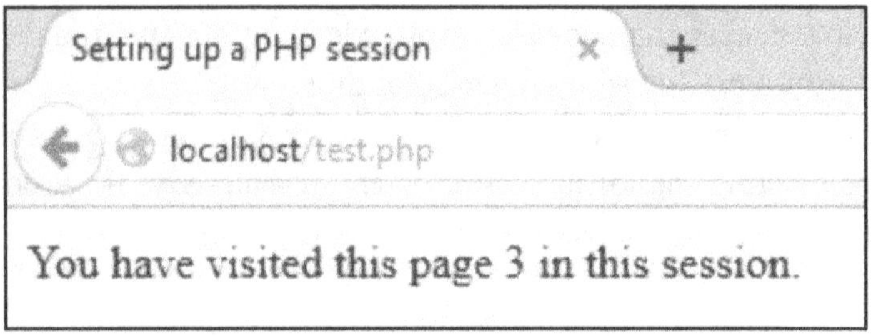

- You can register a variable with the session by passing the name of the variable to session_register(). If register_globals is enabled in the *php.ini* file, the variables are also set directly. Because the array and the variable both reference the same value, setting the value of one also changes the value of the other.
- You can unregister a variable from a session, which removes it from the data store, by calling session_unregister( ).

How to Access Data in the Session?

- Unlike a cookie, you can store any types of data in sessions. You store data as keys and values in the $SESSION[] superglobal array. For example, in the index.php file, you store user string and roles array in the session as follows:

```
<?php
    session_start();
    $_SESSION['user'] = "admin";
    $roles = array("admin", "approver", "editor");
    $_SESSION['roles'] = $roles;
    session_write_close();
?>
<a href="test1.php">Go to profile page</a>
```

- In the profile.php file, you can access session data as follows:

```
<?php
    session_start();
    if(isset($_SESSION['user']))
    {
        echo sprintf("Welcome %s!<br>",$_SESSION['user']);
    }
    if(isset($_SESSION['roles']))
    {
        echo sprintf('Your roles: %s', implode($_SESSION['roles'],','));
    }
?>
```

Output:

```
Welcome admin!
Your roles: admin,approver,editor
```

Destroy a PHP Session: **(April 14)**

- To remove all global session variables and destroy the session, use session_unset() and session_destroy() functions.
- A PHP session can be destroyed by session_destroy() function. This function does not need any argument and a single call can destroy all the session variables.
- If you want to destroy a single session variable then you can use unset() function to unset a session variable.
- Here, is the example to unset a single variable:

```
<?php
   unset($_SESSION['counter']);
?>
```

- Here, is the call which will destroy all the session variables:

```
<?php
session_start();
?>
<html>
<body>
<?php
// remove all session variables session_unset();
// destroy the session session_destroy();
echo "All session variables are now removed, and the session is
destroyed."
?>
</body>
</html>
```

Alternatives to Cookies:

- By default, the session ID is passed from page to page using PHPSESSID cookie. The session ID can also be passed using form fields and URLs.
- Passing the session ID via hidden form fields is extremely awkward, as it forces you to make every link between pages be a form's submit button.
- The URL system for passing around the session ID, however, is very elegant. PHP can rewrite your HTML files, adding the session ID to every relative link. For this to work, PHP must be configured with the -enable-trans-id option when compiled.
- But the performance is decreased, because PHP must parse and rewrite every page. Busy sites must be used cookies, as cookies do not slowdown the website caused by page rewriting.

Custom Storage:

- By default, the session information is stored in files in server's temporary directory.
- Each session's variables are stored in the separate file. The location of the session files can be changed with session Save_path in PHP. ini file.
- The session information is stored in two formats.
  1. PHP's built_in format.
  2. WDDX.
- Here, the session data in a database which will be shared between multiple sites. Here different functions are required for opening new session, closing a session, reading session information, writing session information, destroying a session etc.
- To use the custom session store use the following code:

```
<Directory "/var/html/sample">
php_value session.save_handler user
php_value session.save.path mydb
php_value session.name session_store
</Directory>
```

Combining Cookies and Sessions:

- Using a combination of cookies and session, you can preserve state across visits. When a user leaves the site that state should be forgotten. Any state that should persist between user visits, such as a unique user ID, can be stored in a cookie.
- With the user's ID, you can retrieve the user's more permanent state, such as display preferences, mailing address, and so on, from a permanent store, such as a database.
- Following example allows the user to select text and background colors and stores those values in a cookie. Any visits to the page within the next week send the color values in the cookie.

```
<?php
 if($_POST['bgcolor']) {
   setcookie('bgcolor', $_POST['bgcolor'], time( ) + (60 * 60 * 24 * 7));
 }
   $bgcolor = empty($bgcolor)? 'black': $bgcolor;
?>
  <body bgcolor="<?= $bgcolor?>">
  <form action="<?= $PHP_SELF?>" method="POST">
  <select name="bgcolor">
    <option value="black">Black</option>
    <option value="white">White</option>
    <option value="gray">Gray</option>
    <option value="blue">Blue</option>
    <option value="green">Green</option>
    <option value="red">Red</option>
  </select>
    <input type="submit" />
</form>
</body>
```

Example:

- A PHP script to create a login form with user name and password, once the user login, the second form should be display to accept the user details (roll_no, name, city). If the user does not enter information within specified time limit, expire his session and give the warning.

  login.html File:

```
<html>
   <head> <title> login form </title> </head>
   <body>
   <form method = "POST" action = "login.php">
      Username :
          <input type = "text" name = "user"><br>
      Password :
          <input type = "password" name = "pass"><br><br>
      <input type = "submit" value="Submit">
   </form>
   </body>
</html>
```

login.php File:

```
<?php
    session_start();
    $_SESSION["tm"] = time();
?>
<form method = "GET" action = "new.php">
    Roll No : <input type = "text" name = "rno"><br>
    Name :    <input type = "text" name = "nm"><br>
    City :    <input type = "text" name = "ct"><br><br>
    <input type = "submit" value="Submit">
</form>
```

new.php File:

```
<?php
    session_start();
    $newt=$_SESSION['tm'] + 20;
    if($newt < time())
        echo "Time out";
    else
    {
        echo "Roll No = $_GET[rno] <br>";
        echo "Name = $_GET[nm] <br>";
        echo "City = $_GET[ct]";
    }
    session_destroy( );
?>
```

Output: When you run login.html file, the following screen will be displayed which will ask you to enter username and password.

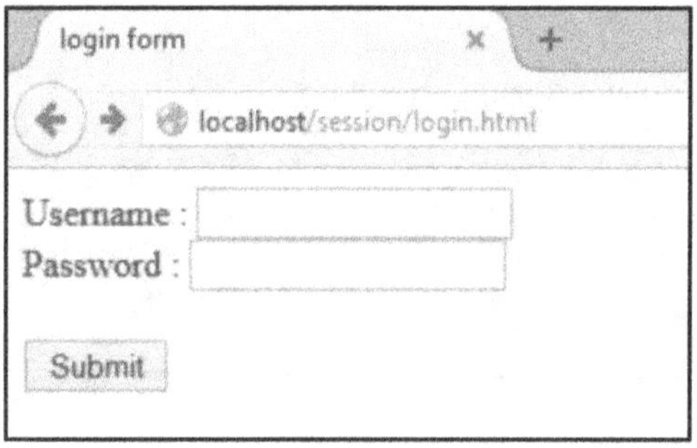

After you enter any username and password, the following screen will be display:

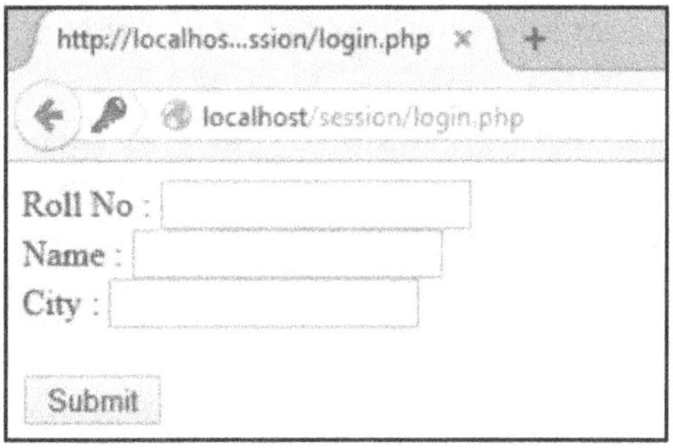

If you fail to enter all the details within 20 second, the following screen will be displayed:

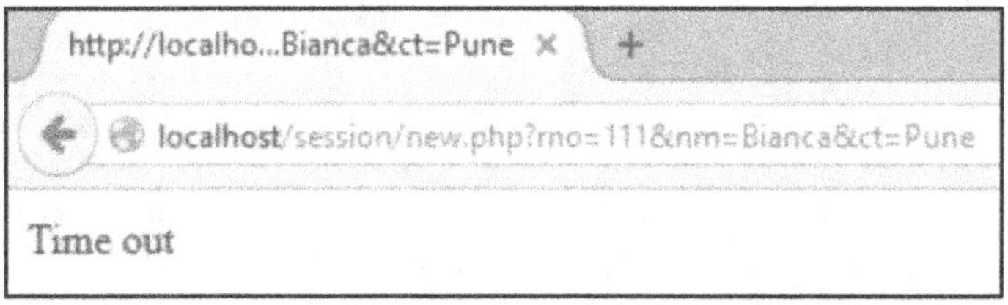

If you enter all the details within 20 second, the following screen will be displayed:

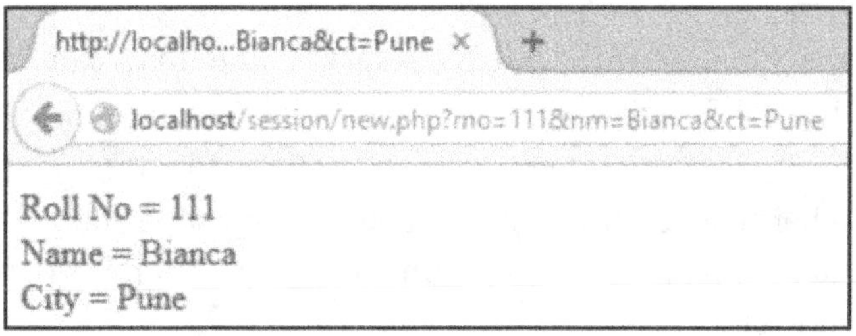

- In login.php file the session 'tm' is set with the current time using time(). When you submit this form after entering all the fields, control goes to new.php file, where session variable 'tm', which now stores the form submission time, is incremented by 20. This total value compared with the current time so that you can find out whether the form is submitted within 20 second or not.

1.6 SSL (April 16)

- Though session IDs are hard to guess, they can also be stolen if they are sent in clear text between your server and a user's browser. HTTP basic authentication also has this problem. For this use SSL to guard against network sniffing.
- SSL stands for Secure Sockets Layer. SSL provides a secure channel over which regular HTTP requests and responses can flow.

- PHP doesn't specifically concern itself with SSL, so you cannot control the encryption in any way from PHP. An https:// URL indicates a secure connection for that document, unlike an http:// URL.
- The HTTPS entry in the $_SERVER array is set to 'on' if the PHP page was generated in response to a request over an SSL connection. To prevent a page from being generated over a non encrypted connection, simply use following:

```
if ($_SERVER{'HTTPS'] !== 'on') {
  die("Must be a secure connection.");
}
```

- A common mistake is to send a form over a secure connection (for example, https://www.nirali.com/form.html), but have the action of the form submit to an http:// URL. Any form parameters entered by the user are sent over an insecure connection—a trivial packet sniffer can reveal them.

SUMMARY

- To keep track of information like server configuration, user request information global variables are used. These global variables allow us to access this information from any page. There are six global arrays like $_GET, $_POST, $_FILES etc.
- Any information related to server is available with $_SERVER array.
- Data passed through forms must be processed by server and that can be made available to server via $_GET or $_POST array.
- Magic quotes is the feature of PHP which automatically adds the quotes and backslashes in user input wherever required provided feature must be enabled.
- Self processing pages provide the flexibility by merging the script and form together in single page which processes itself.
- Sticky forms allow data to be remembered by form which was submitted in previous request.
- Selection of multiple values for one HTML control is done by using [].
- Data inputted by user can be validated by using various strategies before sending it to sever to avoid operation failure at server side.
- Type of HTTP response generated by server for the user can be described by setting different response headers like content type, redirections, expiration and authentication.
- HTTP is stateless protocol. To keep the track of user requests we require maintaining state. Session, Cookie, Hidden form fields and URL rewriting are the techniques used to maintain the state.
- SSL (Secure Socket Layer) provides secure channel over which HTPP requests and responses can be send and received.

PRACTICE QUESTIONS

1. What is variable?
2. Write short note on: Server information.
3. Explain processing forms with example.
4. When to use GET and POST method.
5. What is meant by sticky forms?
6. Describe validation of form with example.
7. What is SSL?
8. How to maintain state in PHP?
9. With the help of program explain how to settling response headers.
10. Write short note on Multivalued parameters.
11. What is cookies? How to create it?
12. What is session? Explain with example.
13. What is SSL?

Ans. Refer to Section 1.6.

14. How we can get the cookie values and destroy the cookies?

Ans. Refer to Section 1.5.1.

15. How to check whether a variable is set with a session?

Ans. Refer to Section 1.5.2.

16. What is form validation? Explain with suitable example.

Ans. Refer to Section 1.3.9.

17. Write Php script to select list of subjects (use multivalued parameter) display on the next page.

Ans.

```
<html>
    <head><title>Personality</title></head>
    <body>
        <form action="<?php echo $_SERVER['PHP_SELF'] ?>" method="GET">
        Select your personality attributes:<br />
        <select name="attributes[]" multiple>
            <option value="os">Operating System</option>
            <option value="cc">Compiler Construction</option>
            <option value="networks">Computer Networks</option>
            <option value="java">Advance Java</option>
            <option value="php">Internet Programming</option>
            <option value="graphics">Computer Graphics</option>
        </select>
        <br>
        <input type="submit" name="s" value="Record Subjects" />
        </form>
    <?php
```

```
        if (array_key_exists('s', $_GET)) {
            $description = join (" ", $_GET['attributes']);
            echo "You have a selected $description subjects.";
        }
?>
</body>
</html>
```

Output:

Before selected subject:

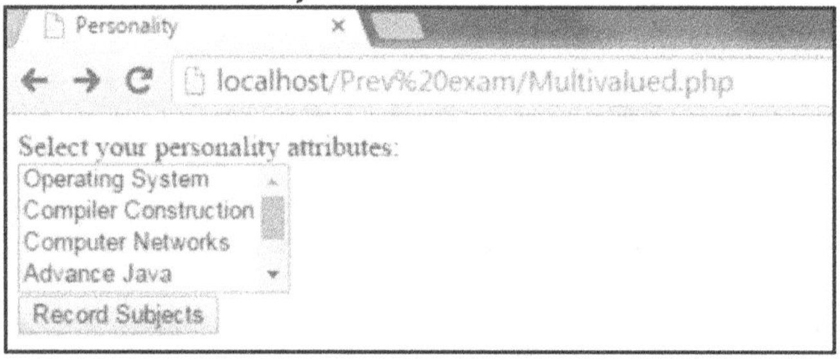

After selected subject:

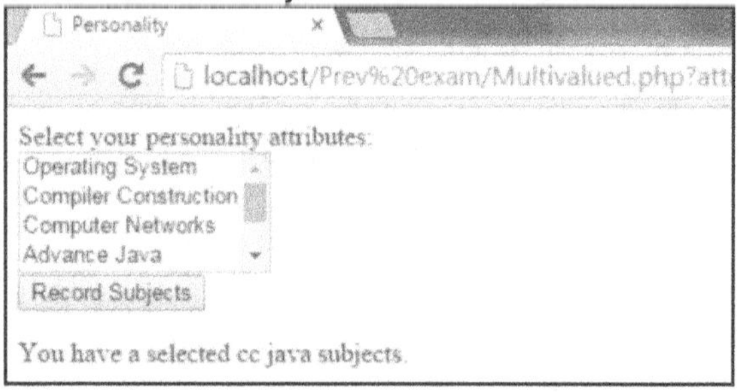

18. Explain in detail the concept of cookies and session.

Ans. Refer to Sections 1.5.1 and 1.5.2.

19. What is sticky form? Explain it with example.

Ans. Refer to Section 1.3.5.

20. Write short note on sessions.

Ans. Refer to Section 1.5.2.

21. Write a PHP script to accept personal details of student (rno, name, class) on first page. On second page accept marks of six subjects (out of 100). On third page print marklist (rno, name, class, marks, total, percentage).

Ans. **5b2.html**

```
<html>
<form action="5b2.php" method="POST">
ENTER THE NAME: <input type="text" name="name">
<br><br>
```

```
ENTER THE CLASS: <input type="text" name="class">
<br><br>
ENTER THE ADDRESS: <input type="text" name="address">
<br><br>
<input type="submit" value="ok">
</form>
</html>
```

5b2.php

```
<?php
setcookie('name',$_POST['name']);
setcookie('class',$_POST['class']);
setcookie('address',$_POST['address']);
?>
<html>
<form action="5b2a.php" method="POST">
<br>
ENTER THE MARKS: <br><br>
SYSPRO: <input type="text" name="syspro" size=3>
<br><br>
NETWORKING: <input type="text" name="networking" size=3>
<br><br>
OOSE: <input type="text" name="oose" size=3>
<br><br>
TCS: <input type="text" name="tcs" size=3>
<br><br>
JAVA: <input type="text" name="java" size=3>
<br><br>
PHP: <input type="text" name="php" size=3>
<br><br>
<input type="submit" value="Result">
</form></html>
```

5b2a.php

```
<?php
echo "<br>NAME: ".$_COOKIE["name"];
echo "<br>CLASS: ".$_COOKIE["class"];
echo "<br>ADDRESS: ".$_COOKIE["address"];
```

```
echo "<br><br>";
echo "<table border=1><tr><th>SUBJECT<th>MARKS</tr>";
echo "<tr><td>SYSPRO<td>".$_POST["syspro"]."</tr>";
echo "<tr><td>NETWORKING<td>".$_POST["networking"]."</tr>";
echo "<tr><td>OOSE<td>".$_POST["oose"]."</tr>";
echo "<tr><td>TCS<td>".$_POST["tcs"]."</tr>";
echo "<tr><td>JAVA<td>".$_POST["java"]."</tr>";
echo "<tr><td>PHP<td>".$_POST["php"]."</tr>";
echo "<br>";
echo "<br><br>";
$total=$_POST["syspro"]+$_POST["networking"]+$_POST["oose"]+$_POST["tcs"]
+$_POST["java"]+$_POST["php"];
$per=$total/6;
echo "<br>TOTAL: ".$total;
echo "<br>PERCENTAGE: ".$per."%";
echo "<br><br>";
?>
```

Output:

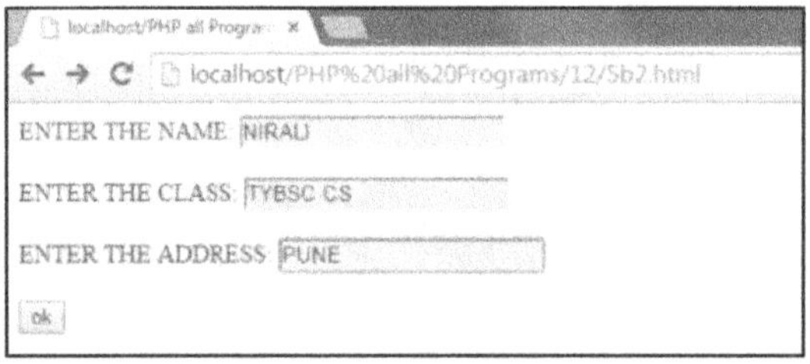

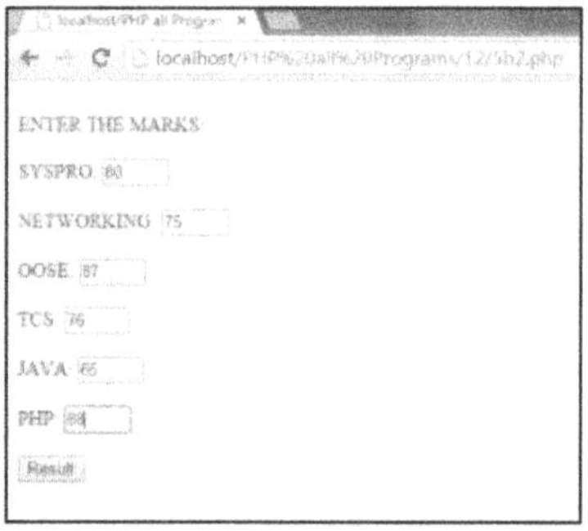

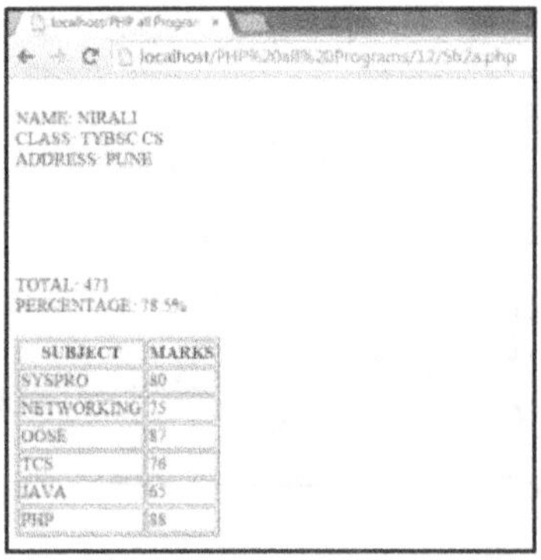

22. Write a PHP script to accept two strings and check if strings are equal using sticky form.

Ans. **Sticky.php**

```
<html>
<head><title>String Comparison</title></head>
<body>
<?php
$s1 = @$_GET['str1'];
$s2 = @$_GET['str2'];
?>
<form action="<?php echo $_SERVER['PHP_SELF'] ?>" method="GET">
String 1:
<input type="text" name="str1" value="<?php echo $s1 ?>" />
<br />
String 2:
<input type="text" name="str2" value="<?php echo $s2 ?>" />
<br />
<input type="submit" name="Check Equality" />
</form>
<?php
if (! is_null($s1) && !is_null($s2)) {
   if(strcmp($s1,$s2)==0){
          echo" Strings are equal";}
   else{
       echo "Strings are not equal";
   }
}
?>
</body>
</html>
```

Output:

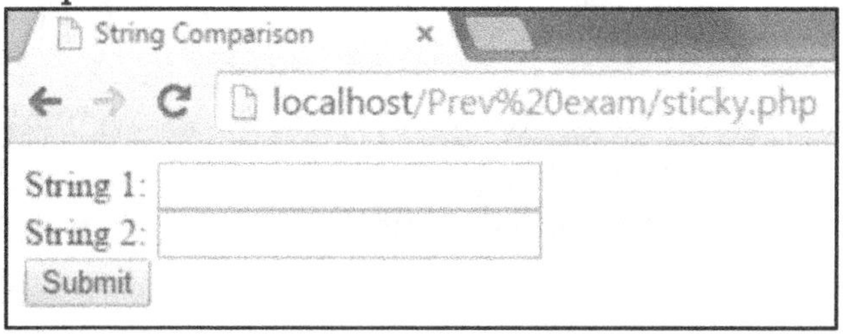

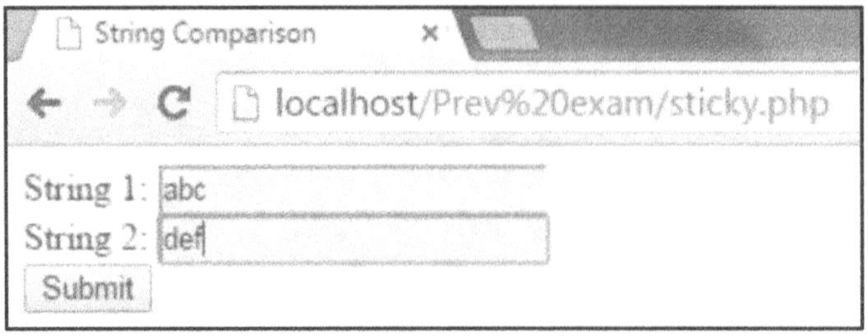

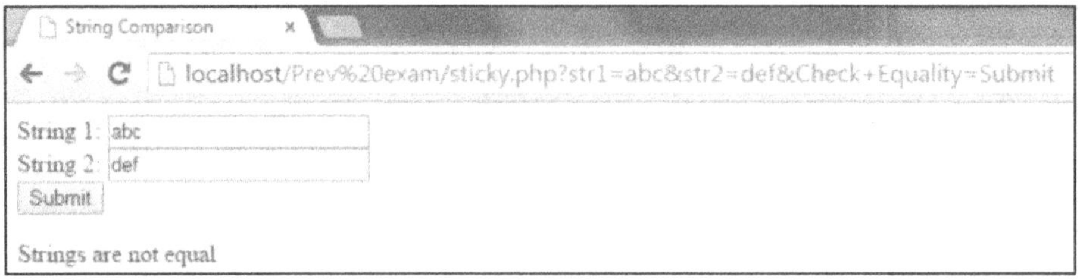

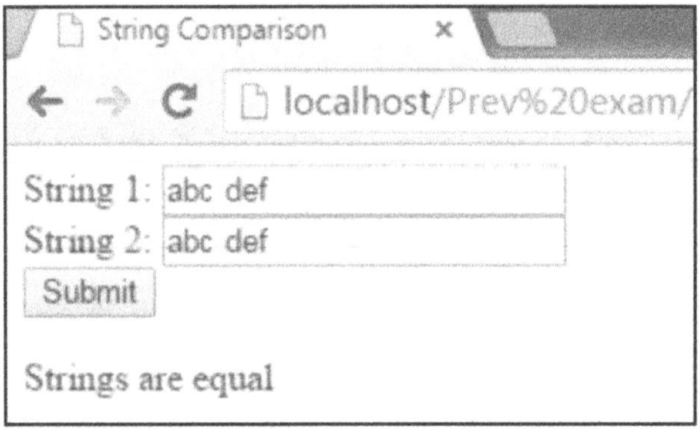

UNIVERSITY QUESTIONS AND ANSWERS

1 Mark Questions:

1. How can you associate a variable with a session? **(April 2013)**

Ans. Refer to Section 1.5.2.

2. How would you destroy session variables both within the current script and the session? **(April 2014)**

Ans. Refer to Section 1.5.2.

3. What is role of $_GET in PHP? **(Oct. 2014)**

Ans. Refer to Section 1.3.1.

5 Mark Questions:

4. Write a short note on cookies. **(April 13, 15)**

Ans. Refer to Section 1.5.1.

5. What is the difference between GET and POST methods in php? Explain it with proper example. **(April 13, 15)**

Ans. Refer to Page 1.8.

6. Write a Php script to accept Employee details (Eno, Ename, Add.) on first page. On second page accept earning (Basic, DA, HRA). On third page Print Employee Information (Eno, Ename, Add, Basic, DA, HRA, total). **(April 2013)**

Ans. 5b2.html

```
<html>
<form action="5b2.php" method="POST">
ENTER THE Emp No: <input type="text" name="no">
<br><br>
ENTER THE Emp Name: <input type="text" name="name">
<br><br>
ENTER THE ADDRESS: <input type="text" name="address">
<br><br>
<input type="submit" value="ok">
</form>
</html>
```

5b2.php

```
<?php
setcookie('name',$_POST['no']);
setcookie('class',$_POST['name']);
setcookie('address',$_POST['address']);
?>
<html>
<form action="5b2a.php" method="POST">
<br>
ENTER THE MARKS: <br><br>
BASIC SALARY: <input type="text" name="basic" size=3>
<br><br>
HRA: <input type="text" name="hra" size=3>
<br><br>
DA: <input type="text" name="da" size=3>
<br><br>
<input type="submit" value="Display Info.">
</form></html>
```

5b2a.php

```
<?php
echo "<br>NAME: ".$_COOKIE["no"];
echo "<br>CLASS: ".$_COOKIE["name"];
echo "<br>ADDRESS: ".$_COOKIE["address"];
echo "<br><br>";
```

```
echo "<table border=1><tr><th>Details</th><th>Values</th></tr>";
echo "<tr><td>Basic</td><td>".$_POST["basic"]."</td></tr>";
echo "<tr><td>HRA</td><td>".$_POST["hra"]."</td></tr>";
echo "<tr><td>DA</td><td>".$_POST["da"]."</td></tr></table>";
echo "<br>";
echo "<br><br>";
$total=$_POST["basic"]+$_POST["hra"]+$_POST["da"];
echo "<br>TOTAL: ".$total;
?>
```

Output:

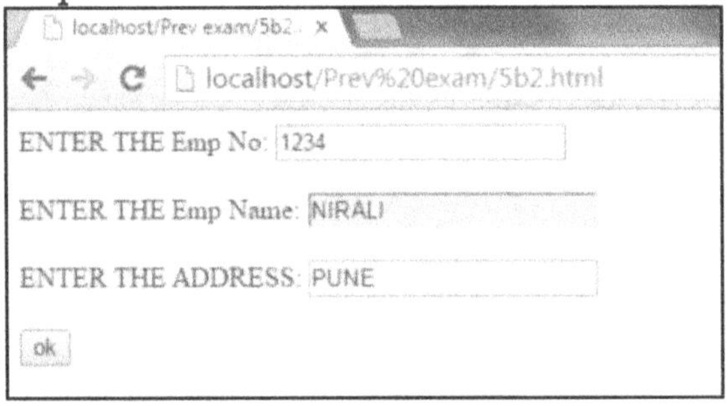

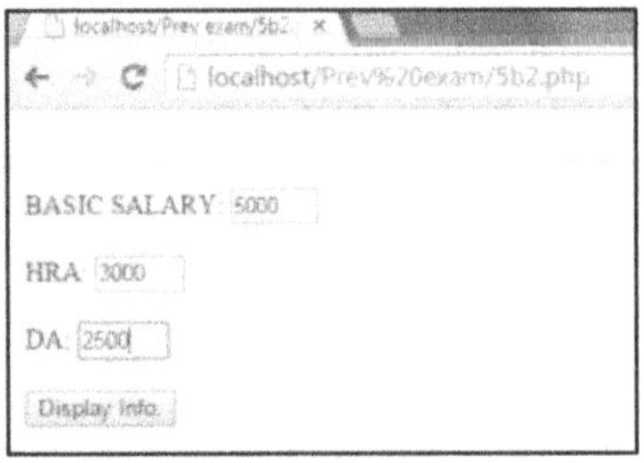

7. Write a script to keep track of number of times the web page has been accessed. **(April 2015)**

Ans. Counter11.html

```
<html>
<head><title>Counter</title></head>
<form method=GET action=counter.php>
```

```
<input type=submit value=submit></input>
</form>
</html>
Counter.php
<?php
    session_start();
    if(isset($_SESSION['cnt']))
    {
        $_SESSION['cnt']+=1;
        echo "You have visited this page".$_SESSION['cnt']."times";
    }
    else
    {
        $_SESSION['cnt']=1;
        echo "You have visited this page {$_session['cnt']} times";
    }
?>
<html>
<body>
<a href="counter.php">Refresh</a>
</body>
</html>
```

Output:

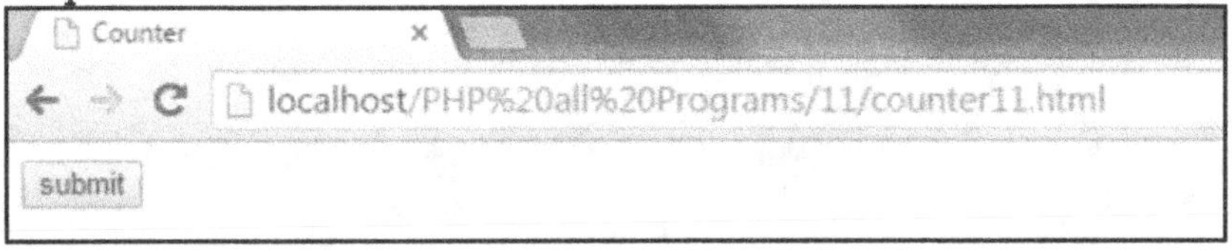

8. Write a php program to convert temperature farhenite to celcius using sticky form. **(Oct. 2014)**

Ans. **Sticky.php**

```
<html>
<head><title>Temperature Conversion</title></head>
<body>
<?php
$fahr = @$_GET['fahrenheit'];
?>
```

```
<form action="<?php echo $_SERVER['PHP_SELF'] ?>" method="GET">
Fahrenheit temperature:
<input type="text" name="fahrenheit" value="<?php echo $fahr ?>" />
<br />
<input type="submit" name="Convert to Celsius!" />
</form>
<?php
if (! is_null($fahr)) {
$celsius = ($fahr - 32) * 5/9;
printf("%.2fF is %.2fC", $fahr, $celsius);
}
?>
</body>
</html>
```

Output:

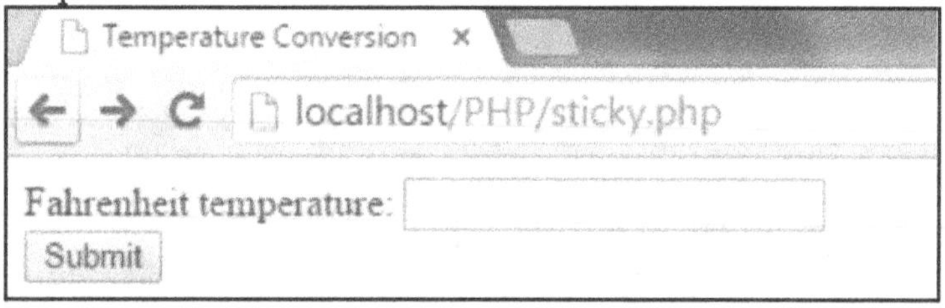

9. Write a php script that uses cookies to remember how long ago a visitor first visited the page. Display value of the page visit in minutes and seconds. (Hint: used time ( ) to find time of cookies). **(Oct. 2014)**

Ans. **Time1.php**

```
<html>
<head><title>Time</title></head>
<body>
<?php
setcookie('access_time',date('H:i:s',time())); //H:i:s is Hr Min Sec
?>
```

```
<form action="<?php echo $_SERVER['PHP_SELF'] ?>" method="GET">
<?php
echo "Current Time: ".date('H:i:s',time());
echo "<br>";
echo "Last access time :";
if(isset($_COOKIE['access_time']))
    echo "".$_COOKIE['access_time'];
echo "<br>";
?>
<input type="submit" name="submit" />
</form>
</body>
</html>
```

Output:

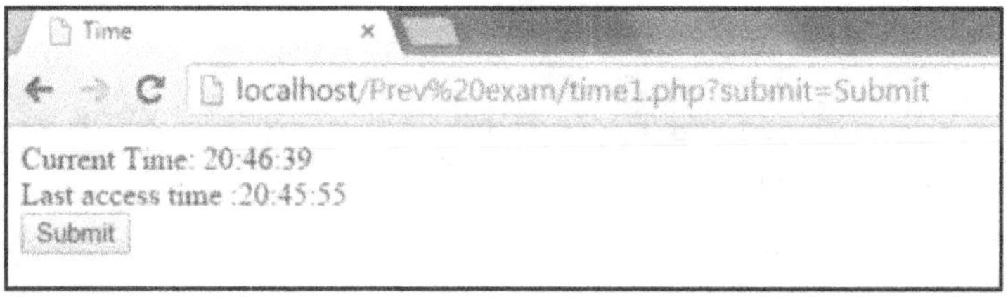

10. What is sticky form? Explain it with suitable example. **(Oct. 2014)**

Ans. Refer to Section 1.3.5.

■■■

CHAPTER 2

Handling Email with PHP

Contents ...

Objectives...

- To Understand Basic Concepts of Email
- To Study Protocols of Email like SMTP, POP3 etc.
- To Learn How to Send a Email through in PHP
- To Understand Error Handling in PHP

2.1 EMAIL BACKGROUND (Oct. 14)

- Email or electronic mail is the fastest method of transferring of messages (called emails or email messages) over computer networks like the Internet.
- PHP built-in support for creating and sending email messages. In PHP, it very easy to send email from within your PHP scripts.
- Originally email was a text-only communication medium. Then it was extended to carry multimedia content attachment called Multipurpose Internet Mail Extensions (MIME). MIME also provides for sending email with attachments.

- Email system is based on client-server architecture. The email server is a machine or group of machines which accepts, forwards, delivers and stores messages. Sender and receiver of the message need not be online at the same time.
- To send an email message in PHP, you use the mail() function. On Unix servers such as Linux and Mac OS X, PHP uses the operating system's built-in Mail Transfer Agent (MTA) to send the email. (Common MTAs include sendmail, postfix, and exim.) On non - Unix servers such as Windows, PHP talks directly to an SMTP mail server (either on the server or on another machine).
- Fig.2.1 shows working of mail system. Which contains following:
  1. **Mail User Agent (MUA):** The MUA is the application the sender(who composes mail) uses to compose and read email, such as Eudora, Outlook, Thunderbird, etc.
  2. **Mail Delivery Agent (MDA):** A mail delivery agent or message delivery agent (MDA) is a computer software component that is responsible for the delivery of e-mail messages to a local recipient's mailbox.
  3. **Mail Transfer Agent (MTA):** A message transfer agent or mail transfer agent (MTA) or mail relay is software that transfers electronic mail messages from one computer to another, using client-server architecture.
  4. **Domain Name System (DNS):** A DNS translates the domain name to IP addresses.

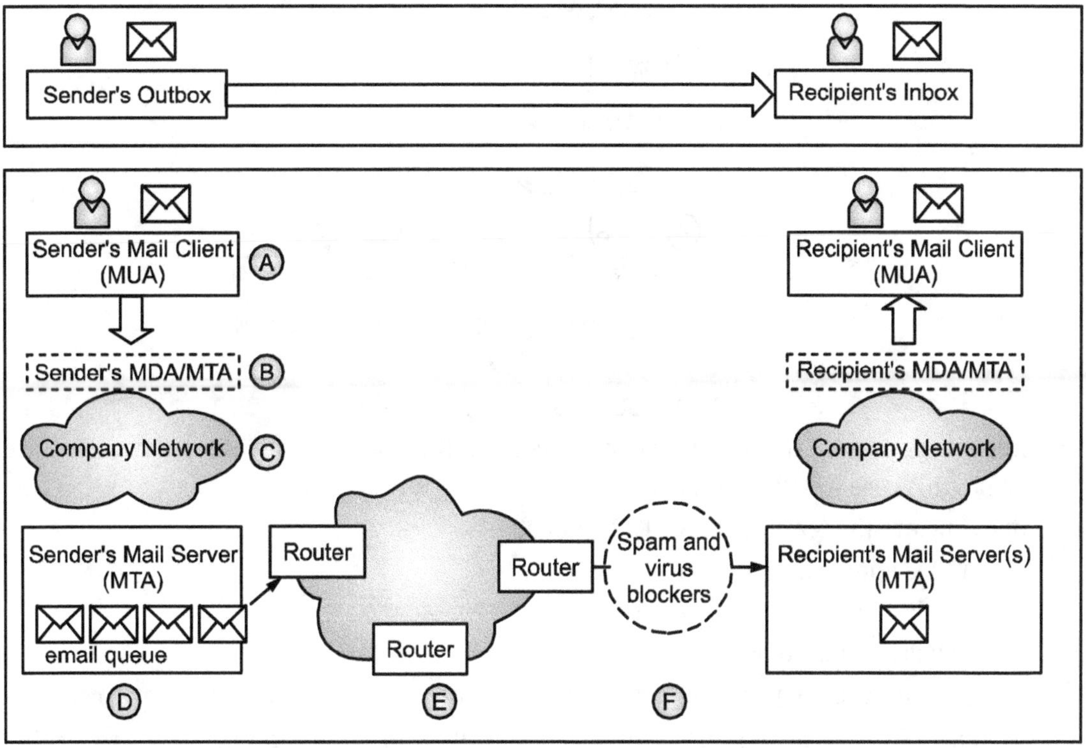

Fig. 2.1: Working of mail system

2.2 INTERNET MAIL PROTOCOLS (Oct. 14, April 16)

- Like any other communications across the Internet, there are protocols involved in mail transmission. These are based on RFCs (Requests For Comment).

1. **SMTP:**

- To send email, SMTP (Simple Mail Transfer Protocol) is used.
- SMTP is the standard protocol for sending emails across the Internet. Port 25 is the default SMTP non-encrypted port.
- The communication model shown in Fig. 2.2 the client uses a SMTP server.
- The server then forward the message to the appropriate receiving SMTP server. Then it will place the message in the appropriate spot i.e. mailbox or popbox.

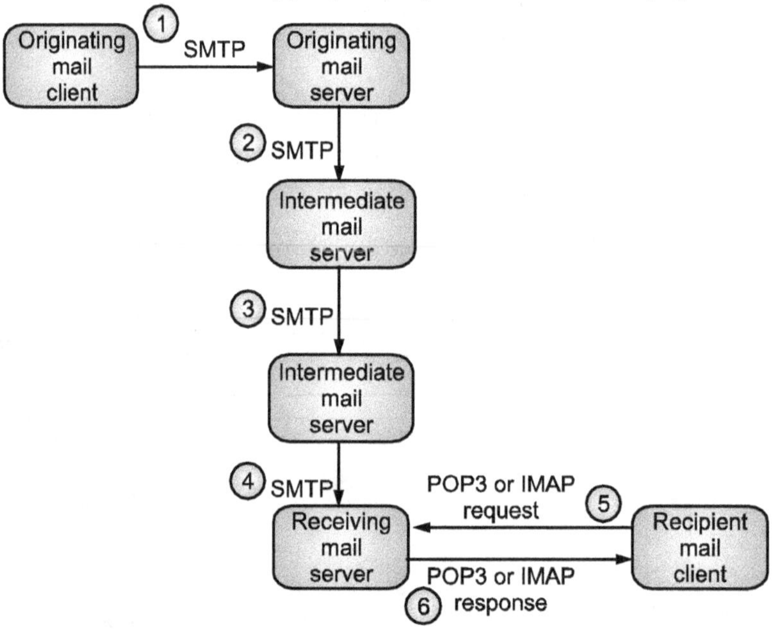

Fig. 2.2: Client used a SMTP Server

- That gets your mail from one server to the next, there are couple of protocols that are used in this case – POP3 and IMAP.
- Following are the features of SMTP Protocol:
  - SMTP is application level protocol.
  - SMTP is connection oriented protocol.
  - SMTP is text based protocol.
  - It handles exchange of messages between e-mail servers over TCP/IP network.
  - Apart from transferring e-mail, SMPT also provides notification regarding incoming mail.

- When you send e-mail, your e-mail client sends it to your e-mail server which further contacts the recipient mail server using SMTP client.
- These SMTP commands specify the sender's and receiver's e-mail address, along with the message to be send.
- The exchange of commands between servers is carried out without intervention of any user.
- In case, message cannot be delivered, an error report is sent to the sender which makes SMTP a reliable protocol.

2. **POP3 (Post Office Protocol 3):**

- POP3 protocol provides a simple, standardized way for users to access mailboxes and download messages to their computers.
- When using the POP protocol all your email messages will be downloaded from the mail server to your local computer. You can choose to leave copies of your emails on the server as well.
- The advantage is that once your messages are downloaded you can cut the internet connection and read your.
- On the other hand you might have transferred a lot of message (including spam or viruses) in which you are not at all interested at this point.
- Following are the features of POP3:
  - POP3 is an application layer internet standard protocol.
  - Since, POP3 supports offline access to the messages, thus requires less Internet usage time.
  - POP3 does not allow search facility.
  - In order to access the messaged, it is necessary to download them.
  - It allows only one mailbox to be created on server.
  - It is not suitable for accessing non mail data.
  - It uses port 110 through Telnet.
  - POP3 server maintains text files for each email account, when a message arrives, the POP3 server appends it to the bottom of the recipient's file.
  - On the successful login, the POP3 server opens user's text file and allow accessing it.

3. **IMAP (Internet Message Access Protocol):** **(April 13)**

- IMAP is a standard protocol for accessing e-mail from your local server.

- IMAP is a client/server protocol in which e-mail is received and held for you by your Internet server. As this requires only a small data transfer this works well even over a slow connection such as a modem. After you request to read a specific email message, then it will be downloaded from the server.
- You can also create and manipulate folders or mailboxes on the server, delete messages etc.
- These perform some sort of authentication before retrieving mail from a remote mail server.
- Following are the features of IMAP:
    - IMAP allows the client program to manipulate the e-mail message on the server without downloading them on the local computer.
    - The e-mail is hold and maintained by the remote server.
    - It enables us to take any action such as downloading, delete the mail without reading the mail.It enables us to create, manipulate and delete remote message folders called mail boxes.
    - IMAP enables the users to search the e-mails.
    - It allows concurrent access to multiple mailboxes on multiple mail servers.

How Combination of These Protocols Works?

- E-mail is delivered over a TCP connection to port 25 of the destination mail server using SMTP. An e-mail daemon, whose job it is to monitor this port, transfers incoming messages from them into the appropriate mailbox.
- If a message cannot be delivered (usually because the named mailbox does not exist on the server) an error report is generated and sent to the incoming message's point of origin.
- The protocol used by a recipient to retrieve mail from their mailbox on the server is POP3, which allows the user to log in and retrieve messages.
- By default, messages that have been downloaded to a recipient's computer are deleted from the server.
- The IMAP is a more sophisticated mail protocol that stores all incoming and outgoing mail on the server so that mail clients with mailboxes on the server can access their e-mail from anywhere.
- Mail is not downloaded to the user's PC, and is only deleted from the client's mailbox if the client specifies that it is to be deleted.

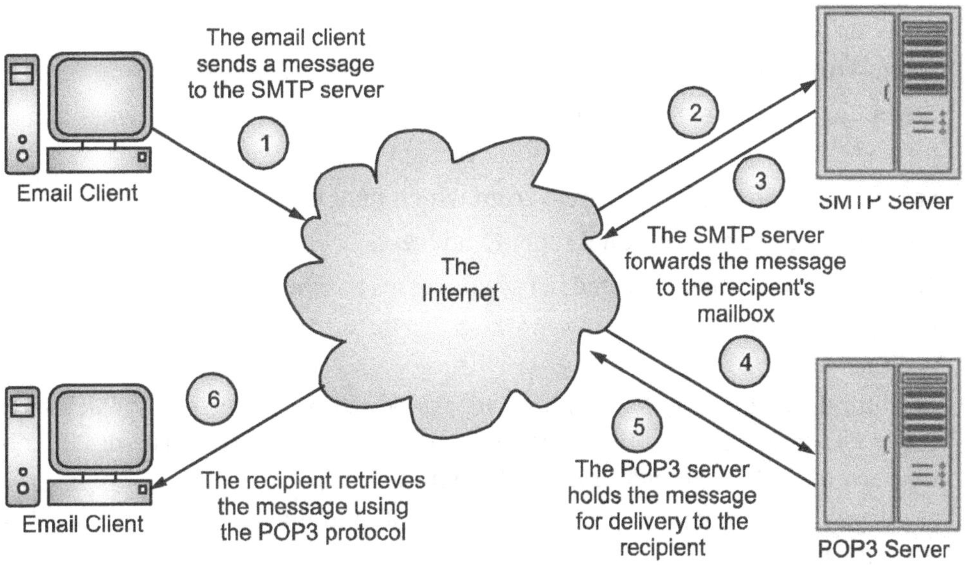

The email client sends a message to the SMTP server
1
2
3
Email Client
SMTP Server
The SMTP server forwards the message to the recipent's mailbox
The Internet
4
6
5
The recipient retrieves the message using the POP3 protocol
The POP3 server holds the message for delivery to the recipient
Email Client
POP3 Server

Fig. 2.3: Internet

- SMTP and POP3 are the protocols most commonly employed in an exchange of email messages.

4. **HTTP:**

- HTTP is the foundation of the modern web. HTTP is at the heart of the Web. It is described in [RFC 1945] and [RFC 2616].
- HTTP is a stateless protocol i.e. HTTP supports only one request per connection. This means that with HTTP the client connects to the server to send one request and then disconnects. This mechanism allows more users to connect to a given server over a period of time.
- Client (also called as HTTP client) and server (also called as HTTP server) communicate by sending messages.

2.3 STRUCTURE OF AN EMAIL MESSAGE

- The structure of Email message consists of Headers followed by body of the message and may also include separate files as attachment.
- RFC 2822 provides definition for the composition of email messages. It defines a message as being composed of ASCII characters divided into lines of characters with each line ending with CRLF (\r\n).
- The header fields are lines of characters separated by a special. The Header field contains field name, a colon, and the field body. The fields order is not important. The only required field is from which contains the origination date and originator address.

- The Header fields are:
    1. **From:** This is required field. It contains the address of the sender.
    2. **Trace:** Includes resent-date, resent-from, resent-to etc. and is used when a message is resent.
    3. **Sender:** Contains a single address from which mail is being sent.
    4. **Reply-to:** Contains an optional reply-to address.
    5. **To:** Contains comma-separated list of addresses to which the message is sent.
    6. **Cc:** Carbon copy (Cc) comma-separated list of addresses to which copies of the message are sent.
    7. **Bcc:** Blind carbon copy (Bcc)comma-separated list of addresses to which copies of the message are sent, while preventing other recipients from seeing or knowing that any other Bcc recipient received the message.
    8. **Message-id:** Optional, but every message should have one. It contain unique message ID.
    9. **In-reply-to:** Optional, one or more message identifier.
    10. **References:** Optional, one or more message Id.
    11. **Subject:** Optional, contains a short string identifying the subject of the message.
    12. **Comments:** Optional, comment about the body of the message.
    13. **Keywords:** Optional, keywords, comma-separated that the user might find important.
    14. **Optional:** Optional, its content is unspecified.

2.4 SENDING EMAIL WITH PHP (April 2016)

- To send email using PHP you must configure the php.ini file with the details of how your system sends email.
- Open the file php.ini and go to the section entitled [mail function].
- Set your SMTP setting:

```
smtp = smtp.my.server.net
```

- Set your sendmail_from seting to reflect your email address:

```
sendmail_from = abc@example.com
```

- Linux users simply need to let PHP know the location of their **sendmail** application. The path and any desired switches should be specified to the sendmail_path directive.
- The configuration for Linux should look something like this:

```
smtp =
sendmail_from =
; for unix only
sendmail_path = /usr/sbin/sendmail -t -i
```

2.4.1 Using the mail( ) Function

- PHP use mail() function to send an email.
- This function requires three mandatory arguments that specify the recipient's email address, the subject of the message and the actual message. Additionally there are other two optional parameters.
- **Syntax:**

```
bool mail (string $to , string $subject , string $message
          [, string $additional_headers [, string $additional_parameters ]] )
```

- Here, is the description for each parameters.

Parameter	Description
to	Required. Specifies the receiver / receivers of the email.
subject	Required. Specifies the subject of the email. This parameter cannot contain any newline characters.
message	Required. Defines the message to be sent. Each line should be separated with a LF (\n). Lines should not exceed 70 characters.
headers	Optional. Specifies additional headers, like From, Cc, and Bcc. The additional headers should be separated with a CRLF (\r\n).
parameters	Optional. Specifies an additional parameter that can be used to pass additional flags as command line options to the program configured to be used when sending mail, as defined by the sendmail_path configuration setting.

Return Values:

- Returns **TRUE** if the mail was successfully accepted for delivery, **FALSE** otherwise.
- Following example will send an email message to xyz@somedomain.com.

```
<?php
   $to = "xyz@somedomain.com";
   $subject = "This is subject";
   $message = "This is simple text message.";
   $header = "From:abc@somedomain.com \r\n";
   if(mail ($to,$subject,$message,$header))
   {
      echo "Message sent successfully...";
   }
   else
   {
      echo "Message could not be sent...";
   }
?>
```

Sending HTML Email:

- When you send a text message using PHP then all the content will be treated as simple text. Even if you will include HTML tags in a text message, it will be displayed as simple text and HTML tags will not be formatted according to HTML syntax. But PHP provides option to send an HTML message as actual HTML message.
- While sending an email message you can specify a Mime version, content type and character set to send an HTML email.
- Following example will send an HTML email message to xyz@somedomain.com copying it to afgh@somedomain.com. You can code this program in such a way that it should recieve all content from the user and then it should send an email.

```
<?php
   $to = "xyz@example.com";
   $subject = "This is subject";
   $message = "<b>This is HTML message.</b>";
   $message .= "<h1>This is headline.</h1>";
   $header = "From:abc@ example.com \r\n";
   $header .= "Cc:afgh@ example.com \r\n";
   $header .= "MIME-Version: 1.0\r\n";
   $header .= "Content-type: text/html\r\n";
   if(mail ($to,$subject,$message,$header))
   {
      echo "Message sent successfully...";
   }
   else
   {
      echo "Message could not be sent...";
   }
?>
```

Example: Sending HTML message to multiple recipients.

```
<?php
// multiple recipients
$to  = 'aidan@example.com' . ', '; // note the comma
$to .= 'wez@example.com';
// subject
$subject = 'Birthday Reminders for August';
```

```
// message
$message = '
<html>
<head>
  <title>Birthday Reminders for August</title>
</head>
<body>
  <p>Here are the birthdays upcoming in August!</p>
  <table>
    <tr>
      <th>Person</th><th>Day</th><th>Month</th><th>Year</th>
    </tr>
    <tr>
      <td>Joe</td><td>3rd</td><td>August</td><td>1970</td>
    </tr>
    <tr>
      <td>Sally</td><td>17th</td><td>August</td><td>1973</td>
    </tr>
  </table>
</body>
</html>
';
// To send HTML mail, the Content-type header must be set
$headers  = 'MIME-Version: 1.0' . "\r\n";
$headers .= 'Content-type: text/html; charset=iso-8859-1' . "\r\n";
// Additional headers
$headers .= 'To: Mary <mary@example.com>, Bianca <bianca@example.com>' .
"\r\n";
$headers .= 'From: Birthday Reminder <birthday@example.com>' . "\r\n";
$headers .= 'Cc: birthdayarchive@example.com' . "\r\n";
$headers .= 'Bcc: birthdaycheck@example.com' . "\r\n";
// Mail it
if(mail ($to,$subject,$message,$header))
   {
      echo "Message sent successfully...";
   }
   else
   {
      echo "Message could not be sent...";
   }
?>
```

2.5 SENDING ATTACHMENTS WITH EMAIL

- To send an email with mixed content requires to set Content-type header to multipart/mixed. Then text and attachment sections can be specified within boundaries.
- Boundary separates the multiple part of the message. It begin with two hyphens (--) followed by a unique number which can not appear in the message part of the email.
- A PHP function md5() is used to create a 32 digit hexadecimal number to create unique number. A final boundary denoting the email's final section must also end with two hyphens (--).
- Attached files should be encoded with the base64_encode() function for safer transmission and are best split into chunks with the chunk_split() function. This adds \r\n inside the file at regular intervals, normally every 76 characters.
- Following is the example which will send a file /tmp/test.txt as an attachment. you can code your program to receive an uploaded file and send it.

```
<html>
<head>
<title>Sending attachment using PHP</title>
</head>
<body>
<?php
  $to = "xyz@example.com";
  $subject = "This is subject";
  $message = "This is test message.";
  # Open a file
  $file = fopen( "/tmp/test.txt", "r" );
  if( $file == false )
  {
     echo "Error in opening file";
     exit();
  }
  # Read the file into a variable
  $size = filesize("/tmp/test.txt");
  $content = fread( $file, $size);
```

```
    # encode the data for safe transit
    # and insert \r\n after every 76 chars.
    $encoded_content = chunk_split( base64_encode($content));

    # Get a random 32 bit number using time() as seed.
    $num = md5( time() );

    # Define the main headers.
    $header = "From:xyz@somedomain.com\r\n";
    $header .= "MIME-Version: 1.0\r\n";
    $header .= "Content-Type: multipart/mixed; ";
    $header .= "boundary=$num\r\n";
    $header .= "--$num\r\n";

    # Define the message section
    $header .= "Content-Type: text/plain\r\n";
    $header .= "Content-Transfer-Encoding:8bit\r\n\n";
    $header .= "$message\r\n";
    $header .= "--$num\r\n";

    # Define the attachment section
    $header .= "Content-Type:  multipart/mixed; ";
    $header .= "name=\"test.txt\"\r\n";
    $header .= "Content-Transfer-Encoding:base64\r\n";
    $header .= "Content-Disposition:attachment; ";
    $header .= "filename=\"test.txt\"\r\n\n";
    $header .= "$encoded_content\r\n";
    $header .= "--$num--";

    # Send email now
    $retval = mail ( $to, $subject, "", $header);
    if( $retval == true )
     {
        echo "Message sent successfully...";
     }
     else
     {
        echo "Message could not be sent...";
     }
?>
</body>
</html>
```

2.6 EMAIL ID VALIDATION AND VERIFICATION (April 15)

- Validation is the process in which we accept data from the user and check it with some predefined standard.
- The email address must follow the RFC 2822 standard.

1. **Validate Email Address using Filters:**

```
<?php
    $email = "xyz@example.com";
if(filter_var($email , FILTER_VALIDATE_EMAIL))
    echo "Email is valid";
else
    echo "Email is not valid";
?>
```

Output:

```
Email is valid
```

2. **Validate Email using Regular Expression Functions:**

- Before checking the email address is valid or not, remove any unnecessary characters from the email address to prevent any malicious attacks by using the htmlspecialchars(), stripslashes(), and strip_tags() functions.
- After that use the regular expression functions ereg() to verify that the email address is in proper format.

```
<?php
    $email_id = "xyz@gmail.com";
    //parse unnecessary characters to prevent exploits
    $email=htmlspecialchars(stripslashes(strip_tags($email_id)));
    //checks to make sure the email address is in a valid format
    if (ereg("^[_a-z0-9-]+(\.[_a-z0-9-]+)*@[a-z0-9]+(\.[a-z0-9]+)*
                                                    (\.[a-z]{2,3})$", $email))
    {
           echo "Email is valid";
    }
}
?>
```

Example: A PHP script to validate given email ID. Design necessary screen layouts.

```
<html>
<head><title>Enter E-mail Data</title></head>
<body>
   <form action="test.php" method="post">
   <table>
      <tr><td>To:</td>
      <td><input type="text" name="to" size="50"></td>
      </tr>
      <tr>
      <td>From:</td>
      <td><input type="text" name="from" size="50"></td>
      </tr>
      <tr>
      <td>Subject:</td><td><input type="text" name="subject" size="50"></td>
      </tr>
      <tr>
      <td valign="top">Message:</td>
      <td>
      <textarea cols="60" rows="10" name="message">
                                          Enter your message here</textarea>
      </td>
      </tr>
      <tr><td></td>
      <td>
      <input type = "Submit" value = "Send" name = "Submit">
      <input type="Reset" value="Reset">
      </td>
      </tr>
   </table>
   </form>
</body>
</html>
```

```
<?php
    $to = $_POST["to"];
    $from = $_POST["from"];
    $subject = $_POST["subject"];
    $message = $_POST["message"];
    if(isset($_POST["Submit"]))
    {
    if (ereg("^[_a-z0-9-]+(\.[_a-z0-9-]+)*@[a-z0-9]+(\.[a-z0-9]+)*
                                                    (\.[a-z]{2,3})$", $to))
        {
            $headers = "From " . $from . "\r\n";
            $mailsent = mail($to, $subject, $message, $headers);
            if ($mailsent)
            {
              echo "Congrats! The following message has been sent: <br><br>";
              echo "<b>To:</b> $to<br>";
              echo "<b>From:</b> $from<br>";
              echo "<b>Subject:</b> $subject<br>";
              echo "<b>Message:</b><br>";
              echo $message;
            }
            else
            {
               echo "There was an error...";
            }
        }
        else
        {
            echo "Email address is invalid";
        }
        }
        ?>
```

Output:

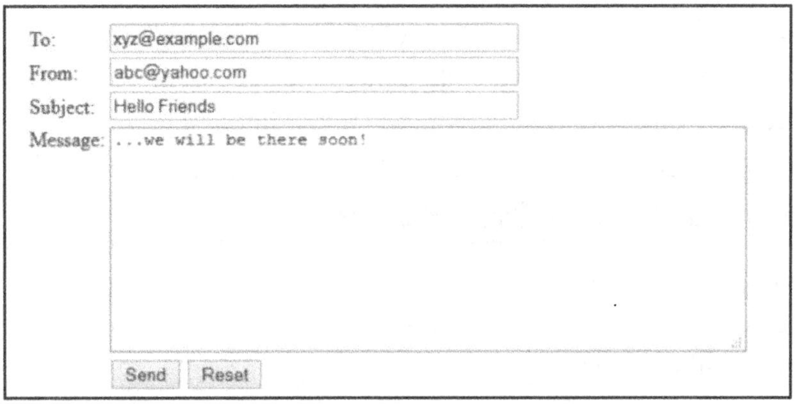

- After you click on Send you will get the following output:
  Congrats! The following message has been sent:
  To: xyz@example.com
  From: abc@yahoo.com
  Subject: Hello Friends
  Message:
  ...we will be there soon!

2.7 PHP ERROR HANDLING

- Error handling is the important part of any program. While creating PHP scripts the errors need to be handled. If your code lacks of error checking, your program may be open to security risks.
- Error handling is the process of catching errors raised by your program and then taking appropriate action.
- It is very simple in PHP to handle errors. An error message with filename, line number and a message describing the error is sent to the browser.
- The first example shows a simple script that opens a text file:

```
<?php
$file=fopen("pragati.txt","r");
?>
```

- If the file does not exist you might get an error message.
- While writing your PHP program you should check all possible error condition and take appropriate action when required.

```
<?php
if(!file_exists("pragati.txt")) {
    die("File not found");
} else {
$file=fopen("pragati.txt","r");
}
?>
```

- Now if the file does not exist you get an error message "File not found" but if the file exists then the file will get open.
- In the above program the error handling mechanism is used, hence, this code is more efficient than the earlier code. The first code is not the right way.
- In the following section some alternative PHP error handler functions are described.

2.7.1 Creating a Custom Error Handler

- In PHP you can define your own error handler function to handle any error.
- Creating a custom error handler is quite simple. We simply create a special function that can be called when an error occurs in PHP.
- To create custom error handler first use the library function set_error_handler(). This function sets a user-defined error handler function.

  Syntax:

```
mixed set_error_handler ( callable $error_handler[, int $error_types =
                                                    E_ALL | E_STRICT ] )
```

  Here, $error_handler contains name of the user defined function, that is used to handle error. Second parameter $error_types is optional.
- The syntax of the user defined function is:

```
bool handler ( int $errno , string $errstr [, string $errfile
                      [, int $errline [, array $errcontext ]]] )
```

- The parameters are described as follows:

Parameter	Description
error_level	Required: Specifies the error report level for the user-defined error. Must be a value number.
error_message	Required: Specifies the error message for the user-defined error.
error_file	Optional: Specifies the file name in which the error occurred.
error_line	Optional: Specifies the line number in which the error occurred.
error_context	Optional: Specifies an array containing every variable and their values in use when the error occurred.

Error Report Levels:

- These error report levels are the different types of error the user-defined error handler can be used for:

Value	Constant	Description
1	E_ERROR	Fatal run-time errors. Execution of the script is halted.
2	E_WARNING	Non-fatal run-time errors. Execution of the script is not halted.
4	E_PARSE	Compile-time parse errors. Parse errors should only be generated by the parser.
8	E_NOTICE	Run-time notices. The script found something that might be an error, but could also happen when running a script normally.
16	E_CORE_ERROR	Fatal errors that occur during PHP's initial startup.
32	E_CORE_WARNING	Non-fatal run-time errors. This occurs during PHP's initial startup.
256	E_USER_ERROR	Fatal user-generated error. This is like an E_ERROR set by the programmer using the PHP function trigger_error().
512	E_USER_WARNING	Non-fatal user-generated warning. This is like an E_WARNING set by the programmer using the PHP function trigger_error().
1024	E_USER_NOTICE	User-generated notice. This is like an E_NOTICE set by the programmer using the PHP function trigger_error().
2048	E_STRICT	Run-time notices. Enable to have PHP suggest changes to your code which will ensure the best interoperability and forward compatibility of your code.
4096	E_RECOVERABLE_ERROR	Catchable fatal error. This is like an E_ERROR but can be caught by a user defined handle.
8191	E_ALL	All errors and warnings, except level E_STRICT (E_STRICT will be part of E_ALL as of PHP 6.0).

Example: Creating a function to handle errors.

```
<?php
    function on_error($num, $str, $file, $line) {
        print "Encountered error $num in $file, line $line: $str\n";
    }
    set_error_handler("on_error");
    print $a;
?>
```

Output:

```
Encountered error 8 in C:\wamp\www\test.php, line 7: Undefined variable: a
```

- The above program first call the function set_error_handler(). Then the set_error_handler() function call on_error() function which display the message with error number, file name, line number and the error message.

2.7.2 Trigger an Error

- In a script where users can input data it is useful to trigger errors when an illegal input occurs. In PHP, this is done by the trigger_error() function.
- In following example an error occurs if the "test" variable is bigger than "1".

```
<?php
    $test=2;
    if ($test>1) {
      trigger_error("Value must be 1 or below");
    }
?>
```

Output:

```
Notice: Value must be 1 or below
in C:\webfolder\test.php on line 6
```

2.7.3 Error Logging

- By default, PHP sends an error log to the server's logging system or a file, depending on how the error_log configuration is set in the php.ini file.
- By using the error_log() function you can send error logs to a specified file or a remote destination.
- Sending error messages to yourself by e-mail can be a good way of getting notified of specific errors.

SUMMARY

- Email is way to transfer digital messages over internet.
- MIME (Multipurpose Internet Mail Extension) is introduced to carry multimedia data via e-mail.
- Internet Mail Protocol is set of standard rules that are followed by communication channel at both the ends.
- Commonly used protocols are POP3 (Post office Protocol 3) (Used to receive e-mails, access mail box and download e-mails), IMAP (Internet Mail Access Protocol) (A standard protocol to receive and access e-mails), SMTP (Simple Mail Transfer Protocol) (Used to send e-mails over the network). HTTP (Hyper Text Transfer Protocol) (This protocol Defines that how e-mails are transmitted and formatted).
- E-mail can be divided in two components i.e., Message Header (describes Sender and Receiver of email and some additional information) and Message Body (contains actual message/information which to be send).
- mail() is the function provided by PHP to send email through PHP scripts. Some configuration is required.
- To send an attachment sending file is required and file needs to converted in compatible format of standard email.
- Sending email requires validation and verification of email address i.e., whether email id is in correct format or not. It can be done by using filters or by using regular expression through eregi().

PRACTICE QUESTIONS

1. What is email?
2. What is SMTP?
3. Which protocols are used to retrieve the mail from server?
4. What is the function of MTA?
5. Which is required field in header message?
6. What is the header field?
7. Which server is used to send the emails?
8. What are the arguments of mail() function?
9. Explain structure of email message.
10. Explain header fields in email message.
11. Explain in brief how to send an email.
12. Write a PHP function to validate the email.
13. Write a complete PHP script to accept email from user and check it is valid or not.

14. State the SMTP protocol.

Ans. Refer to Section 2.2, Point (2).

15. Which are the two parts while message are sent using SMTP?

Ans. Refer to Section 2.2, Point (1).

16. 'SMTP protocol is used to send email'. Justify True/False.

Ans. Refer to Section 2.2, Point (1).

17. Explain the structure of an email message.

Ans. Refer to Section 2.3.

18. Which are the internet protocols used for mail handling? Explain any one in brief.

Ans. Refer to Section 2.2.

UNIVERSITY QUESTIONS AND ANSWERS

1 Mark Questions:

1. Which protocols are used to retreive mail from the server? **(Oct. 2014)**

Ans. Refer to Section 2.2.

5 Mark Questions:

2. When IMAP4 protocol is used in email handling? **(April 2013)**

Ans. Refer to Section 2.2, Point (3).

3. Write a PHP script to accept email address and validate it. Also print domain name of the email and result of validation. **(April 2013)**

Ans. **Emailvalidation.html**

```
<html>
<head><title>email validation</title></head>
<body>
<form action="validate.php" method="GET">
Enter Email ID : <input type="text" name="eid"></input>
<br><input type="submit" name="submit">
</form>
</body>
</html>
```

Validate.php

```
<?php
$emailid=$_GET['eid'];
if(filter_var($emailid, FILTER_VALIDATE_EMAIL))
{
    echo "valid emailid";
    echo "<br>";
    $arr=explode("@",$emailid,2);
    echo "domain name : $arr[1]";
}
else
{
    echo "Invalid EmailId";
}
?>
```

Output:

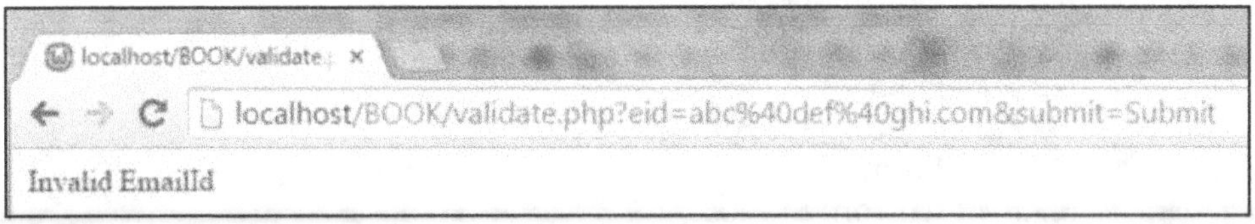

4. Explain E-mail-id validation and verification. **(April 2015)**

Ans. Refer to Section 2.6.

5. Explain how message can be send on Email Server? **(Oct. 2014)**

Ans. Refer to Section 2.1.

■■■

CHAPTER 3

PHP Framework

Contents ...

Objectives...

- To Understand PHP Framework
- To Study Drupal

3.0 INTRODUCTION TO PHP FRAMEWORK

- PHP development is on the rise and more than 50% of web development mostly preferred PHP.
- PHP is an open source, freely available scripting language, ability to work on various OS (Operating System) and ease in integration with several types of databases.
- MVC framework adds up to the beauty of PHP programming and makes it easier for the developer to build robust programs using the classic features of MVC framework.
- However, there are dozens of MVC frameworks at your disposal which can add up to confusion. Therefore, choosing the right PHP framework can be a really daunting task at times.
- Fig. 3.1 shows MVC Framework of PHP.

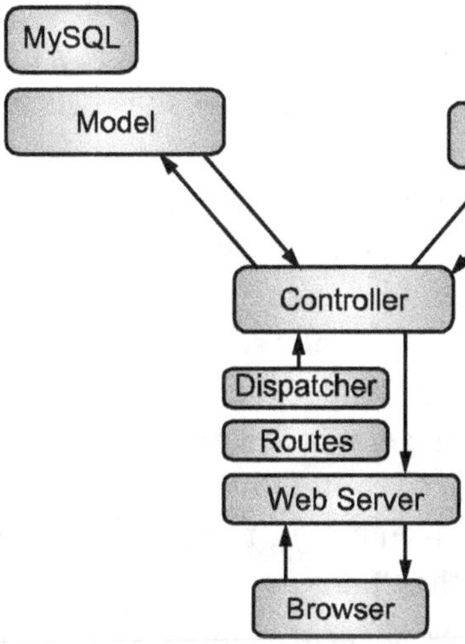

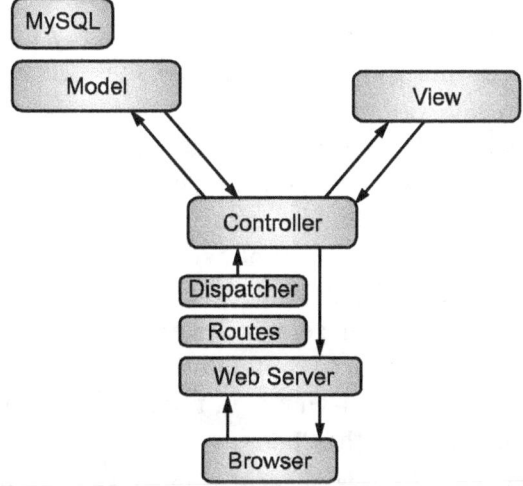

Fig. 3.1: Model View Controller (MVC) Framework

- The Model View Controller architecture primarily reduces the burden of the developers by providing a lucid and presentable coding pattern.
- Its segregation into different parts makes it easier for the programmer to write structured and neat code.
- The segmented feature helps a new developer in understanding the codes easily and also helps in tracing the bugs easily.
- In MVC model:
  1. **Model (M):** This is the one who knows all about data and databases. It is responsible to represent the data in the application.
  2. **View (V):** This section is in-charge of displaying the data to the user. It takes inputs from the Model to display the desired output to the user.
  3. **Controller(C):** Controller acts as an interface between the View and the Model and commands the Model to perform the appropriate action as requested by the user.

3.1 CONTENT MANAGEMENT SYSTEM (CMS)

- A few years back, the only way to develop a website was to write all the HTML and CSS codes by hand. Now a day using content management systems we can develop website quickly without writing HTML and CSS.
- The system will allow you to "build" your website, using a wide selection of different plugins and ad on´s available for the various systems.
- In addition you are able download ready-made themes and templates for your CMS website, and you can then ad content.
- Many content management systems, especially open source, are built using PHP and MySQL.
- Following are some example of content management system:
  1. **Wordpress:** Wordpress is a straight forward and easy to use system, supporting both personal blogs and fully functional websites. There are many Plugins for Wordpress. It is free.
  2. **Drupal:** Drupal is both a framework and a content management system, hence, Drupal is a Content Management Framework.

     Drupal is powerful and all round system. It is build using modules, which can easily be adapted for all your personal needs. There are also a wide selection of plugins and adons available for Drupal. Drupal will take a bit longer to master, compared to other content management systems.
  3. **Joomla:** It is free and open-source content management system for publishing web content. It is built on a model–view–controller web application framework that can be used independently of the CMS.

     Joomla is written in PHP, uses Object-Oriented Programming (OOP), and stores data in a MySQL, or PostgreSQL database. It includes features such as page caching, RSS feeds, printable versions of pages, news flashes, blogs, search, and support for language internationalization.

     There are a many professional themes and plugins available for purchase. Joomla can be used to build a wide range of different website types. Especially static websites including blog features, polls, news feeds and search functions are very easy to manage and implement in Joomla.

3.2 DRUPAL

3.2.1 Introduction

- When you plan to build a website, your site will have content; be it audio or text or animated images etc. A website communicates its content to the world. You will also need to manage this content.

- Although it's possible to develop website using your own system with enough knowledge of the underlying web technologies, Drupal makes creating your website, adding new features, and day-to-day editing of content quick and easy. And finally, your website will have visitors.
- Hence, Drupal is a Content Management System (CMS), which is used to create website with forum, static page, blog and manage the content online.
- Drupal is free and open source software governed by the GNU General Public License.
- Drupal was first released to the public by Dries Buytaert in 2001.The name Drupal is derived from the Dutch word druppel which means "drop."
- Building a website in Drupal is a matter of combining together various "building blocks", in order to customize your website's functionality to your needs. Once website is built, it can be maintained through the use of online forms, without any code having to be changed manually.
- Drupal is free to use, and it has an enormous library of constantly evolving tools that you can use to make your website shine.
- Drupal is also a Content Management Framework (CMF). In addition to providing site building tools for webmasters, it offers ways for programmers and developers to customize Drupal using plug-in modules.

3.2.2 Features

- Drupal provides a number of features. These include:
  1. **Flexible module system:** Modules are plug-ins that can modify and add features to a Drupal site. For almost any functional need, chances are good that either an existing module fits the need exactly or can be combined with other modules to fit the need, or that whatever existing code there is can get you a good chunk of the way there.
  2. **Customizable theming system:** All output in Drupal is fully customizable, so you can bend the look and feel of your site to your will (or, more precisely, to your designer's will).
  3. **Extensible content and entity system:** You can define new types of content (blogs, events, words of the day) on the fly, and even add custom fields for the different content types. Contributed modules can extend this even further by providing new kinds of fields and different ways to manipulate them. Best of all, these fields can also be attached to anything in the system representing itself as an entity, such as users, comments, and taxonomy (categories).
  4. **Innate search engine optimization:** Drupal offers out-of-the-box support for human-readable system URLs, and all of Drupal's output is standards-compliant; both of these features make for searchengine-friendly websites. There are also other contributed modules that take SEO capabilities even further.

5. **Role-based access permissions:** Custom roles and a plethora of permissions allow for fine-grained control over who can access what within the system. And existing modules can take this level of access control even further—down to the individual user level.
6. **Social publishing and Collaboration tools:** Drupal has built-in support for tools such as group blogging, comments, forums, and customized user profiles. The addition of almost any other feature you can imagine—for instance, ratings, user groups, or moderation tools—is only a download away.

3.2.3 How Pages are Built?

- User request a Web page is translated by the Web server into a file on the Web server.
- In Drupal's case, this file retrieves content from the database and assembles a Web page. This is known as the bootstrap process.
- Drupal dumps this content into pages that have been built using modules and designed by themes.
- Once it's assembled, the Web page is returned to the user.
- The Web page will have references to images, style sheets, and interactive scripts. Once the Web browser has the page that Drupal built, it will return to the server to request all of these additional resources.
- Before it is installed, Drupal is just a series of text files written in PHP. When you install Drupal, a relationship is created between these text files and a database on your Web server. The database will store your content and most of the configuration information for your site.
- Within the package of Drupal files there is also a special theme directory that contains design files for your Web site. These are also text files, but they are written in PHP, HTML, CSS, and JavaScript. Packages of design files are referred to as themes. When building a page, Drupal combines these files.

3.2.4 Installing Drupal

1. **Server Requirements:** To run Drupal 7 you need:
   (i) Apache (version 2.0 or Greater).
   (ii) PHP 5 (5.2.0 or Greater), MySQL (5.0 or Greater) or PostgreSQL (8.3 or Greater) or SQLite (3.4.2 or Greater).
2. **Download and extract files:** Download Drupal from http://drupal.org/project/drupal and extract the files (tar or zip). After extracting, move the folder into the Web server's document root (C:\wamp\www or /var/www/html).

3. **Create the configuration file and Grant permissions:** Create a configuration file named settings.php by copying the file named default.settings.php in the sites/default directory.

```
cp sites/default/default.settings.php sites/default/settings.php
```

Give the web server write privileges (644 or) to the configuration file.

```
chmod a+w sites/default/settings.php
```

So that the files directory can be created automatically, give the web server write privileges to the sites/default directory.

```
chmod a+w sites/default
```

4. **Run the script:** Open the web browser and type the URL of the script index.php in the Drupal folder.On the Select an installation profile page, select Standard. Click Save and continue, (See Fig. 3.2).

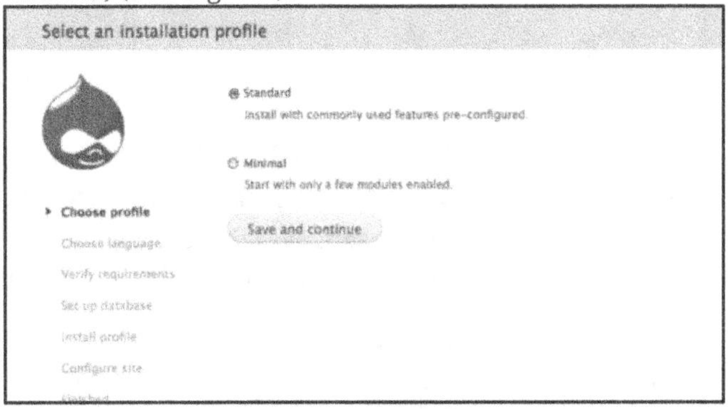

Fig. 3.2: Run the script

On the Choose language page, select English. Click Save and continue.

5. **Create the Drupal database:** You must create a new, empty database for Drupal to use. You must also add a user who has full access to this newly created database.

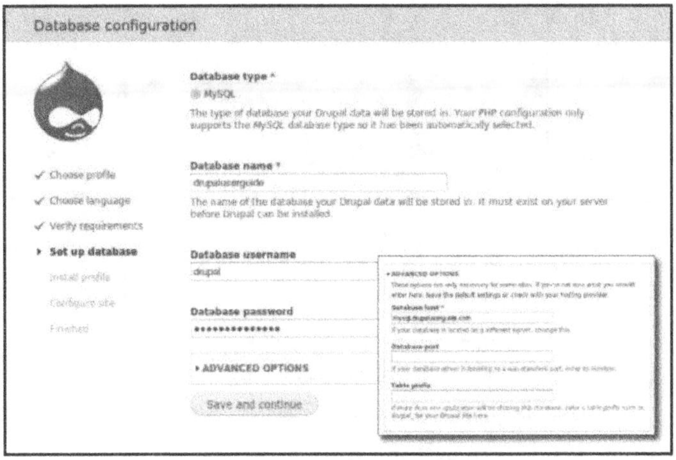

Fig. 3.3: Create the Drupal database

Select Database type; enter your database name, database user name, and its password. If your database host name is something other than localhost, click the advanced link and complete the inset image portion of the form in the Fig. 3.3.

6. With your database information entered, click "Save and continue" to install Drupal. Fig. 3.4 shows the status bar that will appear as your Drupal installation is automatically configured.

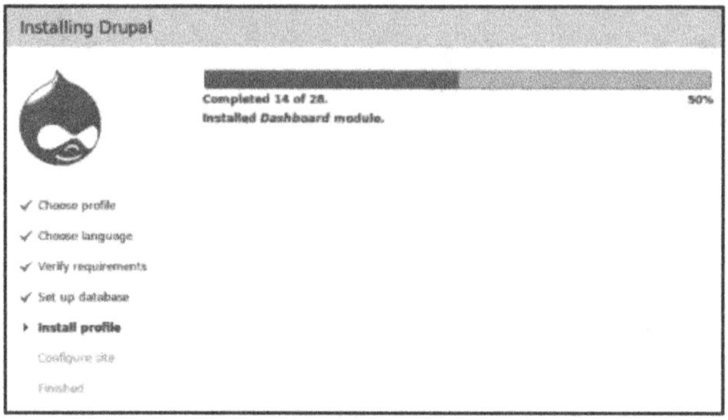

Fig. 3.4: Status bar in Drupal

7. Once, Drupal is installed, you will need to create a site maintenance account and configure some basic administrative settings. Fig. 3.5 shows the site configuration screen. Complete each section using the most appropriate options for your Web site.

Fig. 3.5: Configuration screen

Drupal is now installed and configured for basic use. You will be redirected to the front page of your Web site as shown in Fig. 3.6.

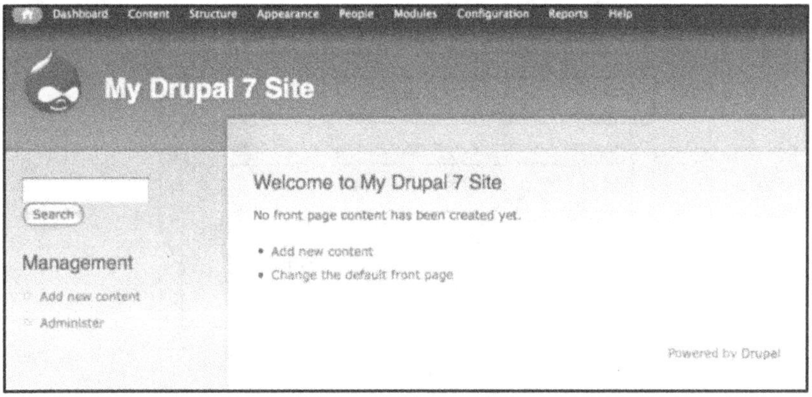

Fig. 3.6: Installed the Drupal

3.2.5 How Does Drupal Work?

- At a conceptual level, the Drupal stack looks like Fig. 3.7. Drupal is a sort of middle layer between the backend (PHP, Database, Web server) and the frontend (what visitors see in their web browsers- HTML, CSS, JavaScript).
- In the bottom layers, things like operating system, web server, database, and PHP are there. The operating system performs low-level tasks such as handling network connections, files, and file permissions.
- Web server provides the web pages of your web site. A database stores all of the website's content, user accounts, and configuration settings. And PHP is used to generate pages dynamically and shuffles information from the database to the web server.
- Drupal itself is composed of many layers. Its lowest layer adds several subsystems, such as user session handling and authentication, security filtering, and template rendering.
- Modules add features to Drupal and generate the contents of any given page. But before the page is displayed to the user, it's run through the theme system, which allows modification as per the designers' needs.
- The theme system outputs page content, usually as XHTML or HTML5.
- CSS is used to control the layout, colors, and fonts of a given page, and JavaScript is thrown in for dynamic elements, such as collapsible fieldsets on forms and drag-and-drop table rows in Drupal's administrative interface.
- Building a website using static HTML files, and the collections of scripts is the "old" way. The "new" way is Drupal's way where you build website using a new set of conceptual building blocks, such as Modules, nodes, blocks, themes etc. These building blocks are explained in the next section.

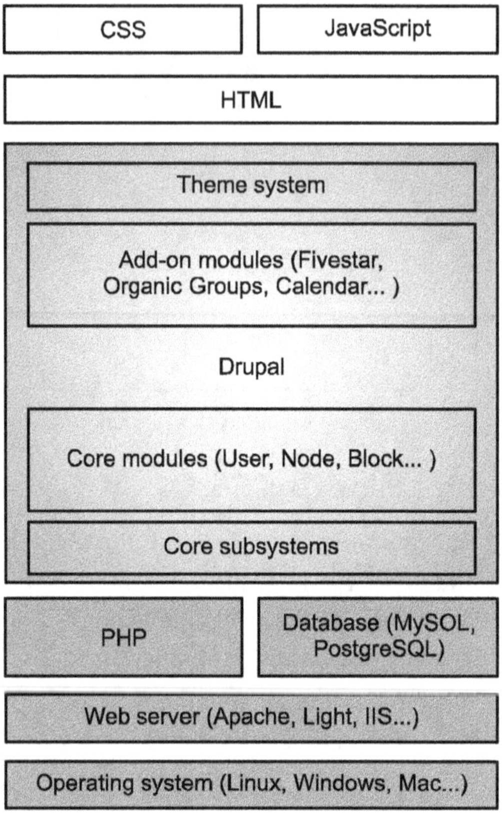

Fig. 3.7: Drupal Structure

3.2.6 Drupal Administration

- You have installed Drupal; it's now time to turn to the administration area of your new Web site. You can perform administrative task such as configuring modules, working with content types, and setting up site navigation etc.
- In every Drupal installation there is both a public version of your Web site and a private, administrative area. Once, you have entered your user name and administrative password, you will have access to the screens described in this section.
- Once, you have logged into your site, you will see a set of toolbars appear across the top of your site. These toolbars are visible only to site visitors who are logged in and have been granted permission to view the toolbar.
- Fig. 3.8 shows the administrative toolbar visible throughout your site.

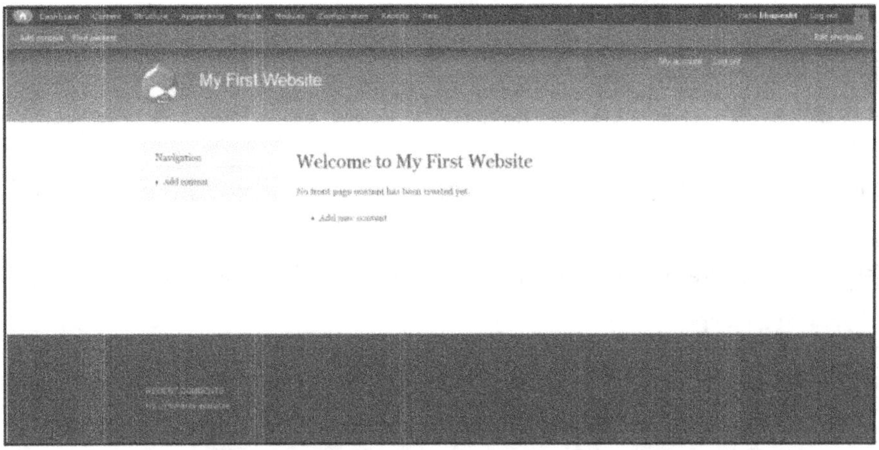

Fig. 3.8: Drupal home page showing administrative toolbar

- There are four parts to the administrative interface. As discussed below:
  1. The **toolbar** is visible across the very top of your Web site. It lists the main sections of the administrative area and provides a link to your account and an option to log out of the Web site. It cannot be customized.
  2. **Shortcuts** are available below the toolbar. This is a list of links within your Web site that you would like to have available. You can use the default links or create a personal set of shortcuts.
  3. The **dashboard** provides you with a summary of what's happening on your Web site. You can configure it to display any available blocks for your Web site.
  4. The **overlay** allows you to edit content, administer modules, and do just about any other administrative task without leaving your current page.

3.2.6.1 Administrative Toolbar

- The administrative toolbar provides links to the nine main sections within the administrative area of the site described as follows:
  1. **Dashboard:** This new feature is highly customizable. It starts with the following components: "Recent content," "Search form," and "Who's new." You can customize the dashboard to include additional, relevant administrative shortcuts.
  2. **Content:** Administer content you have created and comments that visitors have left on your Web site.
  3. **Structure:** To administer menus, content types, and blocks (the stuff that shows up in sidebars), you will use the Structure menu.
  4. **Appearance:** To change your site looks.
  5. **People:** Most basic Web sites are managed by a single person. When your team grows larger or if you have a community site where you have multiple participants, you will spend a lot of time in this area of the administrative section.

6. **Modules:** Drupal itself is a pluggable architectural framework. It allows you to plug in new functionality.
7. **Configuration:** You can change any of the settings you chose during the installation.
8. **Reports:** From this menu option you can view reports, site errors, and available updates.
9. **Help:** You will get references of usage, configuration and modules.

3.2.6.2 Dashboard

- Drupal allows you to completely customize the main administration page using blocks.
- When you create a new menu then for each menu a new block is created.
- Dashboard actually contains blocks.
- Dashboard should be customized to include information that is useful to you.

3.2.6.3 Configuration

- The configuration link is used to alter the setting of your website. There are many configuration screens e.g.,
  1. Configuration > System > Site information
  2. Configuration > Regional and Language > Regional settings
  3. Configuration > Regional and Language > Date and time etc.
- Navigate to the "Site information" configuration screen. The "Site information" configuration screen allows you to customize the following:
  1. **Site name:** The name of your site is included on all page titles.
  2. **Slogan:** This is a subtitle for your site. Depending on your theme, this will display beside or below the site name. The slogan does not typically appear in the page title.
  3. **E-mail address:** This is used to send automated email by the system during the registration process.
  4. **Number of posts on front page:** This number controls the number of items that will appear on the front page of the Web site. Additional posts will be grouped by this number too. For example, if you have 20 posts and "Number of posts on front page" is set to 10, there will be 2 pages of 10 posts each.
  5. **Default front page:** By default this is set to "node," which will publish new content that has been marked as "Promoted to front page."
  6. **Default 403 (access denied) page:** When site visitors do not have sufficient permissions to access a page, they will see a generic "access denied" message. This setting allows you to customize the page that is displayed.

7. **Default 404 (not found) page:** When site visitors arrive at a URL on your site that does not exist, they will see a generic "page not found" message. This setting allows you to customize the page that is displayed. Additional display options, such as the site logo and colours, are adjusted from within the theme.

3.2.7 Web Site Basics

- After you install Drupal, now you can add content to your new Web site. This content type is the basic building block of any Drupal Web site.
- The content type includes a title and some kind of "body" content. Images may also be embedded with the content. Examples of basic content include static pages that rarely change, such as content about the company, a returns policy, shipping information, and legal pages (terms of service or a privacy policy) etc.
- Drupal provides two types of content by default i.e. Article and Basic page.
  1. Article is appropriate for blog like entries on your site.
  2. Basic page is appropriate for pages that are not time-sensitive and that are more "persistent." An example of a Basic page is an About page.

3.2.7.1 Creating Basic Pages

- Most of the pages you create on your Web site are Basic pages. Basic pages are used to create static pages that follow the basic content pattern.
- Basic pages have the following antifeatures:
  1. Are not published to the front page of your Web site?
  2. Do not allow visitors to post comments?
  3. Do not have tagging enabled?
  4. Do not have an image upload widget?
  5. Are not date-stamped?
- To create a Basic page use the following steps:

  Step 1 : From the shortcut menu, click the link "Add content." An overlay will appear.

  Step 2 : You can choose between Article and Basic page.

  Step 3 : Click "Basic page."

  Step 4 : Enter a title and body for your page.

  Step 5 : If you want, you can add a link of your Basic page in the Main Menu after selecting the checkbox "Provide a menu link".

  Step 6 : Scroll to the bottom and click Save.

Fig. 3.9: Creating Basic Page

3.2.7.2 Creating Articles

- Articles are stories may be used as a personal blog or for news articles. Depending on the type of site you have, this may include promotional information about upcoming events or summaries of things that have already passed.
- To create a new front-page story (Article), you will use the content type Article. This content type has the following features.
  1. Summary posted to the front page of the Web site.
  2. Comments enabled.
  3. Option to upload an image to be displayed with the article.
  4. User name of the article author as well as the time it was originally published.
  5. Tags enabled, allowing you to categorize articles.
- To create an article, use the following steps:

  Step 1 : From the shortcut menu, click the link "Add content." An overlay will appear.

  Step 2 : Choose between Article and Basic page.

Step 3 : Click Article. An editing form will appear as in the previously displayed Figure 4.6.

Step 4 : Enter a title and body content.

Step 5 : Enter keywords about your article in the section labeled Tags. This step is optional.

Step 6 : For your first article, you do not need to change any defaults listed at the bottom of the screen. You can scroll past this section.

Step 7 : Scroll to the bottom and click Save.

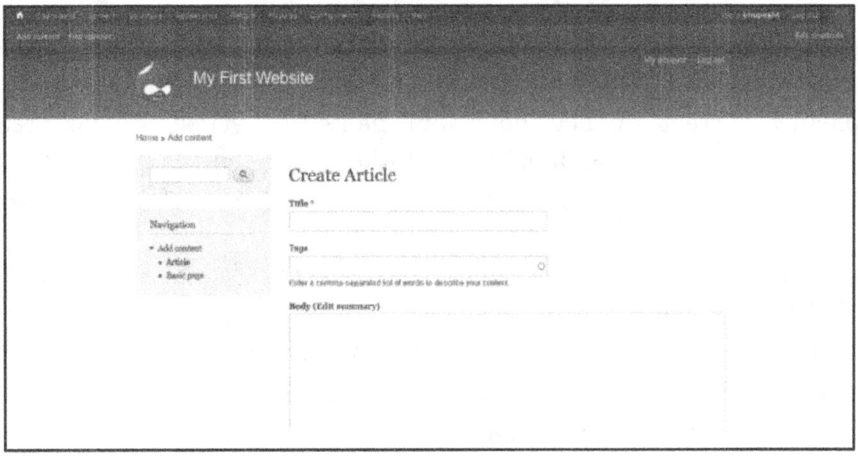

Fig. 3.10: Create Article

- Your article will be added automatically to the front page of the Web site. Beside the title of the new page are two links: View and Edit. To alter the text of your article, click the Edit link. Web site visitors will not see the link to edit your page.

3.2.7.3 Creating Blog Entry

- Blog entries are much like the core content type Article; however, additional functionality is built into the module to permit multiuser blogs. Every user gets a personal blogs.
- By default new blog entries are as follows:
  1. Published and promoted to the front page.
  2. Enabled for comments.
  3. Not version controlled (that is, revisions are not created and saved).
- To create a Blog entry, use the following steps:

Step 1 : From the shortcut menu, click the link "Add content." An overlay will appear.

Step 2 : Click on "Blog entry".

Step 3 : Enter a title and body for your page.

Step 4 : If you want, you can add a link of your Blog entry in the Main Menu after selecting the checkbox "Provide a menu link".

Step 5 : Scroll to the bottom and click Save.

- By default Blog entry link is not enabled. To enable this content type, you must enable the core module Blog from Module Menu. You can easily extend this content type to include an image field and tags.

3.2.7.4 Creating Book Page

- Book pages are used to create static pages that follow the basic content pattern and that have hierarchical content.
- It automatically creates a new navigation block for each new book created. This content type is used for handbooks or tutorials. This content type is well suited to creating structured, multi-page content, such as site resource guides, manuals, and wikis.
- It allows you to create content that has chapters, sections, subsections, or any similarly-tiered structure.
- By dcfault new entries made from this content type are as follows:
  1. Are published but not promoted to the front page?
  2. Accept user-contributed comments?
  3. Are not version controlled (that is, revisions are not created and saved)?
- To create a Book page, use the following steps:

  Step 1 : From the shortcut menu, click the link "Add content". An overlay will appear.

  Step 2 : Click on "Book page".

  Step 3 : Enter a title and body for your page.

  Step 4 : If you want, you can add a link of your Book page in the Main Menu after selecting the checkbox "Provide a menu link".

  Step 5 : Scroll to the bottom and click Save.

- By default Blog entry link is not enabled. To enable this content type, you must enable the core module Book from Module Menu. You can easily extend the content type to include additional fields once it has been enabled.

3.2.7.5 Creating Forum Topic

- A forum topic starts a discussion thread within a forum. People can then discuss this topic by adding their comments to it.
- Forums consist of at least three levels of structure: comments that respond to topics that are sorted into forums.

- By default new forum topics are as follows:
  1. Published but not promoted to the front page,
  2. Enabled for comments, and
  3. Not version controlled (that is, revisions are not created and saved).
- To create a Forum topic, use the following steps:

  Step 1 : From the shortcut menu, click the link "Add content". An overlay will appear.

  Step 2 : Click on "Forum topic".

  Step 3 : Enter subject and body, select a value for Forum.

  Step 4 : If you want, you can add a link of your Forum topic in the Main Menu after selecting the checkbox "Provide a menu link".

  Step 5 : Scroll to the bottom and click Save.
- By default Blog entry link is not enabled. To enable this content type, you must enable the core module Book from Module Menu. Forum topics are sometimes extended to include the ability to upload a relevant file or image for discussion. To control forums hierarchy setting, navigate to Administration > Structure > Forums.

3.2.7.6 Creating Polls

- Poll is used to create simple survey that displays cumulative results.
- A poll is a good way to receive feedback from site users and community members.
- To create a new poll on your site, first enable the Poll module and then complete the following steps:

  Step 1 : From the administration shortcut, click the link "Add content" and choose Poll.

  Step 2 : Enter a question and possible responses (Fig. 3.11). You can change the order of the responses by dragging and dropping the fields into a new position.

  Step 3 : In the poll settings fieldset, you can adjust the poll status to be open or closed.

  Step 4 : You can also set the poll to automatically close after a specific amount of time by altering the drop-down box "Poll duration."

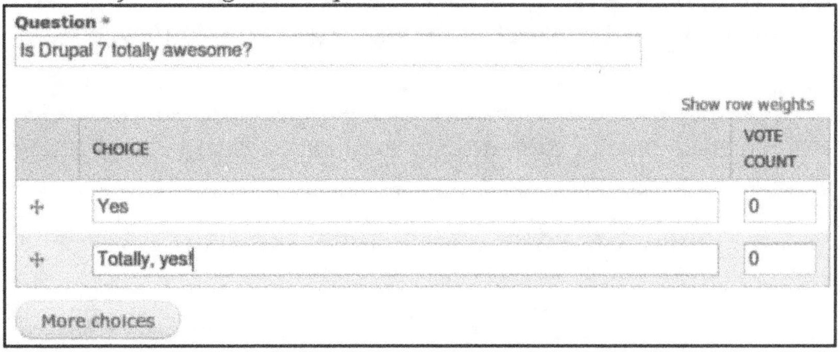

Fig. 3.11: Create Polls

Step 5 : By default site visitors can comment on your poll. If you want to disable this, scroll to the Comment settings, and change the setting to "closed."

Step 6 : You can publish the poll, as a node, to the front page of your site by adjusting the settings within the node. If you prefer to put the poll into a sidebar of your site (Fig. 3.11), navigate to the Blocks administration page (Administration > Structure > Blocks) and change the region for the block labeled "Most recent poll" to one that is appropriate for your theme.

- By default only administrators can read, vote, and view results on polls. To open your polls to a wider audience, navigate to Administer > People > Polls.
- Adjust the permissions for the content type polls and the poll-specific settings:
- "Vote on polls," "Cancel and change own votes," and "View voting results."
- Once, the poll has been created, site visitors can start voting on your site and viewing the results (Fig. 3.12).

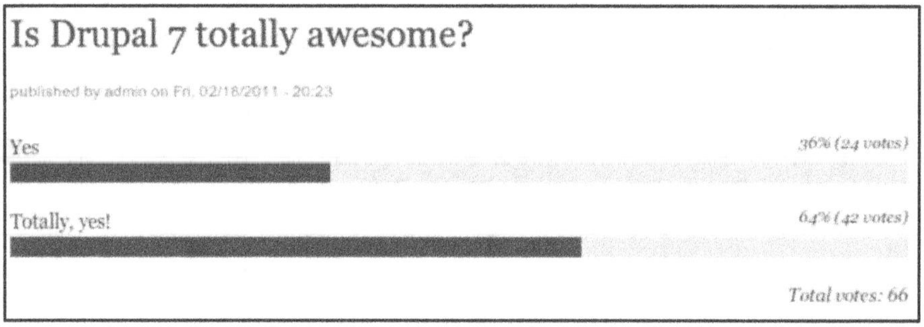

Fig. 3.12: Polls created

3.2.8 Customizing the Display

- You can adjust the display settings for your new site. You can apply themes for your site, which lets you override how everything from a button to an entire page is displayed.
- You can use blocks so that you can place your content in various regions of a site's pages. You can also upload images in your site and use it in different styles.

3.2.8.1 Blocks

- Blocks are smaller chunks of content that you can place in your pages. For examples, block "Who's online," shows a list of users currently logged in; block "User login," displays a login form; and block "Recent comments," shows a list of the newest comments on the site.
- The Navigation bar in the sidebar, the "Powered by Drupal" text at the bottom, and even the entire content area of the page are blocks.

- You can also make your own custom blocks: for example, you might create a block to display an announcement about an upcoming event.
- Blocks are placed in some specific regions in your page, which might include the header, footer, left sidebar, right sidebar, and main content region.

3.2.8.2 Creating Custom Block

- To create a custom block, which can be used as "sidebar" content in any region of your site, complete the following steps:

  Step 1 : Using the administrative dashboard, navigate to Structure > Blocks.

  Step 2 : Click the link "Add block."

  Step 3 : Enter a block description (used in the administrative section only) and the text you want to appear on the Contact page (this goes into the block body).

  Step 4 : Scroll to the fieldset for the region settings. Select the region you would like this block to appear in for your theme (make sure you choose the right theme; all enabled themes will be listed, not just the default theme).

  Step 5 : Scroll to the bottom and click "Save block."

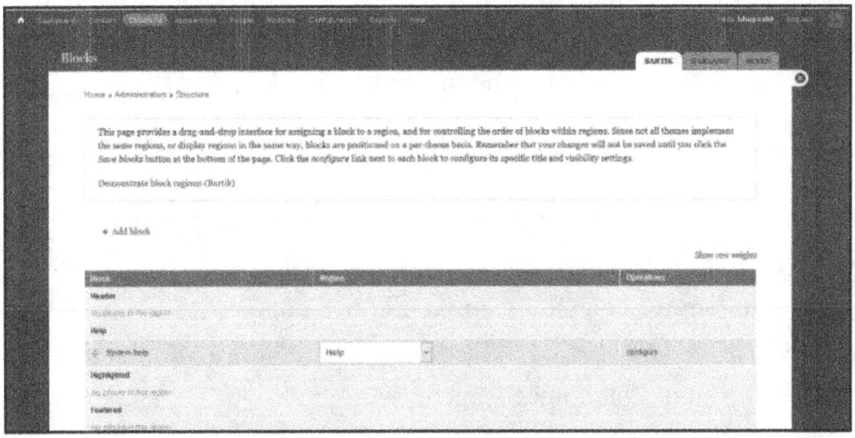

Fig. 3.13: The Block administration page for the Bartik administration theme

- Another way to use a custom block is to add a custom welcome message to the front page of your Web site. To add a custom welcome message to your Web site, complete steps 1 to 3 in the previous exercise and then proceed with the following steps.

  Step 1 : Scroll to the fieldset for the region settings. Select an appropriate region (for example, Content).

  Step 2 : Scroll to the Visibility settings. Select the tab Pages. Enable the option "Only the listed pages." In the large text area below the option you just enabled, type <front> (no quotes, all lowercase, with angle brackets).

  Step 3 : Scroll to the bottom and click "Save block."

- You can make custom content appear in any region on your Web site using blocks.
- Blocks can also be used to feature special content e.g. "PHP books on sale today only!" or use it as a notice area e.g. "School is closed today due to bad weather". You can also add or place any custom HTML into the sidebar of your site e.g. your mailing list sign-up form.

3.2.8.3 Menus

- Menus hold the navigation links to various web pages on a Drupal site.
- Menu provides a reference point to the content types like basic pages, articles and blocks etc.
- By default there are five menus you can place menu items into.
  1. **Main menu:** The Main menu is used on many sites to show the major sections of the site, often in a top navigation bar.
  2. **Management:** The Management menu contains links for administrative tasks.
  3. **Navigation:** The Navigation menu contains links intended for site visitors. Links are added to the Navigation menu automatically by some modules. This menu appears in the Bartik region "Sidebar first" by default.
  4. **User menu:** The User menu contains links related to the user's account, as well as the "'Log out" link.
  5. **Bartik displays** the links in the Main menu as tabs across the top left of the page, (Fig. 3.14).
- **Adding Items to Menus:** To add a menu item for a node on your site, you can use one of two methods.
  1. Edit a specific node and adjust its menu settings.
  2. Use the menu administration system to add a menu item.
- To add subsection menu items, you use either of the same techniques described earlier but change "Parent item" to the menu item in which your new subsection ought to be included.

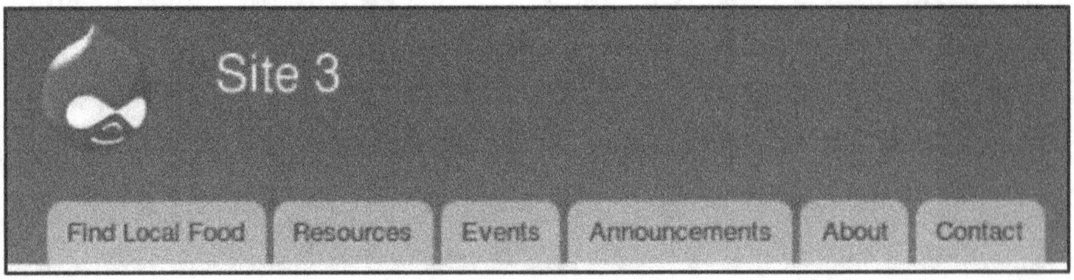

Fig. 3.14: In Bartik, Main menu items are displayed as tabs in the top left of the page

3.2.8.4 Custom Menus

- You can also create custom menus with additional navigation, like Contact, Search, and Login menu.
- To add a custom menu to your site, complete the following steps:

  Step 1 : Using the administrative toolbar, navigate to Structure > Menus.

  Step 2 : Click the link "Add menu."

  Step 3 : Enter a title and a short description of the types of links that ought to be added to this menu.

  Step 4 : Scroll to the bottom of the screen and click Save.
- You can now start adding links to your new menu using "Adding Items to Menus."
- If you want to be able to add nodes to this menu directly, you must add the menu to the list of available menus by completing the following steps for each content type that should be able to be listed in this menu.
  1. Using the administrative toolbar, navigate to Structure > Content types.
  2. Next to the content type you want to configure, click on the link "edit."
  3. Click the vertical tab labeled "Menu settings."
  4. Under the heading "Available menus," enable your new menu.
  5. Under the heading "Default parent item," adjust the drop-down menu so that the correct default menu is selected. By default <Main menu> is selected.
  6. Scroll to the bottom of the screen and click "Save content type."
- Your new menu is now available from the node-editing screen for whichever content type you just altered. You may repeat these steps for any additional content types.
- When you are ready to display the menu on your site, complete the following steps:

  Step 1 : Using the administrative toolbar, navigate to Structure > Blocks.

  Step 2 : Find your new menu in the list of Disabled blocks (near the bottom of the page).

  Step 3 : Drag your menu to the appropriate region (where you want it to be displayed).

  You can just change the region in the drop-down box; however, if you have multiple blocks in the destination region, it might not appear in the right order.

  Step 4 : Scroll to the bottom of the screen and click Save blocks.
- Once, you have saved your new menu link, you can adjust the order of the items in the Main menu by dragging each of the items to a new position in the list as described in the section "Changing the Order of Menu Items." Don't forget to scroll to the bottom of the screen and click "Save configuration" before closing the overlay.

3.2.8.5 Theming

- Themes are the Drupal method for controlling your site's presentation.
- Themes change look and feel of your web site. Using theme you can redesign your site's layout and styling.
- Drupal comes with four themes to get you started:
  1. Bartik.
  2. Seven.
  3. Garland.
  4. Stark.
- **Finding a Theme:** You can apply a theme by downloading a new theme from http://drupal.org/project/themes, or purchasing a commercially available theme, or creating one yourself—once installed and enabled, it takes effect immediately to change the look of your site without the necessity of editing your page content.
- **Theme Configuration:** Themes can be enabled and disabled from the Appearance page (admin/appearance) in the administrative toolbar, shown in Fig. 3.15.
- The Appearance page is divided into Enabled and Disabled themes. The theme marked "Default theme" is the one displayed on the frontend of the site. To set a different theme as the frontend theme, click "Enable and set default" or "Set default," as appropriate.
- Drupal offers a number of configuration features that themes can take advantage of.
- To configure themes, select the Settings tab at Appearance (admin/appearance/settings).

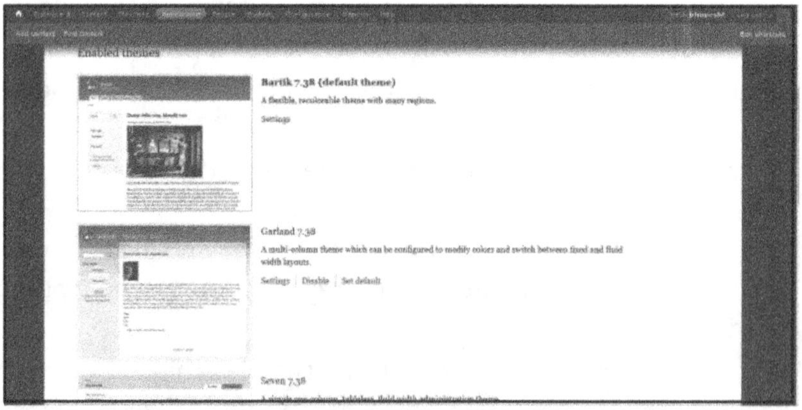

Fig. 3.15: The Appearance administration page

- On these settings pages, you can toggle the display of many page elements, including the site logo, site name, site slogan, user pictures, and others, as shown in Fig. 3.16.

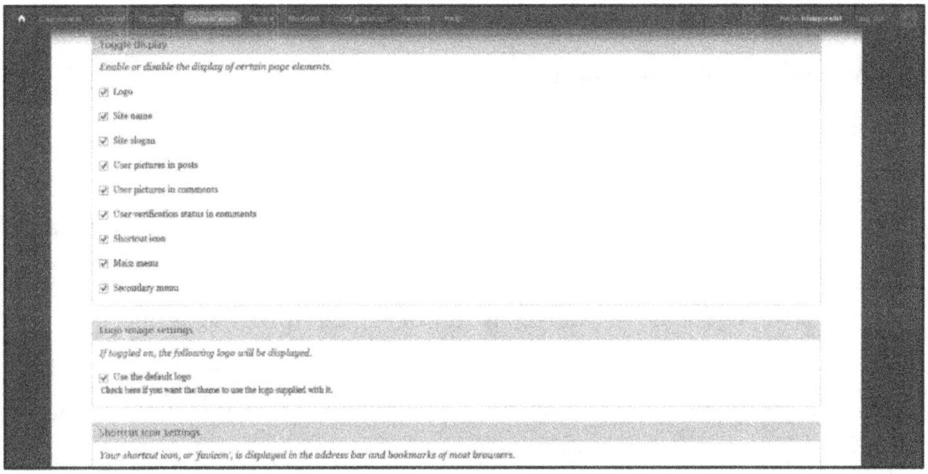

Fig. 3.16: The theme configuration page allows customization of which page elements are displayed

3.2.8.6 Changing Colors

- Use the following steps to recolor the default theme Bartik.

  Step 1 : From the Administrative toolbar, click Appearance. For the theme labelled "default theme," find and click the link titled Settings.

  Step 2 : If you uploaded a new logo in the previous step, you will now see a preview of your site including your logo. You may need to scroll down a bit to see the preview.

  Step 3 : Adjust each of the colors according to your needs. Several color sets are available for you to pick from. These color sets are high contrast and accessible to all Web site visitors.

  Step 4 : When you are happy with the preview, scroll to the bottom of the configuration screen and click "Save configuration."

3.2.9 Creating Modules

- A Drupal module is a collection of files containing some functionality and is written in PHP. Because the module code executes within the context of the site, it can use all the functions and access all variables and structures of Drupal core.
- In fact, a module is no different from a regular PHP file that can be independently created and tested and then used to drive multiple functionalities.
- Drupal have many in-built modules. You can turn site features and functionality on and off by enabling and disabling modules. Also you can download thousands of additional contributed modules from http://drupal.org/project/modules.

- These modules are customizable. Drupal provide hooks that can be used to change the behaviour and output of the modules.
- There are following types hooks:
  1. **Generic hooks,** which allow modules to define additions to Drupal behaviour.
  2. **Alter hooks,** which allow modules to make modifications to existing Drupal behaviour.
  3. **Theme hooks,** which allow themes to modify the output that is sent to the browser.
- Drupal's module system is based on the concept of "hooks". A hook is a PHP function that is named foo_bar(), where "foo" is the name of the module (whose filename is thus foo.module) and "bar" is the name of the hook. Each hook has a defined set of parameters and a specified result type.
- The string "hook" is used as a placeholder for the module name in the hook definitions. For example, if the module file is called example.module, then hook_help() as implemented by that module would be defined as example_help().

3.2.10 Create a Simple Module with a Form and Menu Link

- You can add a form to your website that is accessed through its own URL. For that you need to be created module, form, and the menu hook function.
- Complete the following steps:

Step 1 : **Creating the module structure:** First you need to create a folder for the module. You should put this in "sites/all/modules/{name of your module}". For example “site/all/module/my_module”.

Now, create two empty text files called “my_ module.module" and " my_ module.info" in the “site/all/module/my_form” folder.

These two files are required by your module. The .info file contains information about what your module does, while the .module file contains the actual code including hooks.

Step 2 : **Build the basic module files:** Now put the following code into the my_ module.info file.

```
name = My module

description = Module for form api tutorial

core = 7.x
```

- Put the following code into my_ module.module file. This will create a very basic form that only has one field, a submit button.

```
<?php
function my_ module_form($form, &$form_state) {
  $form['submit_button'] = array(
    '#type' => 'submit',
    '#value' => t('Click Here!'),
  );
  return $form;
}
?>
```

- The process for creating a form is mainly two steps. The first is to build an associative array $form that contains all the fields. The second step is to return that $form variable.
- To add a field, you set the variable $form[{name of your field}] = array(); Each field can then have a number of attributes, such as "#type" and "#value." Most of these attributes are named with a proceeding "#" sign.
- The function t() will output text and is a Drupal function which perform translation.
- Now you can add two more function like my_ module_form_validate, and my_ module_form_submit. These two functions are hook functions that will be called when Drupal validates the form and when it submits the form (assuming it validated).

```
my_ module.module:
<?php
function my_ module_form($form, &$form_state) {
  $form['submit_button'] = array(
    '#type' => 'submit',
    '#value' => t('Click Here!'),
  );
  return $form;
}
function my_ module_form_validate($form, &$form_state) {
}
```

```
function my_ module_form_submit($form, &$form_state) {
//Depending on the type of form you can add the logic
   //to store the details of the form
   //by adding it in a Drupal table.
   //or sending a mail to the admin
   //Storing in a file
   //or pass it to some other service
}
?>
```

- You will note that these three functions take the same variables. $form is the original form information and can be seen as the original structure of the form. $form_state holds all of the submitted values as well as other information, some of which you can add yourself. These two functions need to named similar to the other form, but with "validate" and "submit" at the end.
- The following example shows how to create a complete form, validate and add to navigation.

Example 1: Develop a module in Drupal to design a registration form with the following fields:

Text Field – First Name, Last Name, email, city

List Boxes – Select Country, Date of Birth (Separate Select Boxes for month, day, and year)

Radio Buttons – Gender - Male/Female

Check Boxes – Technology Known – Java, PHP

One Browse button to upload picture.

Perform validation to check if the First Name and Last Name are not empty and the email is valid. If that is not the case display error message and the form will not be submitted.

Display message "Form has been submitted successfully" after clicking on the Submit button.

Also add a Navigation on the Home Page called "Registration".

Solution: site/all/module/registration_module/ registration_module.info file:

```
name = Registration module
description = Registration form to register user
core = 7.x
```

site/all/module/registration_module/registration_module.module file:

```
<?php
function registration_module_menu()
{
$items = array();
$items['registration_module'] = array('title' => t('Registration
                                        form'),'page callback' =>
'drupal_get_form','page arguments' =>
array('registration_module_registration_form'),'access    arguments'    =>
array('access content'),'description' => t('Registration form'),'type' =>
                                                    MENU_CALLBACK);
return $items;
}
function registration_module_form() {
        return drupal_get_form('registration_module_registration_form');
}
function registration_module_registration_form($form_state)
{   $form = array();
   $form['basicdetails']=array(
      '#type'=>'fieldset',
      '#title'=>t('Enter your Basic details below'),
      '#description'=>t('These are all madatory')
    );
   $form['basicdetails']['name']=array(
      '#type'=>'textfield',
      '#title'=>t('Enter your name'),
      '#description'=>t('Your first name goes here')
   );
       $form['basicdetails']['last_name']=array(
           '#type'=>'textfield',
           '#title'=>t('Enter your Last name'),
           '#description'=>t('Your Last name goes here')
         );
```

```
$form['basicdetails']['email']=array(
    '#type'=>'textfield',
    '#title'=>t('Enter your email'),
    '#description'=>t('Your email goes here')
  );
$form['addressdetails']=array(
    '#type'=>'fieldset',
    '#title'=>t('Enter your Address details below'),
    '#description'=>t('These are all madatory')
  );
  $form['addressdetails']['country']=array(
    '#type'=>'select',
    '#title'=>t('Select your country'),
    '#options'=>array('USA','UK','India','France','Japan')
  );
  $form['addressdetails']['city']=array(
    '#type'=>'textfield',
    '#title'=>t('Enter your city'),
    '#description'=>t('Your city name goes here')
  );
  $form['addressdetails']['localaddress']=array(
    '#type'=>'textarea',
    '#title'=>t('Enter address'),
    '#description'=>t('Your Address name goes here')
  );
$form['additionaldetails']=array(
    '#type'=>'fieldset',
    '#title'=>t('Enter your other details below'),
    '#description'=>t('These are all optional')
  );
  $form['additionaldetails']['gender']=array(
    '#type'=>'radios',
    '#title'=>t('Gender'),
    '#options'=>array('Male','Female')
  );
```

```
            $form['additionaldetails']['suscribtion']=array(
                '#type'=>'checkboxes',
                '#title'=>t('Technology Known'),
                '#options'=>array('Java','PHP')
              );
            $form['additionaldetails']['birthdate']=array(
                '#type'=>'date',
                '#title'=>t('Birthdate'),
              );
            $form['#attributes']['enctype'] = 'multipart/form-data';
             $form['additionaldetails']['picture']=array(
                '#type'=>'file',
                '#title'=>t('Upload your picture'),
              );
        $form['submit']=array(
            '#type'=>'submit',
            '#value'=>t('Submit')
          );
          return $form;
}
function registration_module_registration_form_validate($form,
                                                          $form_state) {
  if(empty($form_state['values']['name']))
     form_set_error('name','Name cannot be empty');
  else if(empty($form_state['values']['last_name']))
     form_set_error('last_name','Last name cannot be empty');
  else if(filter_var($form_state['values']['email'],
                                        FILTER_VALIDATE_EMAIL) == false)
    form_set_error('email','Email is not valid');
}
function registration_module_registration_form_submit($form, $form_state)
{
   drupal_set_message("Form has been submitted");
}
?>
```

Now go to Module menu, scroll down, enable the module and click on "Save Configuration", Fig. 3.17.

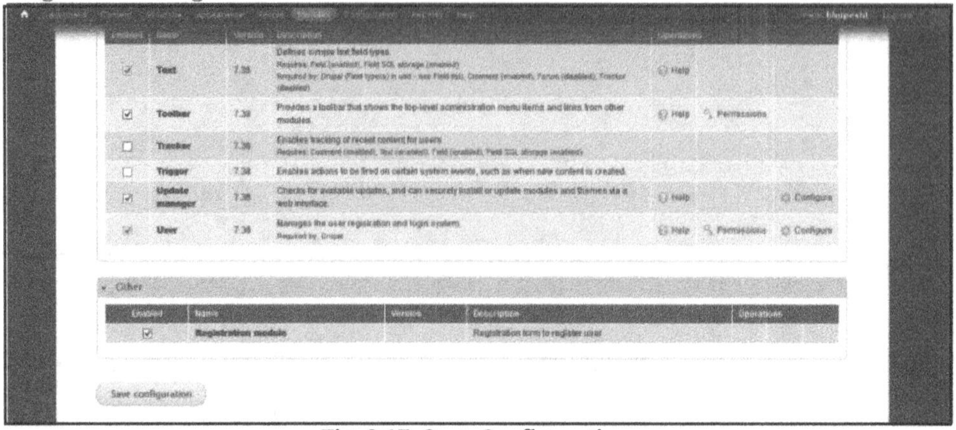

Fig. 3.17: Save Configuration

To add this form to Navigation, go to Structure > Menu.

In the Navigation title click on "add link".

Put title "Registration".

Put path http://localhost/drupal-7.38/?q=registration_module. In place of localhost/Drupal-7.38 you will put your host name and Drupal folder name.

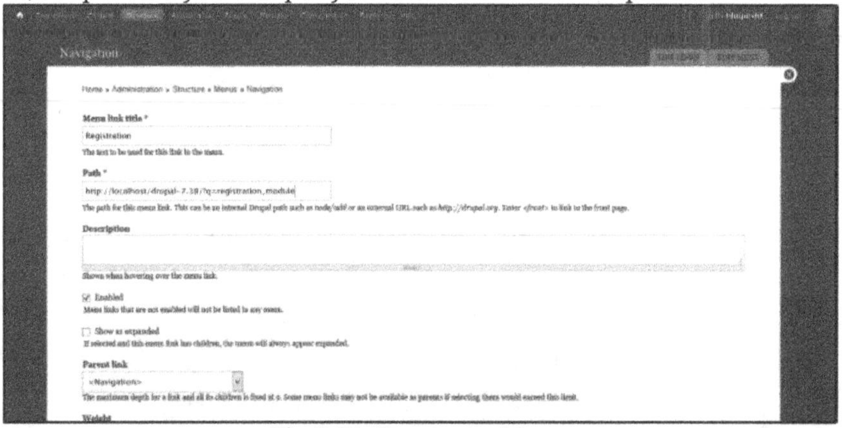

Fig. 3.18: Structure > Menu

Click on "Save".

Go to home page, you will see the navigation "Registration" as shown in Fig. 3.19.

Fig. 3.19: Registration

Click on Registration, you will see the form as shown in the Fig. 3.20.

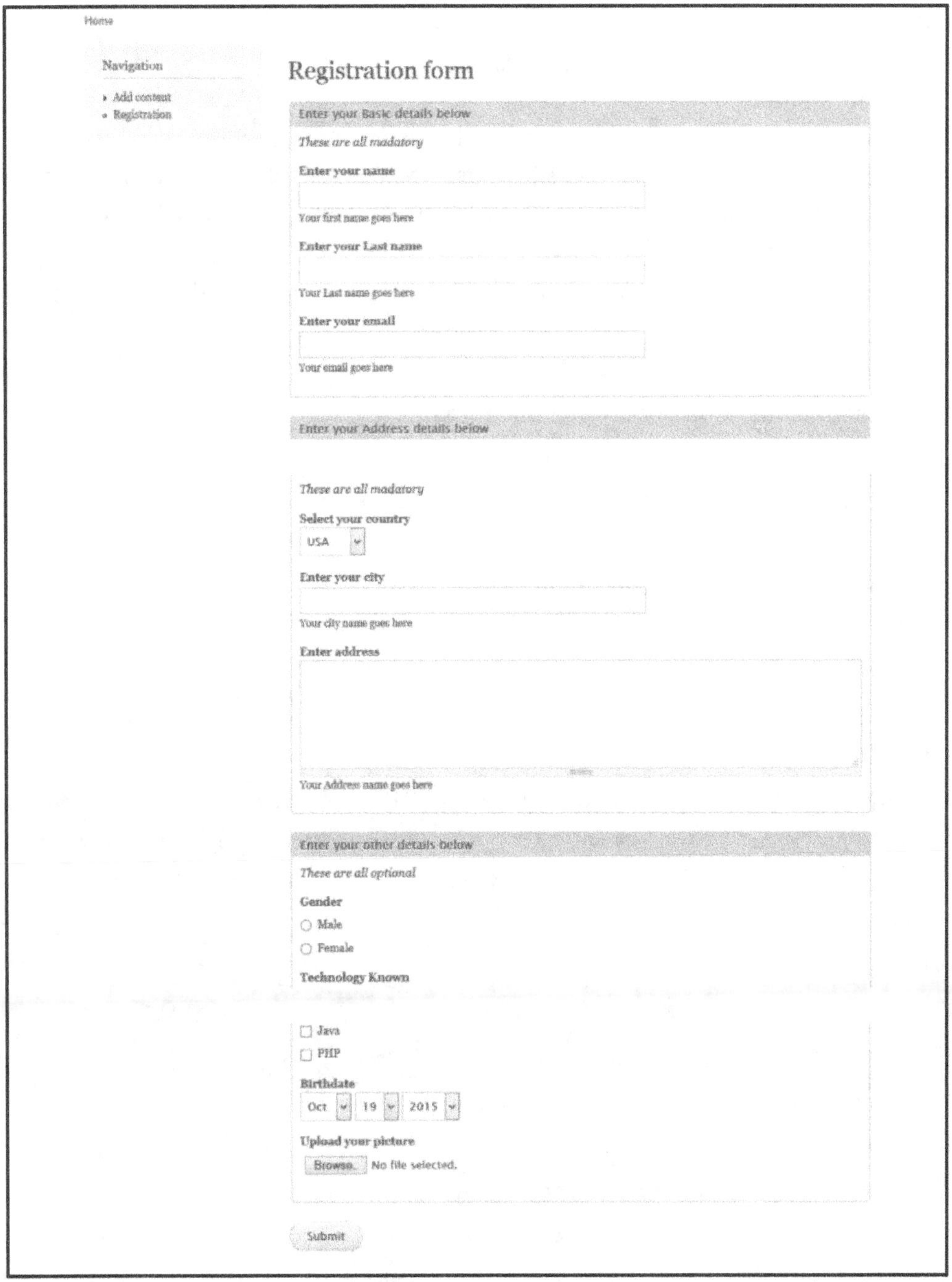

Fig. 3.20: Registration form

- The following example shows how to insert form data into a database and select data from database.

Example 2: Create a module in Drupal To design a form with the following components:

Text Fields - Roll No, Name, and Address

One submit button.

After submitting the form insert a student record into a table named 'student'. Also display a message when the record is inserted successfully, and fetch the name of student from the table and display "Hello: <student name>". Also add a Navigation on the Home Page called "Student Form".

Solution: Create table student in Postgresql database where all the Drupal tables are stored.

```
student(name, rollno, address)
```

site/all/module/my_module/ my_module.info file:

```
name = My module
description = Form to accept student information
core = 7.x
```

site/all/module/my_module/my_module.module file:

```
<?php
function my_module_menu()
{
$items = array();
$items['my_module'] = array('title' => t('My form'),'page callback' =>
'drupal_get_form','page arguments' => array('my_module_my_form'),'access
arguments' => array('access content'),'description' => t('My form'),'type'
=> MENU_CALLBACK);
return $items;
}
function my_module_form() {
    return drupal_get_form('my_module_my_form');
}
function my_module_my_form($form_state)
{   $form['name'] = array('#type' => 'textfield', '#title' => t('Name'),
                                  '#description'=>t('Enter your name'));
$form['rollno'] = array('#type' => 'textfield', '#title' => t('Roll No'),
                                  '#description'=>t('Enter your roll no'));
```

```
$form['address'] = array('#type' => 'textfield', '#title' => t('Address'),
                                    '#description'=>t('Enter your Address'));
$form['submit'] = array('#type' => 'submit', '#value' => 'Submit');
   return $form;
}
function my_module_my_form_submit($form, &$form_state) {
   $name = $form_state['values']['name'];
   $rollno = $form_state['values']['rollno'];
   $address = $form_state['values']['address'];
   db_insert('student')->fields(array('name' => $name,'rollno' =>
                                 $rollno,'address' => $address))->execute();
drupal_set_message(t('Your form has been saved.'));
$q = "SELECT * FROM {student} WHERE name = :name";
$result = db_query($q, array(':name' => $name))->fetchObject();
drupal_set_message("Hello ".$result->name);
}
?>
```

Follow the steps as Example 1.

Before form submit:

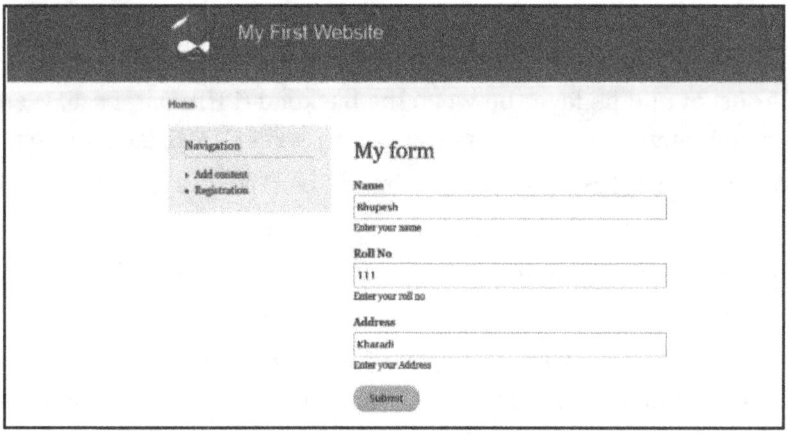

Fig. 3.21: Before form submit

After form submit:

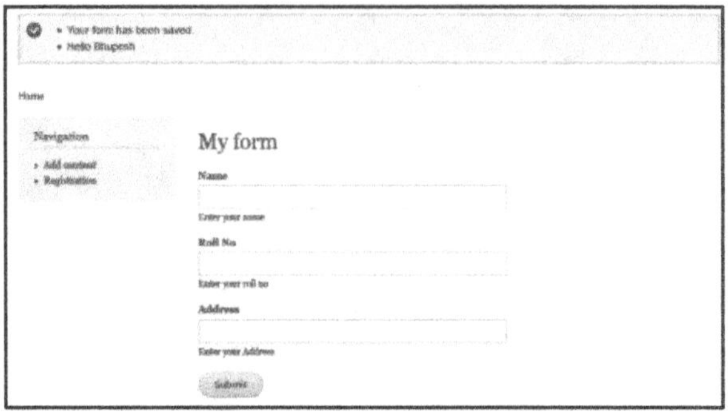

Fig. 3.22: After form submit

SUMMARY

- PHP is an open source, freely available scripting language, ability to work on various OS (Operating System) and ease in integration with several types of databases.
- MVC framework adds up to the beauty of PHP programming and makes it easier for the developer to build robust programs using the classic features of MVC framework.
- The Model View Controller architecture primarily reduces the burden of the developers by providing a lucid and presentable coding pattern.
- Drupal is both a framework and a content management system, hence, Drupal is a Content Management Framework.
- Joomla is free and open-source content management system for publishing web content. It is built on a model–view–controller web application framework that can be used independently of the CMS.
- Drupal was first released to the public by Dries Buytaert in 2001.The name Drupal is derived from the Dutch word druppel which means "drop."
- The Web page will have references to images, style sheets, and interactive scripts.
- Drupal is a sort of middle layer between the backend (PHP, Database, Web server) and the frontend (what visitors see in their web browsers- HTML, CSS, JavaScript).
- Drupal provides two types of content by default i.e. Article and Basic page.
  1. Article is appropriate for blog like entries on your site.
  2. Basic page is appropriate for pages that are not time-sensitive and that are more "persistent."
- Articles are stories may be used as a personal blog or for news articles.
- Blog entries are much like the core content type Article; however, additional functionality is built into the module to permit multiuser blogs. Every user gets a personal blogs.

- Book pages are used to create static pages that follow the basic content pattern and that have hierarchical content.
- A forum topic starts a discussion thread within a forum. People can then discuss this topic by adding their comments to it.
- Poll is used to create simple survey that displays cumulative results.
- Blocks are smaller chunks of content that you can place in your pages.
- Menus hold the navigation links to various web pages on a Drupal site.
- Menu provides a reference point to the content types like basic pages, articles and blocks etc.
- The Main menu is used on many sites to show the major sections of the site, often in a top navigation bar.
- The Navigation menu contains links intended for site visitors.
- Themes are the Drupal method for controlling your site's presentation.
- Themes change look and feel of your web site.
- A Drupal module is a collection of files containing some functionality and is written in PHP.

PRACTICE QUESTIONS

1. What is PHP framework?
2. With the help of diagram describe MVC architecture.
3. What is Drupal?
4. Enlist features of Drupal.
5. Write short note on: Dashboard.
6. How to create basic web pages? Explain with example.
7. What is articles?
8. What is meant by Block? Explain custom blocks in short.
9. What is theming?
10. How to create module?
11. Explain menus in Drupal.
12. List out administrator toolbar of Drupal.

■■■

CHAPTER 4

XML

Contents ...

Objectives...

- To Understand XML
- To Learn XML Document Structure
- To Study PHP and XML
- To Understand SimpleXML
- To Study Dcoument Object Model Concepts

4.1 WHAT IS XML? (April 16; Oct. 14)

- XML – eXtensible Markup Language – lets you create text documents that can hold data in a structured way. Actually XML is a means of storing structured data.
- Although XML is different from a database in many ways, both XML and databases offer ways to format and store structured data. XML is not a language but a specification for creating your own markup languages.
- It is a subset of Standard Generalized Markup Language (SGML, the parent of HTML). XML can exchange data easily from one application to another, even if both the applications are different.
- XML is much like HTML. The difference is:
  1. HTML tags are predefined, XML tags are not predefined.
  2. HTML is used to display data but XML is used to store and transport data.
- The XML - based language can be placed online and any application can read and write it. So, two applications that know nothing about each other can still exchange data. For these reasons XML is rapidly becoming the data exchange standard, and many useful technologies have been created using XML, such as:
  1. Web Services, including languages such as SOAP for exchanging information in XML format over HTTP.
  2. XML - RPC, and the Web Services Description Language (WSDL), used for describing Web Services.
  3. Application file formats, such as OpenOffice's OpenDocument Format (ODF) and Microsoft's Office Open XML (OOXML) that are used to store word processing documents, spreadsheets, and so on.
  4. RSS and Atom news feeds that allow Web applications to publish news stories in a universal format that can be read by many types of software, from news readers and email clients through other Web site applications.
  5. WAP and WML, markup languages for handheld devices.
  6. SMIL, describing multimedia for the web.
- XML is a markup language that defines set of rules for encoding documents in a format that is both human-readable and machine-readable.
- Like HTML, an XML document contains elements and attributes in the form of tags.

Characteristics of XML:

1. **XML is extensible:** XML allows you to create your own self-descriptive tags, or language, that suits your application.

2. **XML is a public standard:** XML was developed by an organization called the World Wide Web Consortium (W3C) and is available as an open standard.
3. **XML carries the data, does not present it:** XML allows you to store the data irrespective of how it will be presented.

- Though XML documents are human - readable, many applications are designed to parse XML documents automatically and work efficiently with their content. PHP has many XML - related functions that can easily be used to work with XML documents.
- You can make your own XML document as easily as this:

```
<?xml version="1.0" ?>
<stockList>
        <item type="fruit">
                <name>apple</name>
                <unitPrice>0.99</unitPrice>
                <quantity>412</quantity>
        </item>
        <item type="vegetable">
                <name>beetroot</name>
                <unitPrice>1.39</unitPrice>
                <quantity>67</quantity>
        </item>
</stockList>
```

- The first line of this document is called the **XML declaration**; it indicates that this document is an XML document, and specifies the version of XML that is used to create the document.
- The second line defines the **root element** of the document (named stockList). There can be only one root element for an XML document.
- The third line defines a **child element named item**, it contains an attribute named type that is set to the value fruit. Apart from elements and attributes, XML also contains plain text such as apple, 0.99 etc.
- From reading this XML document, you can tell that:
  - It stores a list of stock items.
  - There are 412 apples available, and an apple is a fruit and costs $0.99.
  - There are 67 beetroots available, and a beetroot is a vegetable and costs $1.39.
- While creating elements and attributes, their meaning and structure is also specified. This is so that, when you exchange data with another application, both parties to the transaction know exactly what the element and attribute names mean. To do this, you use either a Document Type Definition (DTD) or an XML Schema Definition (XSD).

- Frequently when you create XML documents, you will either use an existing publicly available DTD (or XSD) or the DTD written by yourself.
- Once, you write a DTD, you can publish it on the Web. That means anyone who needs to read or write an XML document compatible with your system has the capability to access the published DTD to make sure the document is valid.

4.2 XML DOCUMENT STRUCTURE

- XML document is a well - formed and valid document.
- A well - formed XML document follows the basic XML syntax rules, and a valid document also follows the rules which are defined in a DTD or an XML schema.
- In other words:
  1. **All XML documents must be well-formed:** A well - formed XML document uses correct XML syntax. Means any elements, attributes, or other constructs are as per the XML specification.
  2. **An XML document can also be valid:** A well - formed document does not need to be valid, but a valid document must be well - formed. An XML document is valid if its elements, attributes, and other contents follow the rules in the DTD or an XML schema.
- By using valid XML documents, applications that know nothing about each other can still communicate effectively — they just have to exchange XML documents, and understand the meaning of the DTD or XML schema against which those documents are validated. This is one of the main features that make XML so powerful.

4.2.1 Major Parts of an XML Document

- A well - formed XML document may contain the following:
- First line of an XML document is an XML version line; possibly include a character encoding declaration. Character encoding declaration is optional. If no character encoding is specified, UTF - 8 is assumed. For example:

```
<?xml version="1.0" encoding="UTF-8"?>
```

- An optional DTD or an XML schema, or a reference to one of these if they are stored externally. This must appear before the document's root element. For example, here's a reference to an external DTD:

```
< !DOCTYPE stockList SYSTEM "http://www.example.com/dtds/stockList.dtd" >
```

- All XML documents must contain one — and only one — root element. This element usually contains one or more child elements, each of which may optionally have one or more attributes.

- An element can contain other child elements or data between its beginning and ending tag, or it may be empty.
- XML documents may contain additional components such as processing instructions (PIs), CDATA sections, comments; entity references; text; and entities.

4.2.2 XML Syntax Rules (April 15)

- A well - formed XML document must follow all the syntax rules of the XML specification, the most common of which are:
  1. There is only one parent element containing all the rest of the elements.
  2. XML elements are declared to be either non - empty, in which case they are designed to contain data; or empty, in which case they cannot contain data. For example, in HTML, the <p>...</p> element is non - empty because it can contain text, whereas the
 (line - break) element is empty because it cannot contain anything.
  3. XML elements must have a closing tag.

     For example:
     ```
     <p>This is a paragraph      - In HTML
     <p>This is a paragraph</p> - In XML
     ```
  4. XML tags are case sensitive.

     For example:
     ```
     <Message>This is incorrect</message>
     <message>This is correct</message>
     ```
  5. XML elements can have attributes in name/value pairs like HTML. In XML the attribute values must always be quoted.

     For example:
     ```
     <books>
          <book id="1">PHP 6</book>
     <books>
     ```
- In an element attribute name can not be repeated.
- XML elements must be properly nested. For example:
  ```
  < !-- Incorrect nesting -- >
  < parent > < child > < /parent > < /child >
  < !-- Correct nesting -- >
  < parent > < child > < /child > < /parent >
  ```
- Names must start with a letter, an underscore, or a colon, but in practice, you should never use colons unless you are dealing with XML namespaces. Names are case-sensitive. Letters, numbers, the hyphen, the underscore, and the period can be used after the first character.
- Comments are delimited in the same way as HTML comments i.e.,
  ```
  < ! - -   and   - - >
  ```

4.2.3 Predefined Character Entities

- Some character have a special meaning in XML If you use '<' character inside an XML element, it will give an error because the character '<' is used as a start of a new element.

  For example: The following code will generate an XML error:

```
<message>If salary < 1000 then</message>
```

- To remove this error, replace '<' with their entity reference.

  For example: The correct code is as follows:

```
<message>If salary &lt; 1000 then</message>
```

- Hence, the entity reference for these predefined characters are as follows:

>	>
<	<
'	'
"	"
&	&

4.2.4 CDATA Sections

- The term CDATA means, Character Data.
- CDATA are defined as blocks of text that are not parsed by the parser, but are otherwise recognized as markup.

  Syntax:

```
<![CDATA[
   characters with markup
]]>
```

- The above syntax is composed of three sections:
  - **CDATA Start section:** CDATA begins with the delimiter `<![CDATA[`
  - **CDATA End section:** CDATA section ends with `]]>` delimiter.
  - **CData section:** Characters between these two delimiters are interpreted as characters, and not as markup. This section may contain markup characters (<, >, and &), but they are ignored by the XML processor.
- The following markup code shows example of CDATA. Here, each character written inside the CDATA section is ignored by the parser.

```
<script>
<![CDATA[
   <message> Welcome to Nirali Prakashan </message>
]] >
</script >
```

- In the above syntax, everything between <message> and </message> is treated as character data and not as markup.

4.2.5 XML Processing

- Processing Instructions (PIs) allow documents to contain instructions for applications.
- Processing instructions (PIs) can be used to pass information to applications.

  Syntax: `<?target instructions?>`

  where, target identifies the application to which the instruction is directed. Instruction is a character that describes the information for the application to process.
- The following line shows a style sheet "niraliprakashan.css" is linked with XML document. So browser will display the XML document according to the CSS.

```
<?xml-stylesheet href="niraliprakashan.css" type="text/css"?>
```

- Here, the target is xml-stylesheet. href="niraliprakashan.css" and type="text/css" are data or instructions that the target application will use at the time of processing the given XML document.

  Example:

```
<?xml version="1.0" ?>
<?xml-stylesheet href="course.css" type="text/css"?>
<Course>
      <Computer Science>
            <Student name> Bianca</Student name>
            <Class name>TYBsc </Class name>
            <percentage>76.4</percentage>
      </Computer Science>
</Course>
```

4.2.6 XML Tree Structure

- An XML document can also be described as a tree structure.
- For example consider the following XML document:

```
<?xml version="1.0"?>
<Company>
  <Employee>
      <FirstName>Tanmay</FirstName>
      <LastName>Patil</LastName>
      <ContactNo>1234567890</ContactNo>
      <Email>tanmaypatil@xyz.com</Email>
      <Address>
```

```
            <City>Bangalore</City>
            <State>Karnataka</State>
            <Zip>560212</Zip>
        </Address>
    </Employee>
</Company>
```

- Following tree structure represents the above XML document:

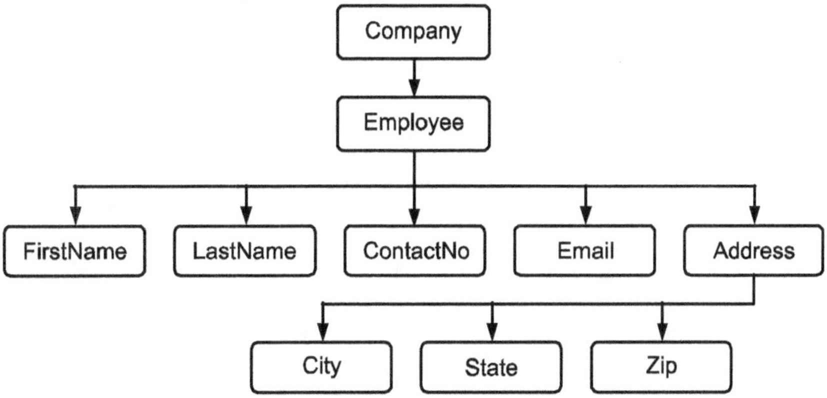

Fig. 4.1: XML Tree structure

- In the Fig. 4.1, there is a root element named as <company>. Inside that, there is one more element <Employee>. Inside the employee element, there are five branches named <FirstName>, <LastName>, <ContactNo>, <Email>, and <Address>. Inside the <Address> element, there are three sub-branches, named <City> <State> and <Zip>.

4.3 PHP AND XML

- PHP has functions and classes to make it easier to work with XML documents. Using PHP you can read XML document, you can also add more element to the document, and also modify and remove elements from the document.
- In the coming section you are going to do the following things with PHP and XML:
  - Reading, or parsing, XML documents using the XML Parser extension.
  - Using the DOM extension to manipulate XML documents via the Document Object Model.
  - Reading, writing, and manipulating XML documents using SimpleXML extension.
- Before you start parsing and using PHP predefined functions, you can generate XML manually i.e. without using PHP built-in function.

- **Example:** A PHP script to generate an XML document.

```
<?php
    header('Content-Type: text/xml');
    print '<?xml version="1.0"?>' . "\n";
    print "<Course>\n";
    $ComputerScience = array(array('StudentName' => 'Bianca',
'ClassName' => 'TYBSc',
'percentage' => '76.4'),
array('StudentName' => 'Bhupesh',
'ClassName' => 'TYBSc',
'percentage' => '72.0'));
    foreach ($ComputerScience as $cs)
    {
        print " <ComputerScience>\n";
        foreach($cs as $tag => $data)
        {
        print " <$tag>" . htmlspecialchars($data) . "</$tag>\n";
        }
        print " </ComputerScience>\n";
    }
        print "</Course>\n";
?>
```

Output:

```
<?xml version="1.0"?>
<Course>
        <ComputerScience>
        <StudentName>Bianca</StudentName>
        <ClassName>TYBSc</ClassName>
        <percentage>76.4</percentage>
</ComputerScience>
<ComputerScience>
        <StudentName>Bhupesh</StudentName>
        <ClassName>TYBSc</ClassName>
        <percentage>72.0</percentage>
        </ComputerScience>
</Course>
```

- In above program a 2D array is created to store the child elements of "Course". Hence, nested for each loop is used to display the elements.

4.4 XML PARSER (April 13, 15, Oct. 14)

- XML parser is used to create, read and manipulate an XML document.
- In PHP there are two major types of XML parsers: **(April 13, Oct. 14)**
  1. **Tree-Based Parsers:** Tree-based parser transforms the XML document into a Tree structure, and then you can access the tree elements individually. Example of tree-based parsers: SimpleXML and DOM.
  2. **Event-Based Parsers:** View an XML document as a series of events. When a specific event occurs, it calls a function to handle it. Event-based parsers do not hold the entire document in Memory; instead, they read in one node at a time and allow you to interact with in real time. Once you move onto the next node, the old one is thrown away. Event based parsers focus on the content of the XML document, not their structure. So it parses faster and consumes less memory. Example of event-based parsers: XMLReader and XML Expat Parser.

4.4.1 Creating a New Parser

- This section shows how to create an Event based parser to read XML documents. For these perform the following steps:

  Step 1 : Create a new parser resource by calling the xml_parser_create() function.

  Step 2 : Create two event handler functions to handle the start and end of an XML element, then register these functions with the parser using the xml_set_element_handler() function.

  Step 3 : Create another event handler function to handle any character (text) data that may be found inside an element, and register this function with the parser using xml_set_character_data_handler() .

  Step 4 : Parse the XML document by calling the xml_parse() function, passing in the parser and the XML string to parse.

  Step 5 : Finally, destroy the parser resource, if it is no longer needed, by calling xml_parser_free().

- These functions and few more functions are described as follows:
  - `xml_parser_create()`: Create an XML parser. Generate a new parser resource, that can be used with other functions.

    ```
    $parser = xml_parser_create();
    ```
  - `xml_parser_free()`: To free up the resource when done.
  - `xml_parse_into_struct()`: Parse XML ddata into an array structure.
  - `xml_get_error_code()`: Get XML parser error code.
  - `xml_error_string()`: Get the textual description of the error based on error code.

- `xml_set_element_handler()`: Set up start and end element handler.
- `xml_set_character_data_handler()`: Set up character data handler.
- `xml_get_current_line_number()`: Gets current line number for an XML parser.
- `xml_parse()`: Start parsing XML document.

- **Example:** First create an XML document.

```
<?xml version="1.0" encoding="UTF-8"?>
<stockList>
    <item type="fruit">
        <name>apple</name>
        <unitPrice>0.99</unitPrice>
        <quantity>412</quantity>
    </item>
    <item type="vegetable">
        <name>beetroot</name>
        <unitPrice>1.39</unitPrice>
        <quantity>67</quantity>
    </item>
</stockList>
```

- Save this XML document as "stock_list.xml". Now you read this document using the following parser script.

```
<pre>
<?php
//Start element handler
function startElementHandler($parser, $element, $attributes)
{
    echo "Start of element: \"$element\"";
    if($attributes)
        echo ", attributes: ";
        foreach($attributes as $name => $value)
            echo "$name=\"$value\" ";
        echo "\n";
}
//End element handler
```

```
function endElementHandler($parser, $element)
{
   echo "End of element: \"$element\"\n";
}
function characterDataHandler($parser, $data)
{
   if(trim($data))
      echo " Character data: \"" . htmlspecialchars($data) . "\"\n";
}
//Error handler:
function parseError( $parser )
{
   $error = xml_error_string( xml_get_error_code( $parser ) );
   $errorLine = xml_get_current_line_number( $parser );
   $errorColumn = xml_get_current_column_number( $parser );
   return "<b>Error: $error at line $errorLine column $errorColumn</b>";
}
// Create the parser and set options
$parser = xml_parser_create();
xml_parser_set_option( $parser, XML_OPTION_CASE_FOLDING, false );
// Register the event handlers with the parser
xml_set_element_handler($parser, "startElementHandler","endElementHandler" );
xml_set_character_data_handler( $parser, "characterDataHandler" );
// Read and parse the XML document
$xml = file_get_contents( "stock_list.xml" );
xml_parse( $parser, $xml ) or die( parseError( $parser ) );
xml_parser_free( $parser );
?>
</pre>
```

Output:

```
Start of element: "stockList"
Start of element: "item", attributes: type="fruit"
Start of element: "name"
Character data: "apple"
End of element: "name"
```

```
Start of element: "unitPrice"
Character data: "0.99"
End of element: "unitPrice"
Start of element: "quantity"
Character data: "412"
End of element: "quantity"
End of element: "item"
Start of element: "item", attributes: type="vegetable"
Start of element: "name"
Character data: "beetroot"
End of element: "name"
Start of element: "unitPrice"
Character data: "1.39"
End of element: "unitPrice"
Start of element: "quantity"
Character data: "67"
End of element: "quantity"
End of element: "item"
End of element: "stockList"
```

- This program have three event handler function `startElementHandler()`, `endElementHandler()`, and `characterDataHandler()`. The function will be called when start of element comes, end of element comes and character data comes respectively and display data accordingly. Finally, the script reads the file to parse into a variable, then calls xml_parse() to parse the variable's contents.
- **Example:** In the following program you read the XML document "stock_list.xml" and parse the XML data into an array.

```
<body>
<h3>Reading XML document</h3>
<pre>
<?php
    $xml_file = "stock_list.xml";
    $xml_parser = xml_parser_create();
    $fp = fopen($xml_file, "r") or die("Could not open");
    $xml_data = fread($fp, 4096);
```

```
        xml_parse_into_struct($xml_parser, $xml_data, $values);
        xml_parser_free($xml_parser);
        print_r($values);
?>
</pre>
</body>
</html>
```

- After you run the program it displays all the elements and their attributes into array structure.

4.5 THE DOCUMENT OBJECT MODEL (April 15, Oct. 14)

- XML Parser can only read XML documents; it can not alter documents or create new documents.
- An alternative approach is to use the Document Object Model (DOM) extension.
- DOM is a way of expressing the various nodes (elements, attributes, and so on) of an XML document as a tree of objects. Then the tree can be traversed and various nodes can be accessed.
- By using various DOM class methods you can also change any of these nodes, and even create a new DOM document from scratch.
- The DOM class description as follows:
    1. `DOMNode`: Represents a single node in the DOM tree. Most DOM classes derive from the DOMNode class.
    2. `DOMDocument`: Stores an entire XML document in the form of a DOM tree. It derives from the DOMNode class, and is effectively the root of the tree.
    3. `DOMElement`: Represents an element node.
    4. `DOMAttr`: Represents an element's attribute.
    5. `DOMText`: Represents a plain - text node.
    6. `DOMCharacterData`: Represents a CDATA (character data) node.
- To start working with a DOM document, you first create a DOMDocument object:

```
$doc = new DOMDocument();
```

- You can then use this object to read in or write out an XML document; examine and change the various nodes in the document; and add or delete nodes from the document's tree.

- **Example:** The following program read the same XML Document "stock_list.xml" using the DOM method.

```
<html><body>
<h3>Reading an XML File with the DOM Extension</h3>
<pre>
<?php
    // Read the XML document into a DOMDocument object
    $doc = new DOMDocument();
    $doc->load("stock_list.xml");
    // Traverse the document
    traverseDocument( $doc );
    //Traverses each node of the DOM document recursively
    function traverseDocument($node)
    {
        switch($node->nodeType)
        {
            case XML_ELEMENT_NODE:
                echo "Found element: \"$node->tagName\"";
                if($node->hasAttributes())
                {
                    echo " with attributes: ";
                    foreach($node->attributes as $attribute)
                    {
                        echo "$attribute->name=\"$attribute->value\" ";
                    }
                }
                echo "\n";
            break;
            case XML_TEXT_NODE:
                if(trim($node->wholeText))
                {
                    echo "Found text node: \"$node->wholeText\"\n";
                }
            break;
```

```
            case XML_CDATA_SECTION_NODE:
                if(trim($node->data))
                {
                    echo "Found character data node:
                                    \"" . htmlspecialchars($node->data) . "\"\n";
                }
            break;
        }
        if($node->hasChildNodes())
        {
            foreach($node->childNodes as $child)
            {
            traverseDocument($child);
            }
        }
    }
?>
</pre>
</body></html>
```

Output:

Reading an XML File with the DOM Extension

```
Found element: "stockList"
Found element: "item" with attributes: type="fruit"
Found element: "name"
Found text node: "apple"
Found element: "unitPrice"
Found text node: "0.99"
Found element: "quantity"
Found text node: "412"
Found element: "item" with attributes: type="vegetable"
Found element: "name"
Found text node: "beetroot"
Found element: "unitPrice"
Found text node: "1.39"
Found element: "quantity"
Found text node: "67"
```

4.5.1 Creating an XML Document using the DOM

- To create a node, you call various methods of the DOMDocument class. Some useful methods are:
  1. `createElement(name [, value ])`: Creates an element node called name and optionally appends a text node to it containing value.
  2. `createTextNode(content)`: Creates a text node that contains content.
  3. `createCDATASection(data)`: Creates a character data node that contains data.
  4. `createComment(data)`: Creates a comment node that contains data.
  5. `appendChild()`: Appends a child element to its root element.
  6. `setAttribute()`: Add attributes to element nodes.
  7. `createAttribute()`: Create new attribute.
  8. `saveXML()`: Converts the DOMDocument object into string.
- **Example:** Following program create an XML document using DOMDocument.

```
<html>
<body>
<h3> Create an XML document with DOMDocument</h3>
<pre>
<?php
    $xml = new DOMDOcument("1.0", "UTF-8");
    echo htmlspecialchars($xml->saveXML());
?>
</pre>
</body>
</html>
```

Output:

Create an XML document with DOMDocument

```
<?xml version="1.0" encoding="UTF-8"?>
```

- The program create an XML document with only version line. First statement creates a DOMDocument object $xml which refers the XML document containing version line. To display the document to the browser you need to convert $xml to string, so that it can be displayed using echo.
- The next example shows how to add elements to the XML document.

- Following is a script to create XML file named "Course.xml".

```
<Course>
      <Computer Science>
            <Student name>.......</Student name>
            <Class name>......</Class name>
            <percentage>.....</percentage>
      </Computer Science>
</Course>
```

- Store the details of a student who are in TYBSc. The solution is given below:

```
<?php
   // Create a DOMDocument object and set nice formatting
   $doc = new DOMDocument("1.0", "UTF-8");
   $doc->formatOutput = true;
   // Create the root "Course" element
   $course= $doc->createElement( "Course" );
   $doc->appendChild( $course);
   // Create the first element (Computer Science)
   $cs = $doc->createElement( "Computer_Science" );
   $course->appendChild( $cs );
   // Create the Student's "name" child element
   $name = $doc->createElement( "Student_Name", "Alok" );
   $cs->appendChild( $name );
   // Create the Student's "Class Name" child element
   $class_name = $doc->createElement( "Class_Name", "TYBSc" );
   $cs->appendChild( $class_name );
// Create the Student's "Percentage" child element
   $percentage = $doc->createElement( "Percentage", "76.4" );
   $cs->appendChild( $percentage );
// Create a file Course.xml and the XML document will be stored in that file
   $doc->save("Course.xml");
   echo "<h4>Course.xml created</h4>";
?>
```

Output:

```
Course.xml created
```

- After adding elements call save() function which is used to save the created XML document into the file specified by the parameter.

4.5.2 Adding Elements to an Existing Document

- The following example reads the "stock_list.xml" file as a DOM document, adds a new item element to the stockList element, and then outputs the modified XML.

```
<html><body>
<h3> Adding an Element to an XML File with the DOM Extension </h3>
<pre>
<?php
// Load the XML file
$doc = new DOMDocument();
$doc-> preserveWhiteSpace = false;
$doc-> load("stock_list.xml");
$doc-> formatOutput = true;
// Get the stockList root element
$stockListElements = $doc-> getElementsByTagName("stockList");
$stockList = $stockListElements-> item(0);
// Create a new "item" element and add it to the stockList
$item = $doc-> createElement("item");
$item-> setAttribute("type", "vegetable");
$stockList-> appendChild($item);
// Create the item's "name" child element
$name = $doc-> createElement("name", "carrot");
$item-> appendChild($name);
// Create the item's "unitPrice" child element
$unitPrice = $doc-> createElement("unitPrice", "0.79");
$item-> appendChild($unitPrice);
// Create the item's "quantity" child element
$quantity = $doc-> createElement("quantity", "31");
$item-> appendChild($quantity);
// Create the item's "description" child element
$description = $doc-> createElement("description");
$item-> appendChild($description);
$cdata = $doc-> createCDATASection("Carrots are crunchy");
$description-> appendChild($cdata);
// Output the XML document, encoding markup characters as needed
echo htmlspecialchars($doc-> saveXML());
?>
</pre>
</body>
</html>
```

Output:

```
Adding an Element to an XML File with the DOM Extension
<?xml version="1.0" encoding="UTF-8"?>
<stockList>
  <item type="fruit">
    <name>apple</name>
    <unitPrice>0.99</unitPrice>
    <quantity>412</quantity>
  </item>
  <item type="vegetable">
    <name>beetroot</name>
    <unitPrice>1.39</unitPrice>
    <quantity>67</quantity>
  </item>
  <item type="vegetable">
    <name>carrot</name>
    <unitPrice>0.79</unitPrice>
    <quantity>31</quantity>
    <description><![CDATA[Carrots are crunchy]]></description>
  </item>
</stockList>
```

- The saveXML() method is used converts the DOMDocument object into string, so that that can be displayed using echo.

4.6 SimpleXML

- Although the DOM extension is a powerful way to work with XML documents, but it contains large number of classes, methods, and properties, so, working with DOM extension can be tedious and time - consuming to code.
- Using SimpleXML is simpler than DOM. SimpleXML extension offers a more straightforward way to manipulate elements within an XML document.
- DOM extension provides more than 15 classes, but SimpleXML has only one class SimpleXMLElement.
- The DOM extension works on the node level, SimpleXML works at the element level, making element manipulation a much more straightforward process.

- Here, is a list of common SimpleXMLElement methods that you can use to manipulate XML documents:
  1. `addAttribute(name, value)`: Adds an attribute named name, with the value of value, to the element.
  2. `addChild(name [, value])`: Adds a child element called name to the element. The child element can be empty, or it can contain the text value. It returns the child element as a new SimpleXMLElement object.
  3. `asXML([filename])`: Generates an XML document from the SimpleXMLElement object. If filename is supplied, it writes the XML to the file; otherwise it returns the XML as a string.
  4. `attributes()`: Returns an associative array of all the attributes in the element, as name= > value pairs.
  5. `children()`: Returns an array of all the element's children, as SimpleXMLElement objects.
  6. `getName()`: Returns the name of the element as a string.
  7. `xpath(path)`: Finds child elements that match the given XPath (XML Path Language) path string.
- In addition, SimpleXML gives you three functions that you can use to import XML data into a SimpleXMLElement object:
  1. `simplexml_import_dom(node)`: Converts the supplied DOM node, into a SimpleXMLElement object.
  2. `simplexml_load_file(filename)`: Loads the XML file with name filename as a SimpleXMLElement object.
  3. `simplexml_load_string(string)`: Loads the supplied XML string as a SimpleXMLElement object.
- With SimpleXML, all the elements in an XML document are represented as a tree of SimpleXMLElement objects. Any given element's children are available as properties of the element's SimpleXMLElement object.
- For example, if $parent is a SimpleXMLElement object representing an element that has a child element called child , you can access that child element's text value directly with:

```
$value = $parent- > child;
```

- To do the same thing with the DOM classes would require several lines of code.

4.6.1 Reading an XML Document

- The following example shows how you can easily read and display the contents of an XML document using SimpleXML:

```
<html>
<body>
<h3> Reading an XML File with the SimpleXML Extension </h3>
<pre>
<?php
   // Read the XML document into a SimpleXMLElement object
   $stockList = simplexml_load_file("stock_list.xml");
   // Display the object
   echo htmlspecialchars($stockList->asXML());
?>
</pre>
</body>
</html>
```

Output:

```
<?xml version="1.0" encoding="UTF-8"?>
<stockList>
  <item type="fruit">
          <name>apple</name>
          <unitPrice>0.99</unitPrice>
          <quantity>412</quantity>
  </item>
  <item type="vegetable">
          <name>beetroot</name>
          <unitPrice>1.39</unitPrice>
          <quantity>67</quantity>
  </item>
</stockList>
```

- In above program first you call simplexml_load_file() function creates a reference to XML document contained by stock_list.xml file. It actually load the root element stockList from the file stock_list.xml.

- The XML document can be displayed to the browser using echo after converting object $stockList into string. htmlspecialchars() function is used so that the XML predefined characters can not be interpreted by the browser, and the browser can display the XML document.

4.6.2 Creating an XML Document with SimpleXML

- The following example shows how to create an XML document using SimpleXML extension.
- A script to create "cricket.xml" file with multiple elements as given below

```
<CricketTeam>
        <Country name = "India">
                <PlayerName >-------- <Player Name >
                <Wickets>--------- </Wickets>
                <Runs>--------</Runs>
        </Country>
</CricketTeam>
```

- Also add country = "England" and its elements.

```
<?php
   // Create the root "CricketTeam" element
   $cricketTeam = new SimpleXMLElement(" <CricketTeam/> ");
   $country = $cricketTeam-> addChild("Country");
   $country -> addAttribute("name", "India");
   $country -> addChild("PlayerName", "M Dhoni");
   $country -> addChild("Wickets", "36");
   $country -> addChild("Runs", "10000");
   $country = $cricketTeam-> addChild("Country");
   $country -> addAttribute("name", "England");
   $country -> addChild("PlayerName", "Alastair Cook");
   $country -> addChild("Wickets", "2");
   $country -> addChild("Runs", "9500");
// Save the created XML document into cricket.xml file
   $cricketTeam -> asXML("cricket.xml");
   echo "<h4>cricket.xml created</h4>";
?>
```

- Open the "criclet.xml" file and see the output.

4.7 CONVERTING BETWEEN SIMPLEXML AND DOM OBJECTS

- It is easy to convert between a SimpleXMLElement object and a DOMElement object, meaning you can work with SimpleXML if you prefer, then switch to the DOM when you need to do something that SimpleXML can not do.
- The two key functions here are:
    1. `simplexml_import_dom(node)`: Converts the supplied DOM node, node , into a SimpleXMLElement object.
    2. `dom_import_simplexml(element)`: Converts the supplied SimpleXMLElement object, element , into a DOM node
- **Example:** The program shows the DOM object is converted into SImpleXML object.

```
<?php
$xmlstr = <<< XML
<php_programs>
    <program name = "Cart">
        <price> 100 </price>
    </program>
    <program name = "Survey">
        <price> 500 </price>
    </program>
</php_programs>
XML;
    $dom = new DOMDocument;
$dom->loadXML($xmlstr);
$s_dom = simplexml_import_dom($dom);
echo "The price of the first program is " . $s_dom->program[0]->price;
?>
```

Output:

```
The price of the first program is 100
```

- In above program one string variable $xmlstr is created which stores the XML document. Then DOM object is created and the XML is loaded into it.
- Now simplexml_import_dom() function converts the DOM object into the SimpleXML object $s_dom. Finally, using SimpleXML method the price of the first program "Cart" is displayed.

4.8 CHANGING A VALUE WITH SIMPLE XML

- Not only you can read the part of an XML document into a SimpleXML object, you can change data in the in-memory document.
- All you need to do is properly address the data you want to change and then set it equal to the value you want it to have.
- **Example:**

```
<?php
$xmlstr = <<< XML
<php_programs>
    <program name = "Cart">
        <price> 100 </price>
    </program>
    <program name = "Survey">
        <price> 500 </price>
    </program>
</php_programs>
XML;
    $first_xml_string = Simplexml_load_string($xmlstr);
    $first_xml_string→program[0]→price = '250';
    echo "<pre>";
    var_dump($first_xml_string);
    echo "</pre>";
    ?>
```

Output:

```
SimpleXMLElement Object
(
    [program] => Array
        (
            [0] => SimpleXMLElement Object
                (
                    [@attributes] => Array
                        (
                            [name] => Cart
                        )
                    [price] => 250
                )
```

```
            [1] => SimpleXMLElement Object
                (
                    [@attributes] => Array
                        (
                            [name] => Survey
                        )
                    [price] =>  500
                )
        )
)
```

SUMMARY

- XML is Extensible Markup Language which simplifies data sharing. It designed to carry and display data. XML is self descriptive.
- XML is well formed and valid document. Well formed document is the document that follows the XML specifications and valid document ensures that DTD (Data Type Definitions) is associated with document type.
- XML and PHP are combined to build web applications. PHP uses set of XML extensions and functions to transform XML mark-up and traverse XML document so as to share data between web applications.
- Most of the browsers have a built in XML parser. XML parser converts XML into JavaScript object.
- XML-DOM defines a standard for accessing and manipulating documents.
- The XML DOM defines the objects, properties and methods of all XML elements.
- Simple XML Extension is PHP Extension with set of functions to access and manipulate XML. It is provided to handle XML and to convert it into an object.

PRACTICE QUESTIONS

1. What is XML?
2. Explain the source of XML document.
3. Write note on: XML parser with example.
4. Explain few PHP DOM extension functions.
5. Explain few simple xml extension functions.
6. Write short note on: PHP and XML.
7. Explain the term document object model in detail.
8. Describe SimpleXML with example.
9. With the help of program explain XML tree structure.
10. How to change value using simple XML? Explain with example.
11. What is parser in XML? Enlist its type.

12. What are the uses of XML?

Ans. Refer to Section 4.1.

13. What is DOM?

Ans. Refer to Section 4.5.

14. “XML is case sensitive”. Justify T/F.

Ans. Refer to Section 4.1.

15. Explain the XML document structure.

Ans. Refer to Section 4.2.

16. How to define elements and attributes in XML?

Ans. Refer to Section 4.1.

17. Write any two applications of XML.

Ans. Refer to Section 4.1.

18. What is DomDocument ()?

Ans. Refer to Section 4.5.

19. What are the different kinds of parsers used in XML?

Ans. Refer to Section 4.4.

20. Write PHP script to read emp. XML file (contains emp-no, emp-name, salary, designation) and print employee details in tabular format. (use Simple XML).

Ans.

```
<?xml version="1.0" encoding="utf-8"?>
<employee>
  <emp>
    <empno>111</empno>
    <empname>John</empname>
    <salary>10000</salary>
    <designation>Accountant</designation>
  </emp>
  <emp>
    <empno>120</empno>
    <empname>Dane</empname>
    <salary>15000</salary>
    <designation>Asst. Manager</designation>
  </emp>
  <emp>
    <empno>122</empno>
    <empname>Wiely</empname>
    <salary>17000</salary>
    <designation>Manager</designation>
  </emp>
```

```
  <emp>
    <empno>100</empno>
    <empname>Robert</empname>
    <salary>12000</salary>
    <designation>Sr. Accountant</designation>
  </emp>
</employee>
XML.html
<html>
   <head><title>XML</title></head>
   <body>
   <form action="xml.php" method="get">
      Select XML File:
      <input type="file" name="fname" />
      <br><br>
      <input type="submit" name="submit" value="Read and Display">
   </form>
   </body>
</html>
<?php
   $fname=$_GET['fname'];
   $xml=simplexml_load_file($fname) or die("Error: Cannot create
object");
   echo "Contents of $fname in tabular format : <br><br>";
   echo"<table border=1><tr><th>Emp
No.</th><th>Name</th><th>Designation</th><th>Sal</th></tr>";
   foreach($xml->children() as $books) {
         echo "<tr><td>".$books->empno . "</td> ";
         echo "<td>".$books->empname . "</td> ";
         echo "<td>".$books->salary . "</td>";
         echo "<td>".$books->designation. "</td></tr>";
   }
   echo "</table>"
?>
```

Output:

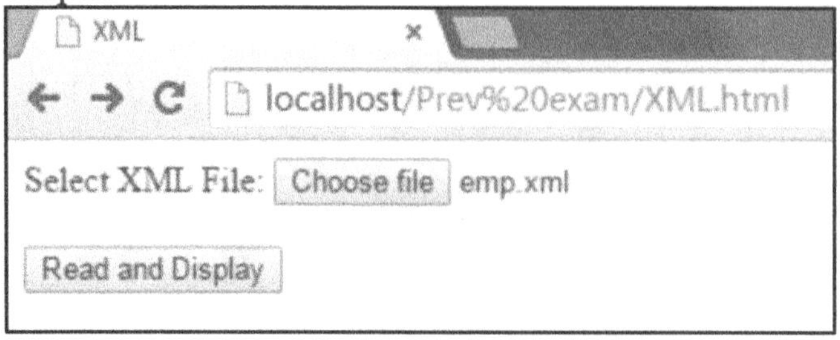

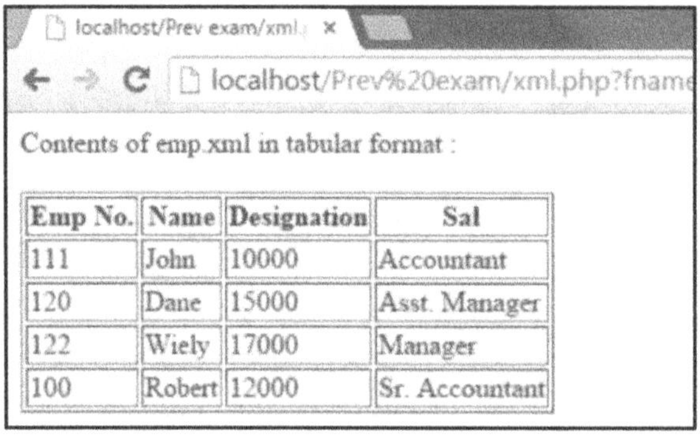

21. Explain any five advantages of XML over HTML.

Ans. Refer to Section 4.1.

22. Write a php script to read item-XMl file (contain INo, Iname, I-desc, Price) and print item details in tabular format (use simple XML).

Ans. **Item.xml**

```
<?xml version="1.0" encoding="utf-8"?>
<product>
    <item>
        <ino>1</ino>
        <iname>Dove</iname>
        <desc>Soap</desc>
        <iprice>55</iprice>
    </item>
    <item>
        <ino>2</ino>
        <iname>Iphone 6</iname>
        <desc>Mobile</desc>
        <iprice>65000</iprice>
    </item>
    <item>
```

```
        <ino>3</ino>
        <iname>T-Shirt</iname>
        <desc>Apparel</desc>
        <iprice>450</iprice>
    </item>
    <item>
        <ino>4</ino>
        <iname>Timex</iname>
        <desc>Wrist Watch</desc>
        <iprice>2500</iprice>
    </item>
</product>
```

XML.html

```
<html>
    <head><title>XML</title></head>
    <body>
    <form action="xml.php" method="get">
        Select XML File:
        <input type="file" name="fname" />
        <br><br>
        <input type="submit" name="submit" value="Read and Display">
    </form>
    </body>
</html>
<?php
    $fname=$_GET['fname'];
    $xml=simplexml_load_file($fname) or die
                                ("Error: Cannot create object");
    echo "Contents of $fname in tabular format : <br><br>";
    echo"<table border=1><tr><th>Item No.</th><th>Name</th><th>
                            Description</th><th>Price</th></tr>";
    foreach($xml->children() as $books) {
            echo "<tr><td>".$books->ino . "</td> ";
            echo "<td>".$books->iname . "</td> ";
            echo "<td>".$books->desc . "</td>";
            echo "<td>".$books->iprice . "</td></tr>";
    }
    echo "</table>"
?>
```

Output:

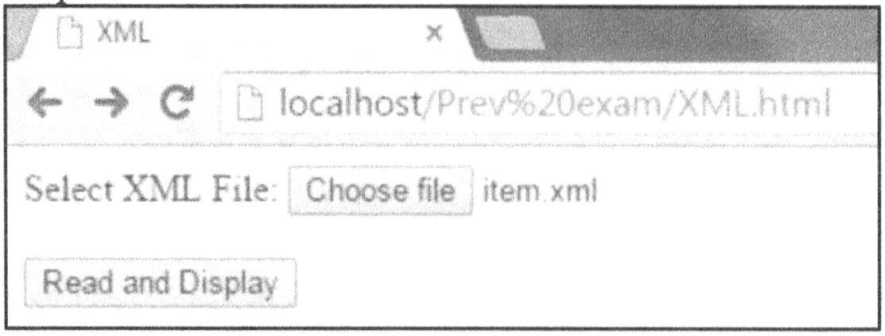

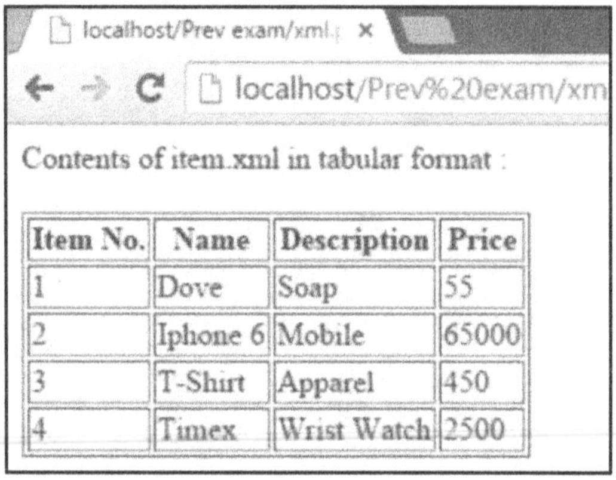

23. Write a PHP script to read book.XML and print book details in tabular format using simple XML. (Content of book.XML are (bookcode, bookname, author, publisher, price).

Ans. **Books.xml**

```
<?xml version="1.0" encoding="utf-8"?>
<bookstore>
  <book category="COOKING">
    <code >02011</code>
    <name lang="en">Everyday Italian</name>
    <author>Giada De Laurentiis</author>
    <year>2005</year>
    <price>30.00</price>
  </book>
  <book category="CHILDREN">
    <code >0156</code>
    <name lang="en">Harry Potter</name>
    <author>J K. Rowling</author>
    <year>2005</year>
    <price>29.99</price>
  </book>
```

```
    <book category="WEB">
      <code >2017</code>
      <name lang="en-us">XQuery Kick Start</name>
      <author>James McGovern</author>
      <year>2003</year>
      <price>49.99</price>
    </book>
    <book category="WEB">
      <code >5397</code>
      <name lang="en-us">Learning XML</name>
      <author>Erik T. Ray</author>
      <year>2003</year>
      <price>39.95</price>
    </book>
  </bookstore>
```

XML.html

```
<html>
   <head><title>XML</title></head>
   <body>
   <form action="xml.php" method="get">
      Select XML File:
      <input type="file" name="fname" />
      <br><br>
      <input type="submit" name="submit" value="Read and Display">
   </form>
   </body>
</html>
```

Xml.php

```
<?php
   $fname=$_GET['fname'];
   $xml=simplexml_load_file($fname)    or    die("Error:    Cannot    create
object");
   echo "Contents of $fname in tabular format : <br><br>";
   echo"<table
border=1><tr><th>Code</th><th>TItle</th><th>Author</th><th>Year</th><th>P
rice</th></tr>";
   foreach($xml->children() as $books) {
         echo "<tr><td>".$books->code . "</td> ";
         echo "<td>".$books->name . "</td> ";
         echo "<td>".$books->author . "</td>";
         echo "<td>".$books->year . "</td>";
         echo "<td>".$books->price . "</td></tr>";
   }
   echo "</table>"
?>
```

Output:

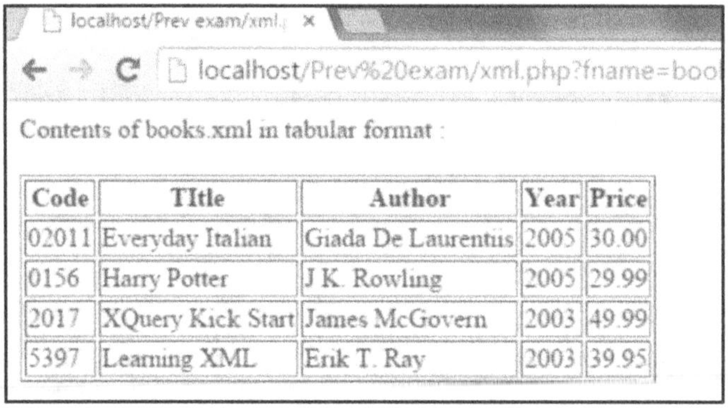

UNIVERSITY QUESTIONS AND ANSWERS

1 Mark Questions:

1. Write any two applications of XML. **(Oct. 2014)**

Ans. Refer to Section 4.1.

2. What is XML Parser? **(April 2012, 2015)**

Ans. Refer to Section 4.4.

3. Give names of two XML parsers. **(April 2013, Oct. 2014)**

Ans. Refer to Section 4.4.

5 Mark Questions:

4. Write a PHP script to read student.xml file which contains student roll no, name, address, college, and course. Print student's details of specific course in tabular format after accepting course as input. **(April 2013)**

Ans. Student.xml

```
<?xml version="1.0" encoding="utf-8"?>
<college>
<student>
    <rno>1</rno>
    <name>John</name>
    <addr>PUNE</addr>
    <collegename>Science College</collegename>
    <course>BSC CS</course>
```

```
</student>
<student>
    <rno>2</rno>
    <name>Bob</name>
    <addr>Mumbai</addr>
    <collegename>Arts College</collegename>
    <course>BA</course>
</student>
<student>
    <rno>3</rno>
    <name>Wiely</name>
    <addr>Nashik</addr>
    <collegename>Commerce</collegename>
    <course>BCOM</course>
</student>
<student>
    <rno>4</rno>
    <name>Sam</name>
    <addr>Satara</addr>
    <collegename>Management College</collegename>
    <course>BCA</course>
</student>
</college>
```

XML.html

```
<html>
    <head><title>XML</title></head>
    <body>
    <form action="xml.php" method="get">
        Select XML File:
        <input type="file" name="fname" />
        <br><br>
        <input type="submit" name="submit" value="Read and Display">
    </form>
    </body>
</html>
<?php
    $fname=$_GET['fname'];
    $xml=simplexml_load_file($fname) or die
                                        ("Error: Cannot create object");
    echo "Contents of $fname in tabular format : <br><br>";
    echo"<table border=1><tr><th>Roll No. </th> <th> Name </th> <th>
                  Address </th> <th> College</th><th>Course</th></tr>";
```

```
        foreach($xml->children() as $books) {
                echo "<tr><td>".$books->rno . "</td> ";
                echo "<td>".$books->name . "</td> ";
                echo "<td>".$books->addr . "</td>";
                echo "<td>".$books->collegename . "</td>";
                echo "<td>".$books->course . "</td></tr>";
        }
        echo "</table>"
?>
```

Output:

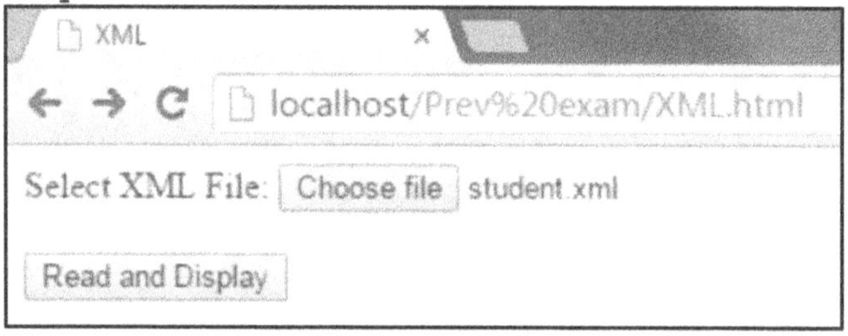

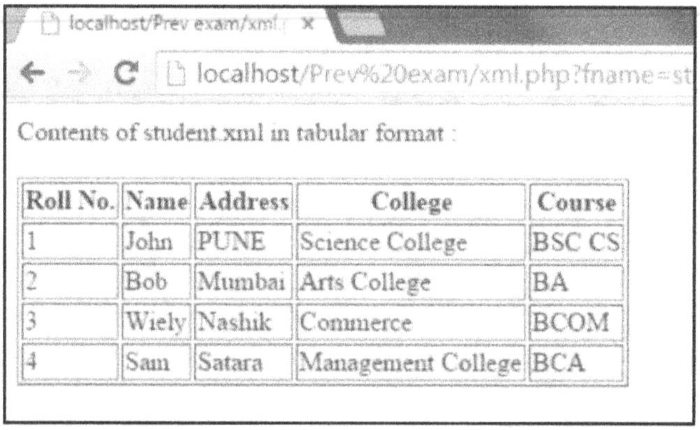

Roll No.	Name	Address	College	Course
1	John	PUNE	Science College	BSC CS
2	Bob	Mumbai	Arts College	BA
3	Wiely	Nashik	Commerce	BCOM
4	Sam	Satara	Management College	BCA

5. Write a note on DOM. **(April 2015)**

Ans. Refer to Section 4.5.

6. Explain rules to write XML elements and attributes with example. **(April 2015)**

Ans. Refer to Section 4.2.2.

7. What is DOM and how does it relate to XML? **(Oct. 2014)**

Ans. Refer to Section 4.5.

8. Write a php script to read Account. XML file which contains Account-No, name, address, branch, Account type, balance. Print Account details of specific branch in tabular format after accepting branch as input. **(Oct. 2014)**

Ans. Account.xml

```xml
<?xml version="1.0" encoding="utf-8"?>
<bank>
<account>
    <acno>1111</acno>
    <name>bob</name>
    <addr>mumbai</addr>
    <branch>dadar</branch>
    <actype>savings</actype>
    <bal>10000</bal>
</account>
<account>
    <acno>2222</acno>
    <name>sam</name>
    <addr>satara</addr>
    <branch>cbs</branch>
    <actype>current</actype>
    <bal>50000</bal>
</account>
<account>
    <acno>3333</acno>
    <name>wiely</name>
    <addr>nashik</addr>
    <branch>mg road</branch>
    <actype>current</actype>
    <bal>76000</bal>
</account>
<account>
    <acno>4444</acno>
    <name>john</name>
    <addr>pune</addr>
    <branch>jm road</branch>
    <actype>savings</actype>
    <bal>16000</bal>
</account>
</bank>
```

XML.html

```
<html>
    <head><title>XML</title></head>
    <body>
    <form action="xml.php" method="get">
        Select XML File:
        <input type="file" name="fname" />
        <br><br>
        <input type="submit" name="submit" value="Read and Display">
    </form>
    </body>
</html>
```

Xml.php

```
<?php
    $fname=$_GET['fname'];
    $xml=simplexml_load_file($fname)   or   die("Error:   Cannot   create
object");
    echo "Contents of $fname in tabular format : <br><br>";
    echo"<table border=1><tr><th>Account No.</th><th>Name</th><th>
          Address</th><th>Branch</th><th>Type</th><th>Balance</th></tr>";
    foreach($xml->children() as $books) {
          echo "<tr><td>".$books->acno . "</td> ";
          echo "<td>".$books->name . "</td> ";
          echo "<td>".$books->addr . "</td>";
          echo "<td>".$books->branch . "</td>";
          echo "<td>".$books->actype . "</td>";
          echo "<td>".$books->bal . "</td></tr>";
    }
    echo "</table>"
?>
```

Output:

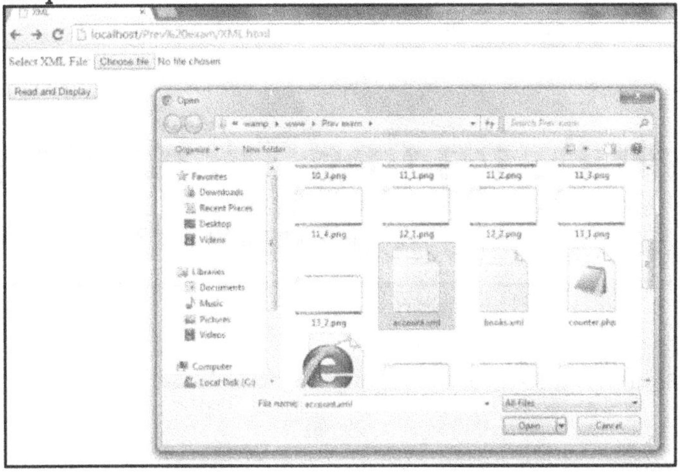
Select XML File: Choose file No file chosen
Read and Display

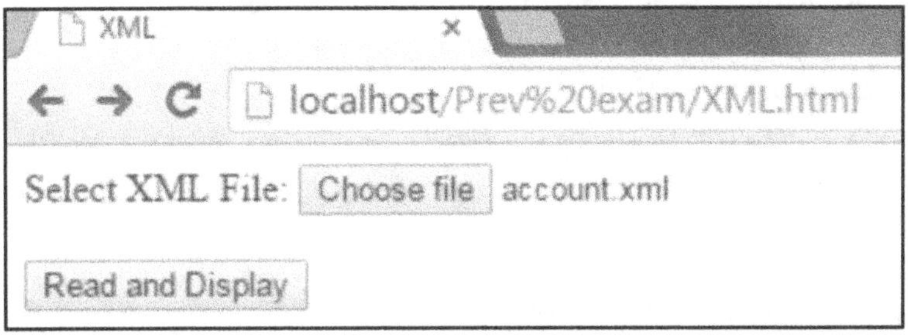
XML
localhost/Prev%20exam/XML.html
Select XML File: Choose file account.xml
Read and Display

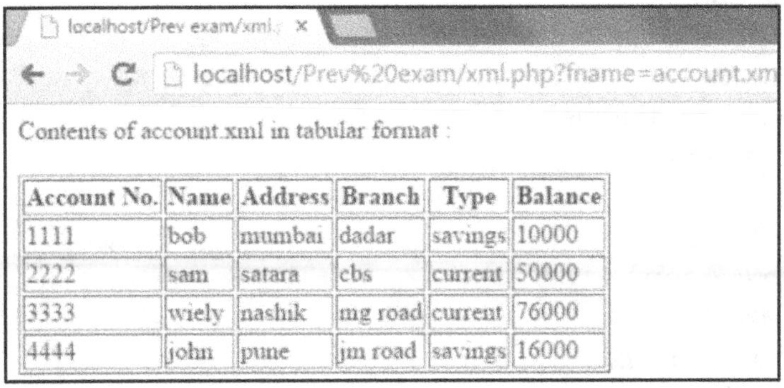
localhost/Prev exam/xml.
localhost/Prev%20exam/xml.php?fname=account.xm
Contents of account.xml in tabular format :
Account No. Name Address Branch Type Balance
1111 bob mumbai dadar savings 10000
2222 sam satara cbs current 50000
3333 wiely nashik mg road current 76000
4444 john pune jm road savings 16000

■■■

CHAPTER 5

Web Designing Technologies (JavaScript-DHTML)

Contents ...

Objectives...

- To Study Basic Concepts of JavaScript and DHTML
- To Study JavaScript Control Statements and Loop Statements
- To Understand JavaScript Functions and Strings
- To Learn JavaScript Pop-up Boxes and Events

5.1 OVERVIEW OF JAVASCRIPT AND DHTML

- JavaScript is a scripting language designed primarily for adding interactivity to Web pages and creating Web applications.
- Script means list of actions for the something to perform.
- A scripting language is a language that interprets scripts at runtime. Scripts are usually embedded into other software environments.
- Scripting languages are of two types:
  1. Client-side scripting languages, and
  2. Server-side scripting languages.
- Client-server script runs at user's end i.e. the browser execute the scripts. JavaScript is an example of a client side script that is interpreted by the client browser.
- Where as server-side scripting language is executed on a web server. PHP is a server side script that is interpreted on the server.

5.1.1 JavaScript

- JavaScript is a lightweight, interpreted programming language.
- JavaScript is very easy to implement because it is integrated with HTML. It is open and cross-platform.
- JavaScript most commonly used as a part of web pages, whose implementations allow client-side script to interact with the user and make dynamic pages. It is an interpreted programming language with object-oriented capabilities.

5.1.1.1 Features of JavaScript

- Features of JavaScript are listed below:
  1. JavaScript is an object-based scripting language.
  2. It is light weighted.
  3. JavaScript is a scripting language and it is not java.
  4. JavaScript is interpreter based scripting language.
  5. JavaScript gives HTML designers a programming tool.
  6. JavaScript can put dynamic text into an HTML page.
  7. JavaScript can react to event.
  8. JavaScript can read and write HTML document.
  9. JavaScript can be used to validate data.
  10. JavaScript is object based language as it provides predefined objects.
  11. Most of the JavaScript control statements syntax is same as syntax of control statements in C language.

5.1.1.2 Advantages and Disadvantages of JavaScript

Advantages:

1. **Less server interaction:** We can validate user input before sending the page to the server. Which means less load on our server.
2. **Immediate feedback to the visitors:** They do not have to wait for a page reload to see if they have forgotten to enter something.
3. **Increased interactivity:** We can create interfaces that react when the user put mouse on that interface.
4. **Richer interfaces:** We can use JavaScript to include such items as drag-and-drop components and sliders to give a Rich Interface to our site visitors.
5. **Speed:** Being client-side, JavaScript is very fast because any code functions can be run immediately instead of having to contact the server and wait for an answer.
6. **Simplicity:** JavaScript is relatively simple to learn and implement.
7. **Versatility:** JavaScript plays nicely with other languages and can be used in a huge variety of applications. Unlike PHP or SSI scripts, JavaScript can be inserted into any web page regardless of the file extension. JavaScript can also be used inside scripts written in other languages such as Perl and PHP.
8. **Server load:** Being client-side reduces the demand on the website server.

Disadvantages:

1. Client-side JavaScript does not allow the reading or writing of files. This has been kept for security reason.
2. JavaScript cannot be used for Networking applications because there is no such support available.
3. JavaScript does not have any multithreading or multiprocessing capabilities.
4. **Security:** Because the code executes on the users' computer, in some cases it can be exploited for malicious purposes. This is one reason some people choose to disable JavaScript.
5. **Reliance on End User:** JavaScript is sometimes interpreted differently by different browsers. Whereas, server-side scripts will always produce the same output, client-side scripts can be a little unpredictable. Don't be overly concerned by this though - as long as you test your script in all the major browsers you should be safe.

5.1.2 DHTML

- DHTML stands for Dynamic HyperText Markup Language.
- DHTML uses collection of technologies together to create interactive and animated web sites. It uses combination of a static markup language (such as HTML), a client-side scripting language (such as JavaScript), a presentation definition language (such as CSS), and the Document Object Model.
- DHTML allows scripting languages to change variables in a web page's definition language, which in turn affects the look. DHTML has dynamic characteristic. It generates a unique page with each page load.
- DHTML allows programmers to add effects to their web pages that are otherwise difficult to achieve.
- DHTML is the combination of HTML, CSS and JavaScript it perform the following task:
  1. Animate text and images in their document, independently moving each element from any starting point to any ending point, following a predetermined path or one chosen by the user.
  2. Embed a ticker that automatically refreshes its content with the latest news, stock quotes, or other data.
  3. Use a form to capture user input, and then process, verify and respond to that data without having to send data back to the server.
  4. Include rollover buttons or drop-down menus.
- DHTML is the combination of several built-in browser features in fourth generation browsers that enable a web page to be more dynamic.

- DHTML is NOT a scripting language (like JavaScript), but merely a browser feature- or enhancement- that gives your browser the ability to be dynamic. What you really want to learn is not DHTML itself, but rather, the syntax needed to use DHTML.
- The technology of DHTML is currently at its development stage, with NE, IE 5 differing quite greatly in their implementation of this great technology. It's currently not possible to write one DHTML code and expect it to function in both browsers properly.

5.2 OBJECT ORIENTATION AND JAVASCRIPT

- JavaScript features powerful, flexible OOP capabilities. In JavaScript, you can write code that can be re-used and that is encapsulated.
- JavaScript is all about objects. Windows and buttons, forms and images, links and anchors are all objects. Programming languages like Java, C++, and Python that focus on objects are called Object-Oriented Programming (OOP) languages.
- JavaScript is called an Object-Based Language because it doesn't technically meet the criteria of the more heavy-duty languages, but it certainly behaves as an object-oriented language.
- In the real world, you may see a book or a car as an object. JavaScript can represent data such as a string or a number as an object, and JavaScript lets you create your own objects also. Object-oriented languages, such as C++ and Java, bundle up data and behaviour and call it an object. So does JavaScript.
- JavaScript sees your browser window as an object, a window that can be resized, opened, closed, and so on. It sees all the frames, documents, images, and widgets inside the window as objects. And these objects have properties and methods.
- JavaScript supports several types of objects, as follows:
  1. User-defined objects defined by the programmer.
  2. Core or built-in objects, such as Date, String, and Number.
  3. Browser objects, the BOM.
  4. The Document objects, the DOM.
- Core objects are built right into the language. JavaScript provides built-in objects that deal with the date and time, math, strings, regular expressions, numbers, and other useful entities.
- The core objects are consistent across different implementations and platforms, and were standardized by the ECMAScript 1.0 specification, allowing programs to be portable.

- JavaScript programs are associated with a browser window and the document displayed in the window. The window is a browser object and the document is an HTML object.
- In the browser object model, sometimes called BOM, the window is at the top of the tree, and below it are objects: window, navigator, frames[], document, history, location, and screen.

5.3 BASIC SYNTAX (JS DATATYPES AND JS VARIABLES) (April 13)

- JavaScript is case sensitive language.
- Two types of comments used in JavaScript:
  1. Multi line comment i.e.,

     /* --------------------

     ---------------- */
  2. Single line comment i.e.,

     // ----------------------
- { } are used to indicate a block of code.
- ; is optional at the end of the statement.
- JavaScript can be implemented using JavaScript statements that are placed within the <script>... </script> HTML tags in a web page.
- You can place the <script> tags, containing your JavaScript, anywhere within you web page, but it is normally recommended that you should keep it within the <head> tags.
- The <script> tag alerts the browser program to start interpreting all the text between these tags as a script. **(April 13)**
- A simple syntax of your JavaScript will appear as follows:

```
<script ...>
 JavaScript code ...
</script>
```

- The script tag takes two important attributes:
  1. **Language:** This attribute specifies what scripting language you are using. Typically, its value will be javascript.
  2. **Type:** This attribute is what is now recommended to indicate the scripting language in use and its value should be set to "text/javascript".
- So your JavaScript segment will look like:

```
<script language="javascript" type="text/javascript">
 JavaScript code ...
</script>
```

- <script> and </script> informs browser that everything in between is a scripting language. The attribute type, is given a value "text/javascript", specifying that the scripting language is javascript.

Embedding JavaScript:

- Javascript can be added in the <body> or in the <head> sections of an HTML code.

1. **Example of Embedding JavaScript in <head> Tag:**

```
<html>
<head>
<title>Javascript Example </title>
<script type="text/javascript">
   document.write("My First Javascript");
</script>
</head>
</html>
```

Output:

```
My first Javascript
```

- In document.write document is the part of browser where we see webpage content, document.write will write the text in parentheses (round brackets) to the browser document. In our case, the text "My First Javascript" will be written. The double quotes are important when we want to print/write the text in is. And every statement in JavaScript ends with a semi-colon(;).

2. **Example shows Embedded JavaScript in <body > Tag:**

```
<html>
<body>
This is body.
<script type="text/javascript">
   document.write("Hello World!");
</script>
</body>
</html>
```

Output:

```
This is body.
Hello World!
```

3. Embedding a JavaScript using External File:

- First create "myScript.js" file write the following JavaScript code in it.

```
document.write("This is JavaScript");
```

- Now create an HTML file and put the following code. In this HTML the JavaScript is embedded externally.

```
<html>
<body>
    This is body <br>
    <script type="text/javascript" src="myScript.js"></script>
</body>
</html>
```

Output:

```
This is body
This is JavaScript
```

5.3.1 JavaScript Datatypes (April 2016)

- One of the most fundamental characteristics of a programming language is the set of data types it supports. These are the type of values that can be represented and manipulated in a programming language.
- JavaScript provides different data types to hold different types of values. There are two types of data types in JavaScript.
    1. Primitive data type, and
    2. Non-primitive (Reference) data type.
- There are five types of primitive data types in JavaScript. They are as follows:

Data Type	Description
String	Represents sequence of characters e.g. "hello".
Number	Represents numeric values e.g. 100.
Boolean	Represents boolean value either false or true.
Undefined	Represents undefined value.
Null	Represents null i.e. no value at all.

- The non-primitive data types are as follows:

Data Type	Description
Object	Represents instance through which we can access members.
Array	Represents group of similar values.
RegExp	Represents regular expression.

5.3.2 Regular Expression

- A regular expression is a sequence of characters that forms a search pattern.
- When you search for data in a text, you can use this search pattern to describe what you are searching for.
- A regular expression can be a single character, or a more complicated pattern.
- Regular expressions can be used to perform all types of text search and text replace operations.

  Syntax: `/pattern/modifiers;`

  Example: `var patt = /niraliprakashan/i;`

  Example explained:

  `/ niraliprakashan/i` is a regular expression.

  `niraliprakashan` is a pattern (to be used in a search).

  `i` is a modifier (modifies the search to be case-insensitive).

5.3.3 Variables

- Variables are "containers" for storing information.
- JavaScript variables are used to hold values (a = 5) or expressions (x = y + z) in them.

  Syntax: `var variable_name = value;`
- We define variables in JavaScript using a keyword var. variable_name is name of the variable which holds some value.

  Example: `var x = 10;`
- In the above statement, we assigned value "10" to a variable x.
- There are some rules for variable names in JavaScript:
  1. A variable must start with an alphabet or an underscore.
  2. The subsequent characters can be digits (0-9) or alphabets or an underscore.
  3. As JavaScript is case-sensitive, number is not same as Number.
- Some valid examples of variable names in JavaScript are given below:

  `simple_Interest, _name, number1`
- Some invalid examples of variable names are given below:

  `23Amar, &MyName, Mega%tron`

1. **Variable Scope:**

- The scope of a variable is the region of our program in which it is defined.
- JavaScript variable will have only two scopes:

  (i) **Global variables:** A global variable has global scope which means it is defined everywhere in our JavaScript code.

(ii) Local variables: A local variable will be visible only within a function where it is defined. Function parameters are always local to that function.

- Global variables are accessible from anywhere in the program. On other hand, Local variables are accessible only in the function they are defined.

Example:

```
<html>
    <head>
    <title>Javascript Local and Global Variables Example</title>
    </head>
    <body>
    <script type="text/javascript">
    var a = 10; //global variable
    function test(){
        document.write("a = "+a); //access inside function
        var b = 20; // local variable
        document.write("<br/>");
        document.write("b = "+b); //access inside function
        document.write("<br/>");
    }
    test();
    document.write("a = "+a); //acces outside function
    document.write("b = "+b); //not acces outside function
    </script>
    </body>
</html>
```

Output:

```
a = 10
b = 20
a = 10
```

- We declared a=10; outside the function, hence its a global variable, and can be accessed from anywhere in the program. In the above example, we accessed it from inside the function and as well as outside the function using document.write("a = "+a); statement.
- We declared b=20; inside the function, hence its a local variable, and can be accessed only within the function but from the outside the function it is not accessible.

5.4 PRIMITIVES, OPERATIONS AND EXPRESSIONS

- An operator is used to transform one or more values into a single resultant values and the values to which the operator is applied is referred as operands.
- JavaScript language supports following type of operators:
  1. Arithmetic operators,
  2. Comparison operators,
  3. Logical (or Relational) operators,
  4. Assignment operators, and
  5. Conditional (or ternary) operators.

1. Arithmetic Operators:

- Arithmetic operators are used to perform arithmetic between variables and/or values.
- Following table shows arithmetic operators supported by JavaScript language. Assume variable A holds 10 and variable B holds 20 then:

Sr. No.	Operator	Description	Example
1.	+ (Addition Operator)	Adds two operands.	A + B = 30
2.	– (Subtraction Operator)	Subtracts second operand from the first.	A – B = –10
3.	* (Multiplication Operator)	Multiply both operands.	A * B = 200
4.	/ (Division Operator)	Divide numerator by denumerator.	B / A = 2
5.	% (Modulus Operator)	Modulus operator and remainder of after an integer division.	B % A = 0
6.	++ (Increment Operator)	Increases integer value by one.	A++ = 11
7.	-- (Decrement Operator)	Decreases integer value by one.	A-- = 9

2. Comparison Operators:

- Comparison operators are used to compare a condition and are always inside conditional statements. A comparison evaluate to their true or false. These true and false values are called Booleans.

- Following table shows comparison operators supported by JavaScript and assume variable A holds 10 and B holds 20.

Sr. No.	Operator	Description	Example
1.	== (Equal To Operator)	This operator checks if the value of two operands are equal or not, if yes then condition becomes true.	(A == B) is not true.
2.	!= (Not Equal To Operator)	This operator checks if the value of two operands are equal or not, if values are not equal then condition becomes true.	(A != B) is true.
3.	> (Greater Than Operator)	This operator checks if the value of left operand is greater than the value of right operand, if yes then condition becomes true.	(A > B) is not true.
4.	< (Less Than Operator)	This operator checks if the value of left operand is less than the value of right operand, if yes then condition becomes true.	(A < B) is true.
5.	>= (Less Than or Equal To Operator)	This operator checks if the value of left operand is greater than or equal to the value of right operand, if yes then condition becomes true.	(A >= B) is not true.
6.	<= (Greater Than or Equal To Operator)	This operator checks if the value of left operand is less than or equal to the value of right operand, if yes then condition becomes true.	(A <= B) is true.

3. **Logical Operators:**

- Using logical operators, we can test two or more conditions in one line code.
- There are following logical operators supported by JavaScript and assume variable A holds 10 and variable B holds 20 then:

Sr. No.	Operator	Description	Example
1.	&& (Logical AND Operator)	If both the operands are non zero then condition becomes true.	(A && B) is true.
2.	|| (Logical OR Operator)	If any of the two operands are non zero then then condition becomes true.	(A || B) is true.
3.	! (Logical NOT Operator)	Use to reverses the logical state of its operand. If a condition is true then Logical NOT operator will make false.	!(A && B) is false.

4. **Bitwise Operators:**

- Bitwise operators act upon the individual bits of their operands.
- Following table gives bitwise operators supported by JavaScript and assume variable A holds 2 and variable B holds 3 then:

Sr. No.	Operator	Description	Example
1.	& (Bitwise AND operator)	It performs a Boolean AND operation on each bit of its integer arguments.	(A & B) is 2.
2.	| (Bitwise OR Operator)	It performs a Boolean OR operation on each bit of its integer arguments.	(A | B) is 3.
3.	^ (Bitwise XOR Operator)	It performs a Boolean exclusive OR operation on each bit of its integer arguments. Exclusive OR means that either operand one is true or operand two is true, but not both.	(A ^ B) is 1.
4.	~ (Bitwise NOT Operator)	It is a is a unary operator and operates by reversing all bits in the operand.	(~B) is -4 .

contd. ...

5.	<< (Bitwise Shift Left Operator)	It moves all bits in its first operand to the left by the number of places specified in the second operand. New bits are filled with zeros. Shifting a value left by one position is equivalent to multiplying by 2, shifting two positions is equivalent to multiplying by 4, etc.	(A << 1) is 4.
6.	>> (Bitwise Shift Right with Sign Operator)	It moves all bits in its first operand to the right by the number of places specified in the second operand. The bits filled in on the left depend on the sign bit of the original operand, in order to preserve the sign of the result. If the first operand is positive, the result has zeros placed in the high bits; if the first operand is negative, the result has ones placed in the high bits. Shifting a value right one place is equivalent to dividing by 2 (discarding the remainder), shifting right two places is equivalent to integer division by 4, and so on.	(A >> 1) is 1.
7.	>>> (Bitwise Shift Right with Zero Operator)	This operator is just like the >> operator, except that the bits shifted in on the left are always zero.	(A >>> 1) is 1.

5. Assignment Operators:

- Assignment operators are used to assign values to JavaScript variables.
- There are following assignment operators supported by JavaScript.

Sr. No.	Operator	Description	Example
1.	= (Simple Assignment Operator)	Assigns values from right side operands to left side operand.	C = A + B will assignee value of A + B into C.
2.	+= (Add and Assign-ment Operator)	It adds right operand to the left operand and assign the result to left operand.	C += A is equivalent to C = C + A.
3.	-= (Subtract and Assignment Operator)	It subtracts right operand from the left operand and assign the result to left operand.	C -= A is equivalent to C = C - A.
4.	*= (Multiply and Assignment Operator)	It multiplies right operand with the left operand and assign the result to left operand.	C *= A is equivalent to C = C * A.
5.	/= (Divide and Assignment Operator)	It divides left operand with the right operand and assign the result to left operand.	C /= A is equivalent to C = C / A.
6.	%= (Modulus and Assignment Operator)	It takes modulus using two operands and assign the result to left operand.	C %= A is equi-valent to C = C % A.

6. Conditional Operators (?:):

- There is an operator called conditional operator. This first evaluates an expression for a true or false value and then execute one of the two given statements depending upon the result of the evaluation.
- The conditional operator has following syntax:

Sr. No.	Operator	Description	Example
1.	?:	Conditional Expression	If Condition is true? Then value X: Otherwise value Y.

7. typeof Operator:

- The typeof is a unary operator that is placed before its single operand, which can be of any type. Its value is a string indicating the data type of the operand.

- The typeof operator evaluates to "number", "string", or "boolean" if its operand is a number, string, or boolean value and returns true or false based on the evaluation.
- Here, is the list of return values for the typeof Operator:

Type	String Returned by typeof
Number	"number"
String	"string"
Boolean	"boolean"
Object	"object"
Function	"function"
Undefined	"undefined"
Null	"object"

Expressions:

- An expression is any valid set of literals, variables, operators, and expressions that evaluates to a single value.
- The value may be a number, a string, or a logical value. Conceptually, there are two types of expressions i.e., those that assign a value to a variable, and those that simply have a value.
- For example, the expression x = 7 is an expression that assigns x the value 7. This expression itself evaluates to 7. Such expressions use assignment operators.
- On the other hand, the expression 3 + 4 simply evaluates to 7; it does not perform an assignment. The operators used in such expressions are referred to simply as operators.

5.5 JS CONTROL STATEMENTS

- While writing a program, there may be a situation when we need to adopt one path out of the given two paths. So we need to make use of conditional statements that allow our program to make correct decisions and perform right actions.
- JavaScript supports conditional statements which are used to perform different actions based on different conditions.
- In JavaScript we have the following conditional statements:
  1. **if Statement:** Use this statement to execute some code only if a specified condition is true.
  2. **if...else Statement:** Use this statement to execute some code if the condition is true and another code if the condition is false.

3. **if...elseif....else Statement:** Use this statement to select one of many blocks of code to be executed.
4. **switch Statement:** Use this statement to select one of many blocks of code to be executed.

5.5.1 if Statement

- The if statement is the fundamental control statement that allows JavaScript to make decisions and execute statements conditionally.
- We can use the if statement to execute some code only if a specified condition is true.

Syntax:

```
if(condition)
{
execute this statement;
}
```

Example:

```
<!DOCTYPE html>
<head><title>If statement</title></head>
<body>
<script type="text/javascript">
var x = 7;
var y = 7;
if(x==y)
{
   document.write("Both are equal");
}
</script>
</body>
</html>
```

Output:

```
Both are equal
```

5.5.2 if...else Statement

- We can use the if....else statement to execute some code if a condition is true and another code if the condition is not true.
- The keyword if executes a statement only if the condition is true. It does not do anything if the condition is false.

Syntax:

```
if(condition)
{
execute this statement;
}
else
{
execute this statement;
}
```

Example:

```
<script>
var a=40;
if(a%2==0)
{
    document.write("a is even number");
}
else{
    document.write("a is odd number");
}
</script>
```

Output:

```
a is even number
```

5.5.3 if... elseif... else Statement

- The if...else if... statement is the one level advance form of control statement that allows JavaScript to make correct decision out of several conditions.

Syntax:

```
if(condition)
{
    execute this statement;
}
else if(condition)
{
    execute this statement;
}
else
{
    execute this statement;
}
```

Example:

```
<!DOCTYPE html>
<body>
<script type="text/javascript">
var your_age = 14;
var friends_age = 16;
if(your_age >= 18)
{
   document.write("Get a drivers license");
}
else if(friends_age >= 18) {
   document.write("Let our friend drive the car");
}
else {
   document.write("Kids, stick to bicycle");
}
</script>
</body>
</html>
```

Output:

```
Kids, stick to bicycle
```

5.5.4 switch Statement

- Switch statement is used to execute one of the statements from many blocks of statements.
- Switch statement is like enhanced if-else if-else statement, only less confusing and more easy and simple to use.

Syntax:

```
switch(value/expression)
{
case "value1":
execute this statement1;
break;
```

```
case "value2":
execute this statement2;
break;
---
---
---
default:
executes this statement;
}
```

Example:

```
<!DOCTYPE html>
<body>
<script>
var x;
var d=new Date().getDay();
switch (d)
 {
 case 0:
 x="Today it's Sunday";
 break;
 case 1:
 x="Today it's Monday";
 break;
 case 2:
 x="Today it's Tuesday";
 break;
 case 3:
 x="Today it's Wednesday";
 break;
 case 4:
 x="Today it's Thursday";
 break;
 case 5:
 x="Today it's Friday";
 break;
```

```
 case 6:
 x="Today it's Saturday";
 break;
 default:
 x="Looking forward to the Weekend";
 }
document.write(x);
</script>
</body>
</html>
```

Output:

```
Today it's Sunday
```

5.5.5 Loops

- It is often the case that we want to do something fixed number of times or until a particular condition has been met. In JavaScript, this repetitive operation is done using loops.
- Loops can execute a block of code a number of times.
- JavaScript supports following kinds of loops:
  1. **for:** Loops through a block of code a number of times.
  2. **for/in:** Loops through the properties of an object.
  3. **while:** Loops through a block of code while a specified condition is true.
  4. **do/while:** Loops through a block of code while a specified condition is true.

5.5.5.1 for Loop

- The 'for' loop is the most compact form of looping. It includes the following three important parts:
  1. **The loop initialization** where we initialize our counter to a starting value. The initialization statement is executed before the loop begins.
  2. **The test statement** which will test if a given condition is true or not. If the condition is true, then the code given inside the loop will be executed, otherwise the control will come out of the loop.
  3. **The iteration statement** where you can increase or decrease your counter.

Syntax:

```
for(initialize; condition; increment)
{
execute statements;
}
```

Example:

```
<!DOCTYPE html>
<head>
<script type="text/javascript">
for(var x=6; x<=10; x++)
{
    document.write("The number is: " +x);
    document.write("<br/>");
}
</script>
</head>
</html>
```

Output:

```
The number is: 6
The number is: 7
The number is: 8
The number is: 9
The number is: 10
```

5.5.5.2 for/in Loop

- JavaScript for/in statement loops through the properties of an object.

Syntax:

```
for (variablename in object){
    statement or block to execute ...
}
```

- In each iteration, one property from object is assigned to variablename and this loop continues till all the properties of the object are exhausted.

Example:

```
<html>
<body>
<script>
var x;
var txt="";
var person={fname:"John",lname:"Doe",age:25};
```

```
for (x in person)
{
document.write(person[x] + " ");
}
</script>
</body>
</html>
```

Output:

```
John Doe 25
```

5.5.5.3 while Loop

- The purpose of a while loop is to execute a statement or code block repeatedly as long as an expression is true. Once, the expression becomes false, the loop terminates.

Syntax:

```
initialize;
while (condition)
{
execute statement;
increment;
}
```

Example:

```
<!DOCTYPE html>
<head>
<script type="text/javascript">
var number = 3;
while (number <= 10)
{
document.write("The number is: " +number);
document.write("<br/>");
number++;
}
</script>
</head>
</html>
```

Output:

```
The number is: 3
The number is: 4
The number is: 5
The number is: 6
The number is: 7
The number is: 8
The number is: 9
The number is: 10
```

5.5.5.4 do/while Loop

- Sometimes, we want some statements to be executed atleast once even if the condition is false for the first time. To do this we use a do-while loop.

Syntax:

```
do{
 Statements to be executed;
} while (expression);
```

Example:

```
<html>
<body>
<script>
var x="",i=0;
do
 {
 x=x + "The number is " + i + "<br>";
 i++;
 }
while (i<5)
document.write(x);
</script>
</body>
</html>
```

Output:

```
The number is 0
The number is 1
The number is 2
The number is 3
The number is 4
```

5.5.6 Loop Control Statements

- JavaScript provides full control to handle loops and switch statements. There may be a situation when you need to come out of a loop without reaching at its bottom.
- There may also be a situation when you want to skip a part of your code block and start the next iteration of the look.
- To handle all such situations, JavaScript provides break and continue statements. These statements are used to immediately come out of any loop or to start the next iteration of any loop respectively.

5.5.6.1 break Statement

- break statement indicates the end of that particular case.
- break statement was used to "jump out" of a switch() statement.
- The break statement can also be used to jump out of a loop.
- The break statement breaks the loop and continues executing the code after the loop (if any).

Syntax:

```
break;
```

Example:

The following example illustrates the use of a break statement with a while loop. Notice how the loop breaks out early once x reaches 5 and reaches to document.write (..) statement just below to the closing curly brace:

```
<html>
    <body>
        <script type="text/javascript">
            <!--
            var x = 1;
            document.write("Entering the loop<br /> ");
            while (x < 20)
            {
                if (x == 5){
                    break; // breaks out of loop completely
                }
                x = x + 1;
                document.write( x + "<br />");
            }
```

```
            document.write("Exiting the loop!<br /> ");
            //-->
        </script>
        <p>Set the variable to different value and then try...</p>
    </body>
</html>
```

Output:

```
Entering the loop
   2
   3
   4
   5
Exiting the loop!
Set the variable to different value and then try...
```

- We already have seen the usage of break statement inside a switch statement.

5.5.6.2 continue Statement

- The continue statement breaks one iteration (in the loop), if a specified condition occurs, and continues with the next iteration in the loop.

  Syntax: `continue;`

Labels:

- JavaScript statements can be labeled. To label JavaScript statements we proceed the statements with a colon(:).

```
label:
statements
```

- The break and the continue statements are the only JavaScript statements that can "jump out of" a code block.

Syntax:

```
break labelname;
continue labelname;
```

- The continue statement (with or without a label reference) can only be used inside a loop.
- The break statement, without a label reference, can only be used inside a loop or a switch.
- With a label reference, it can be used to "jump out of" any JavaScript code block.

Example:

```
<!DOCTYPE html>
<body>
<script>
cars=["Ritz","Alto","Bravo","Ford"];
list:
{
document.write(cars[0] + "<br>");
document.write(cars[1] + "<br>");
document.write(cars[2] + "<br>");
break list;
document.write(cars[3] + "<br>");
document.write(cars[4] + "<br>");
document.write(cars[5] + "<br>");
}
</script>
</body>
</html>
```

Output:

```
Ritz
Alto
Bravo
```

5.6 JS FUNCTIONS

- Like any other advance programming language, JavaScript also supports all the features necessary to write modular code using functions.
- A function is a block of code that will be executed when "someone" calls it.
- Function is a block of statements that performs certain task.
- Functions are of two types' pre-defined/built-in functions and user-defined functions.
- Built-in functions are the functions that are already defined in the javascript. Examples are write(), alert(), prompt() etc.
- User-defined functions are defined by a user. Sometimes, this functions are simple, and sometimes they are quite complex.

Function Definition:

- The most common way to define a function in JavaScript is by using the function keyword, followed by a unique function name, a list of parameters (that might be empty), and a statement block surrounded by curly braces.

Syntax:

```
<script type="text/javascript">
function function_name(parameter-list)
{
    statements ...
}
</script>
```

Calling a Function:

- A function can be called from any section of our code.

  Syntax: `functionName();`

Example:

```
<!DOCTYPE html>
<head>
<title>Javascript Function Example </title>
</head>
<body>
<script type="text/javascript">
function test(){ //defining function
var a = 40;
document.write(a);
}
test();   //calling function
</script>
</body>
</html>
```

Output:

```
40
```

- We have defined a function test using keyword function. In the function block we have assigned a value 40 to variable a. The next line is document.write() statement.
- This function test() will not print 40 to the screen all by itself. It has to be called, which we are doing using the statement test();

Function Parameters:

- In the previous point, we defined a function test() without any values in the round brackets.
- In practical situations, we might need to add some values (parameters) in the round brackets.

Syntax:

```
function functionName(para_1, para_2...para_n)
{
    statements to be executed;
}
```

Example:

```
<!DOCTYPE html>
<head>
<title>Javascript Function Parameters</title>
</head>
<body>
<script type="text/javascript">
function add(x,y){
result = x+y;
document.write("addition is: "+result);
document.write("<br/>");
}
add(10,10);
add(23,12);
</script>
</body>
</html>
```

Output:

addition is: 20
addition is: 35

return Statement:

- A JavaScript function can have an optional return statement. This is required if we want to return a value from a function. This statement should be the last statement in a function.

- For example, we can pass two numbers in a function and then we can expect from the function to return their multiplication in our calling program.

  Syntax: `return value;`

Example:

```
<!DOCTYPE html>
<head>
<title>Javascript Return statement</title>
</head>
<body>
<script type="text/javascript">
function areaRect(L,B){
var area = L*B;
return area;
}
x=areaRect(6,8);
document.write(x);
</script>
</body>
</html>
```

Output:

```
48
```

- areaRect(6,8); calls the function and passes values 6 and 8.
- The function calculates the area, and returns it (in our case, 48).
- Now, after the function has returned a value, areaRect(6,8) is 48. This value 48, is assigned to x.
- The statement document.write(x) will print 48 in the webpage.

Example: This program shows a button. After you click on the button, the function show() will be called and it displays the output "Hello World".

```
<!DOCTYPE html>
<head>
<script type="text/javascript">
    function show()
    {
        document.write("Hello World");
    }
```

```
</script>
</head>
<body>
    <form>
        <input type="button" value="Click Me" onclick="show()">
    </form>
</body>
</html>
```

Output:

After you click on button displays `Hello World.`

- This program performs event handling i.e. onclick event.

Example:

```
<!DOCTYPE html>
<head>
<script>
function myFunction()
{
    var x = "Hello " + document.getElementById("n1").value;
    document.getElementById("demo").innerHTML=x;
}
</script>
</head>
<body>
    <p>Enter your name and Click the button</p>
    <input type="text" name="name1" id="n1">
    <button onclick="myFunction()">Click it</button>
    <p id="demo"></p>
</body>
</html>
```

Output:

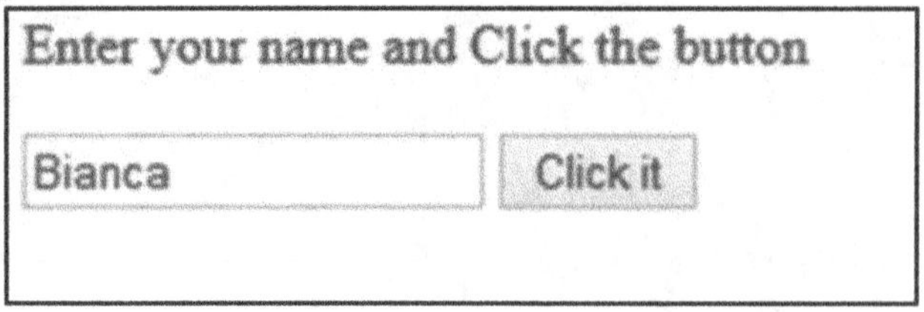

- After you click on the button you will get the following output:

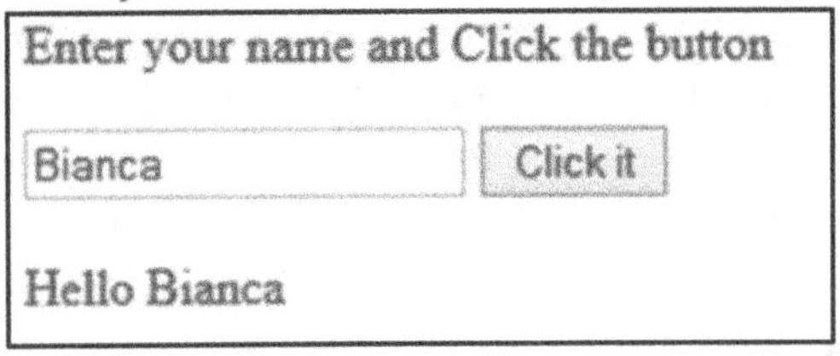

- In this program displays a form with a text field and a button. After you click on the button function myFunction() will be called the property of the document object getElementById()will get value entered in the text field. Another property innerHTML will put the contents of variable x into the place specified by the id "Demo".

5.7 JAVASCRIPT HTML DOM EVENTS (April 2016)

- Every web page resides inside a browser window which can be considered as an object.
- A Document object represents the HTML document that is displayed in that window.
- The Document object has various properties that refer to other objects which allow access to and modification of document content.
- The way that document content is accessed and modified is called the Document Object Model, or DOM.
- The Objects are organized in a hierarchy as shown in Fig. 5.1.
- This hierarchical structure applies to the organization of objects in a Web document.
  - **Window Object:** Top of the hierarchy. It is the outmost element of the object hierarchy. The window object represents an open window in a browser. An object of window is created automatically by the browser.
  - **Navigator Object:** The JavaScript navigator object is the object representation of the client Internet browser or web navigator program that is being used. Navigator object is the top level object to all others. The navigator object contains information about the browser.
  - **Document Object:** Each HTML document that gets loaded into a window becomes a document object. The document contains the content of the page. The document object is itself a property of the window object. This makes sense, because all documents in a Web browser are displayed in a window.
  - **Form Object:** Everything enclosed in the <form>...</form> tags sets the form object.
  - **Form control elements:** The form object contains all the elements defined for that object such as text fields, buttons, radio buttons, and checkboxes.

- The **History Object**, also a property of the window objects, represents the history list in the window. The history object is automatically created by the JavaScript runtime engine and consists of an array of URLs. These URLs are the URLs the user has visited within a browser window. The history object is part of the Window object and is accessed through the window.history property. The history list contains the most recent pages we have visited during the current browser session, those that we can get to with the Back and Forward buttons.
- The **Location Object**, also a property of the window, represents the location of the current document (usually shown in the location bar, also known as the address bar) in the browser window. The location object is actually a JavaScript object, not an HTML DOM object. The location object is automatically created by the JavaScript run-time engine and contains information about the current URL. The location object is part of the Window object and is accessed through the window.location property.

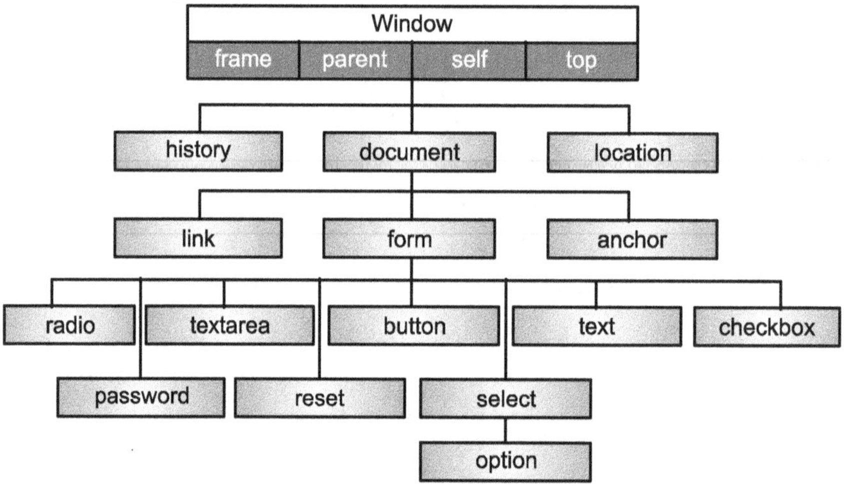

Fig. 5.1: Hierarchy of DOM

- The navigator object represents the browser and is one of two top-level objects, its name is rather Netscape biased, "browser" would be a non-biased name, but then Netscape was the company that created the JavaScript language, so we think that entitles them to some liberties. The window object is the other top-level object.

JavaScript DOM Objects:

1. **The anchors Array:**
   - The anchors array is an array of anchor objects and it is a property of the document object.
   - This objects are reflections of a elements that have a name attribute:

```
<a name="anchorName">anchorText</a>
```

2. **The button Object:**
   - It is a reflection of an input element with a type attribute of "button".

```
<input type="button">
```

   - Button objects are members of the containing form object's elements array.

3. **The checkbox Object:**
   - This object is a reflection of an input element with a type attribute of "checkbox".

```
<input type="checkbox">
```

   - Checkbox objects are members of the containing form's elements array.

4. **The Document Object:**
   - This object contains information about the currently displayed document and its properties are derived from the document's body element.

```
<body>document contents</body>
```

   The elements Array:
   - It contains references to input elements in a form.
   - We cannot add elements to this array, replace elements in the array or remove elements from the array. The elements array is a form object property.

5. **The form Object:**
   - This object collects input from the user and may send the input to a server and it is a reflection of a form element:

```
<form>form contents</form>
```

   - Each and every form object is a member of the containing document object's forms array.

The forms Array:
   - It is a property of the containing document object and contains references to all of the form objects in the document, in source order.
   - We cannot add a form to the array, replace a form in the array, or remove a form from the array.

6. **The frame Object:**
   - This object is a reflection of a frame element:

```
<frame>
```

   The frames Array:
   - A frames array contains the non-empty frames within a frame or a window.

7. **The hidden Object:**
   - This object is a reflection of an input element with a type attribute of "hidden".

```
<input type="hidden">
```

8. **The link Object:**
   - This object is a reflection of an a element that has an href attribute.
     ```
     <a href=url>anchorText</a>
     ```
   - All links are members of the document's links array in source order.

The links Array:
   - It contains references to all the links in the document, in source order.
   - We cannot remove a link from the array or replace a link in the array and we can create another links with the string object's link() method.

9. **The password Object:**
   - This object is a reflection of an input element with a type attribute of "password".
     ```
     <input type="password">
     ```
     The data entered by the user is not visible to the display each and every character appears as an asterisk (*) and it is not visible programmatically.
     Password objects are members of the containing form object's elements array.

10. **The radio Object:**
   - This object represents a set of input elements of type "radio" with the same name attribute:
     ```
     <input type="radio" name=radioName>
     ```
     Each button is a radio object is a member of the containing form object's elements array.

11. **The reset Object:**
   - This object is a reflection of an input tag with a type attribute of "reset".
     ```
     <input type="reset">
     ```
     Reset objects are members of the containing form object's elements array.

12. **The select Object:**
   - This object is a reflection of a SELECT element of form.
     ```
     <select><option>...</select>
     ```
     Select objects are members of the containing form object's elements array.

   The options Array:
   - This is a property of select objects and it allows we to manipulate the options of the select object. Individual options objects are reflections of option elements.
     ```
     <option>, text to be displayed ............
     ```

13. **The submit Object:**
   - This object is a reflection of an input element with a type attribute of "submit".
     ```
     <input type="submit">
     ```
   - Submit objects are members of the containing form object's elements array.

14. The text Object:

- This object is a reflection of an input element with a type attribute of "text".

```
<input type="text">
```

- Text object are members of the containing form object's elements array.

15. The textarea Object:

- This object is a reflection of textarea element like:

```
<textarea> text to be displayed…….</textarea>
```

5.8 EVENT HANDLING IN JAVASCRIPT

1. Events:

- JavaScript-enabled Web pages are typically event driven. Events are actions that occur on the webpage.
- Events are signals generated when specific action occurs.
- JavaScript is aware of these signals are scripts can be built to react to these events.

2. Event Handler:

- Event handlers execute JavaScript code to respond to events whenever they occur.
- Event handlers are scripts, in the form of attributes of specific HTML tags, which we as the programmer can write.
- The general form of an event handler is:

```
<html_tag other_attributes eventhandler = "JavaScript program">
```

- Event handler is actually a call to a function defined in the header of the document or a single JavaScript command. While any JavaScript statements, methods or functions can appear inside the quotation marks of event handler.

3. Creating an Event Handler:

- We do not need the <script> tag to define an event handler. Instead, we add an event attribute to an individual HTML tag.
- For example, here is a link that includes an OnMouseOver event handler.

```
<a href=http://www.pragati.com/ OnMouseOver="window.alert
                    ("We moved over the link");">Click here </a>
```

Here, <a> is tag, which specifies a statement to be used as OnMouseOver event handler for the link and this statement displays an alert message when the mouse moves over the link.

- We can use JavaScript statements like the previous one in an event handler, but if we need more than one statement, its good idea to use a function as the event handler like this:

```
<a href = "#bottom" OnMouseOver = "DoIt();">
```

- Move the mouse over this link </a>
- This example calls a function called DoIt() when the user moves the mouse over the link.

Event Handlers with JavaScript:

- Instead of specifying an event handler is an HTML document, we can use JavaScript to assign a function as an event handler. This allows us to set event handlers.
- To define event handler in this way, first define a function and then assign it is an event handler. Events are occurrences generated by the browser, such as loading a document or by the user such as moving the mouse.
- They are the user and browser activities to which we may respond dynamically with a scripting language like JavaScript.

1. onclick Event:

- onclick is the most frequently used event type which occurs when a user clicks mouse left button.
- We can put our validation, warning and so on against this event type.

Example:

```
<!DOCTYPE html>
<head>
<script type="text/javascript">
function sayHello() {
 alert("Hello JavaScript!")
}
</script>
</head>
<body>
<input type="button" onclick="sayHello()" value="Say Hello" />
</body>
</html>
```

Output:

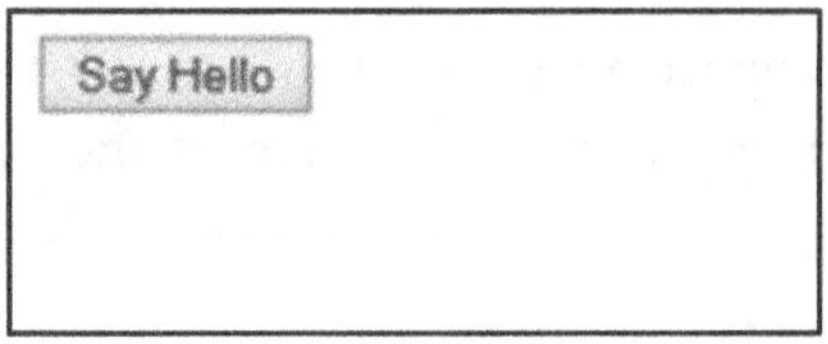

- After you click you will get the following alert box:

2. **onsubmit Event:**

- This event occurs when we try to submit a form. So we can put our form validation against this event type.
- Following is a simple example showing its usage. Here, we are calling a validate() function before submitting a form data to the webserver. If validate() function returns true the form will be submitted otherwise it will not submit the data.

Example:

```
<!DOCTYPE html>
<head>
<script type="text/javascript">
<!--
function validation() {
 all validation goes here
 .........
 return either true or false
}
//-->
</script>
</head>
<body>
<form method="POST" action="t.cgi" onsubmit="return validate()">
.......
<input type="submit" value="Submit" />
</form>
</body>
</html>
```

3. onmouseover and onmouseout Events:

- These two event types will help us to create nice effects with images or even with text as well.
- The onMouseover event occurs when you bring mouse over any element and the onMouseout occurs when we take our mouse out from that element.

Example:

```
<!DOCTYPE html>
<head>
<script type="text/javascript">
    function over() {
    alert("Mouse Over");
    }
    function out() {
    alert("Mouse Out");
    }
</script>
</head>
<body>
    <p>Bring our mouse inside the division to see the result:</p>
    <div onmouseover="over()" onmouseout="out()">
        <h2> This is inside the division </h2>
    </div>
</body>
</html>
```

Output: You will see the following screens:

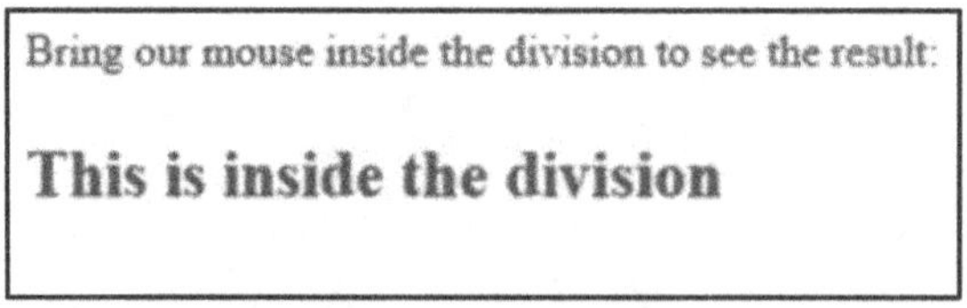
Bring our mouse inside the division to see the result:
This is inside the division

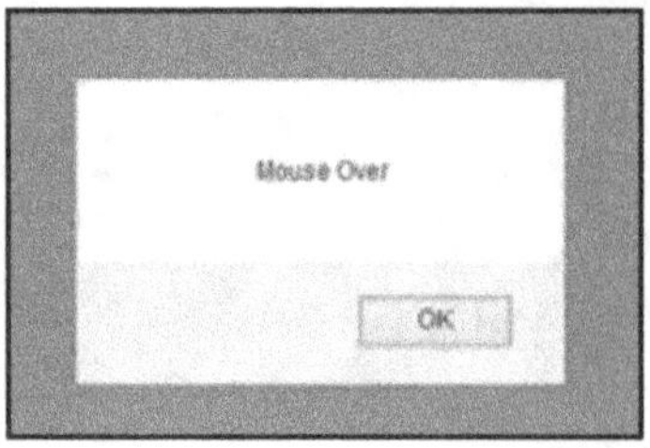
Mouse Over
OK

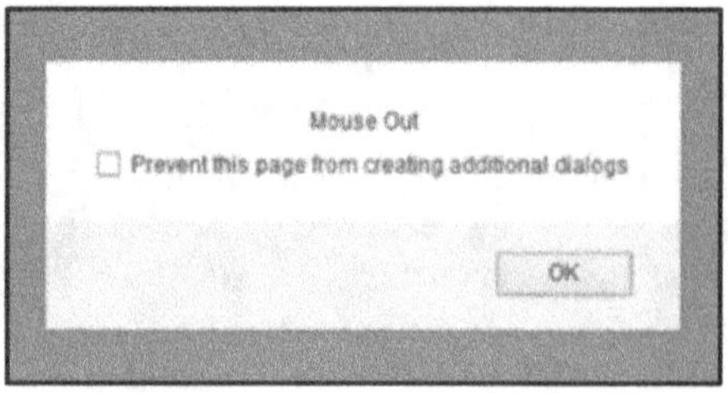
Mouse Out
Prevent this page from creating additional dialogs
OK

4. onload and onunload Events:

- These two events are triggered when the user enters or leaves the page.
- The onload event can be used to check the visitor's browser type and browser version, and load the proper version of the web page based on the information.
- The onload and onunload events can be used to deal with cookies.

Example:

```
<!DOCTYPE html>
<body onload="checkCookies()">
<script>
function checkCookies()
{
if (navigator.cookieEnabled==true)
    {
    alert("Cookies are enabled")
    }
else
    {
    alert("Cookies are not enabled")
    }
}
</script>
<p>An alert box should tell we if our browser has enabled cookies or
not.</p>
</body>
</html>
```

Output:

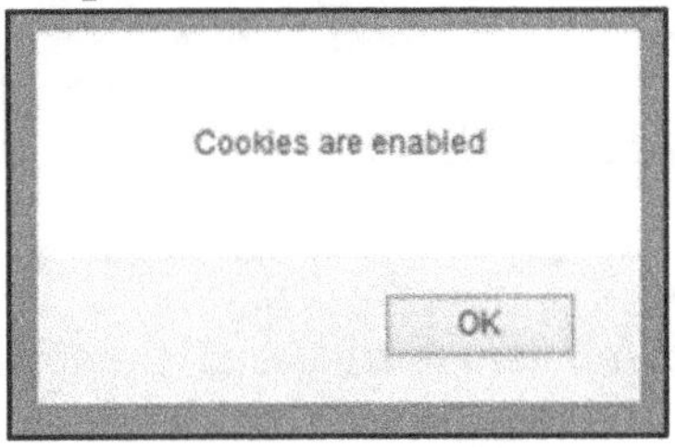

- The above output will come if your browser has enabled cookies.

5. onchange Event:

- This event are often used in combination with validation of input fields.
- Following is an example of how to use the onchange. The upperCase() function will be called when a user changes the content of an input field.

Example:

```
<!DOCTYPE html>
<head>
<script>
function myFunction()
{
   var x=document.getElementById("fname");
   x.value=x.value.toUpperCase();
}
</script>
</head>
<body>
   Enter our name: <input type="text" id="fname" onchange="myFunction()">
   <p>When we leave the input field, a function is triggered which transforms the input text to upper case.</p>
</body>
</html>
```

Output: You will see the following screens:

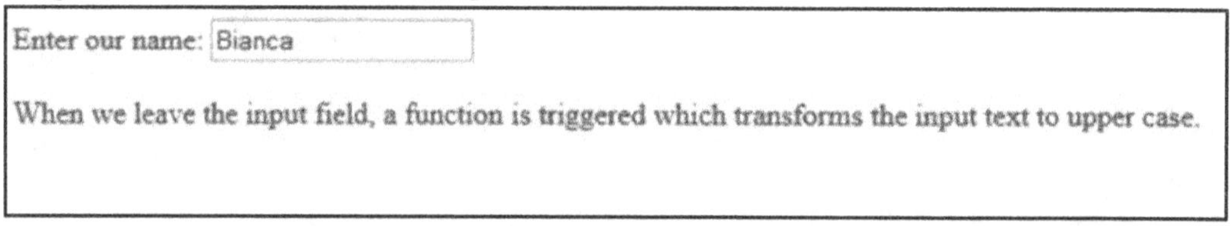
Enter our name: Bianca
When we leave the input field, a function is triggered which transforms the input text to upper case.

- When you the text field you will get the following screen.

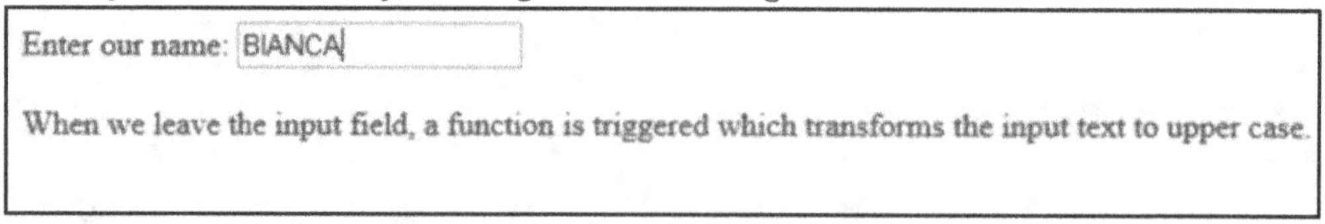
Enter our name: BIANCA
When we leave the input field, a function is triggered which transforms the input text to upper case.

6. onmousedown, onmouseup and onclick Events:

- These three events are all parts of a mouse-click.
- First when a mouse-button is clicked, the onmousedown event is triggered, then, when the mouse-button is released, the onmouseup event is triggered, finally, when the mouse-click is completed, the onclick event is triggered.

Example:

```
<!DOCTYPE html>
<head>
<script>
    function mDown(obj)
    {
        obj.style.backgroundColor="#1ec5e5";
        obj.innerHTML="Release Me"
    }
    function mUp(obj)
    {
        obj.style.backgroundColor="#D94A38";
        obj.innerHTML="Thank You"
    }
</script>
</head>
<body>
    <div onmousedown="mDown(this)" onmouseup="mUp(this" style="background
        color:#D94A38;width:90px;height: 20px;padding:40px;">Click Me</div>
</body>
</html>
```

5.9 JS STRINGS

- The JavaScript string is an object that represents a sequence of characters.
- The string object is used for storing and manipulating text.
- A string can be any text inside quotes and we can use simple or double quotes as:

```
var carname="Alto XC60";
var carname='Alto XC60';
```

- The String object let's you work with a series of characters and wraps Javascript's string primitive data type with a number of helper methods.
- Because Javascript automatically converts between string primitives and String objects, you can call any of the helper methods of the String object on a string primitive.

- There are two ways to create string in JavaScript i.e., By string literal and By string object (using new keyword).

1. **By String Literal:**

- The string literal is created using double quotes. The syntax of creating string using string literal is given below:

```
var stringname="string value";
```

Example:

```
<script>
var str=" Hello JavaScript ";
document.write(str);
</script>
```

2. **By String Object (Using new Keyword):**

- The syntax of creating string object using new keyword is given below:

```
var stringname=new String("string literal");
```

Here, new keyword is used to create instance of string.

- The string parameter is series of characters that has been properly encoded.

Example:

```
<script>
var stringname=new String("Hello JavaScript ");
document.write(stringname);
</script>
```

String Properties:

Sr. No.	Property	Description
1.	`constructor`	This property returns a reference to the String function that created the object.
2.	`length`	This property returns the length of the string.
3.	`prototype`	This property allows you to add properties and methods to an object.

5.10 JS STRING METHODS

- Following table lists methods of string in JS:

Sr. No.	Method Name	Description
1.	`charAt()`	This method returns the character at the specified index.
2.	`charCodeAt()`	This method returns a number indicating the Unicode value of the character at the given index.
3.	`concat()`	This method combines the text of two strings and returns a new string.
4.	`indexOf()`	This method returns the index within the calling String object of the first occurrence of the specified value, or –1 if not found.
5.	`lastIndexOf()`	This method returns the index within the calling String object of the last occurrence of the specified value, or –1 if not found.
6.	`localeCompare()`	This method returns a number indicating whether a reference string comes before or after or is the same as the given string in sort order.
7.	`match()`	This method used to match a regular expression against a string.
8.	`replace()`	This method used to find a match between a regular expression and a string, and to replace the matched substring with a new substring.
9.	`search()`	This method executes the search for a match between a regular expression and a specified string.
10.	`slice()`	This method extracts a section of a string and returns a new string.
11.	`split()`	This method Splits a String object into an array of strings by separating the string into substrings.
12.	`substr()`	This method returns the characters in a string beginning at the specified location through the specified number of characters.

contd. ...

13.	`substring()`	This method returns the characters in a string between two indexes into the string.
14.	`toLocaleLowerCase()`	This method returns the characters within a string are converted to lower case while respecting the current locale.
15.	`toLocaleUpperCase()`	This method returns the characters within a string are converted to upper case while respecting the current locale.
16.	`toLowerCase()`	This method returns the calling string value converted to lower case.
17.	`toString()`	This method returns a string representing the specified object.
18.	`toUpperCase()`	This method returns the calling string value converted to uppercase.
19.	`valueOf()`	This method returns the primitive value of the specified object.

Examples:

1. **The length of a string (a String object) is found in the built in property length().**

```
<!DOCTYPE html>
<body>
<script>
   var txt = "Hello JavaScript!";
   document.write("<p>" + txt.length + "</p>");
</script>
</body>
</html>
```

Output:

```
17
```

2. **The indexOf() method returns the position (as a number) of the first found occurrence of a specified text inside a string.**

```
<!DOCTYPE html>
<head>
<script>
```

```
    function myFunction()
    {
        var str=document.getElementById("p1").innerHTML;
        var n=str.indexOf("locate");
        document.getElementById("p2").innerHTML=n+1;
    }
</script>
</head>
<body>
    <p id="p1">Click the button to locate where "locate" first occurs.</p>
    <p id="p2">0</p>
    <button onclick="myFunction()">Click it</button>
</body>
</html>
```

Output:

You will see the following screens:

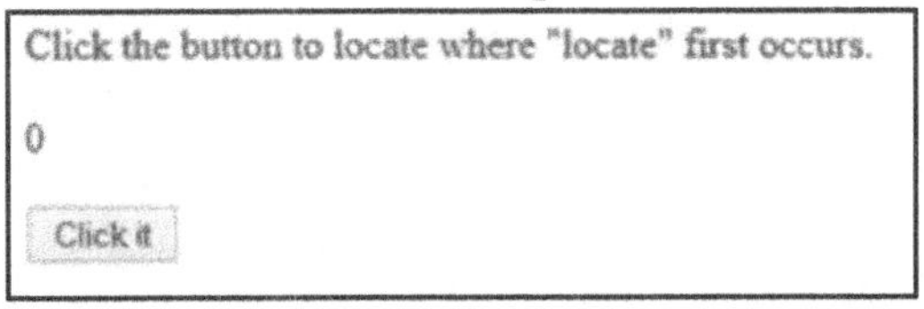

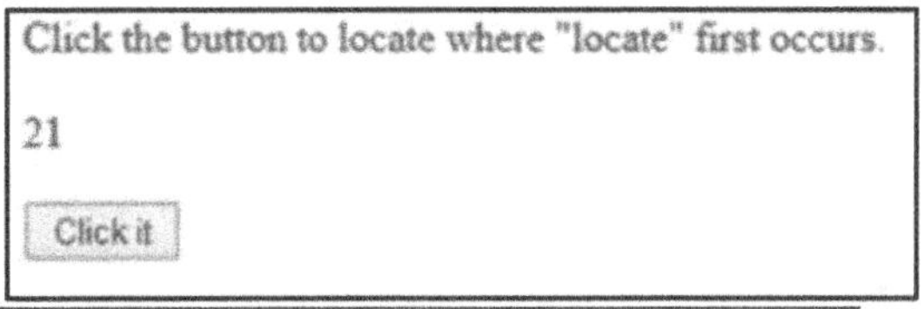

3. **The match() method can be used to search for a matching content in a string.**

```
<!DOCTYPE html>
<body>
<script>
    var str="Hello JavaScript world!";
    document.write(str.match("world") + "<br>");
    document.write(str.match("World") + "<br>");
    document.write(str.match("world!"));
</script>
</body>
</html>
```

Output:

```
world
null
world!
```

4. **The replace() method replaces a specified value with another value in a string.**

```
<!DOCTYPE html>
<head>
<script>
   function myFunction()
   {
      var str=document.getElementById("demo").innerHTML;
      var n=str.replace("Nirali Prakashan","Pragati");
      document.getElementById("demo").innerHTML=n;
}
</script>
</head>
<body>
   <p>Click the button to replace "Nirali Prakashan" with "Pragati" in the paragraph below:</p>
   <p id="demo">Please visit Nirali Prakashan!</p>
   <button onclick="myFunction()">Click it</button>
</body>
</html>
```

Output:

You will get the following screens:

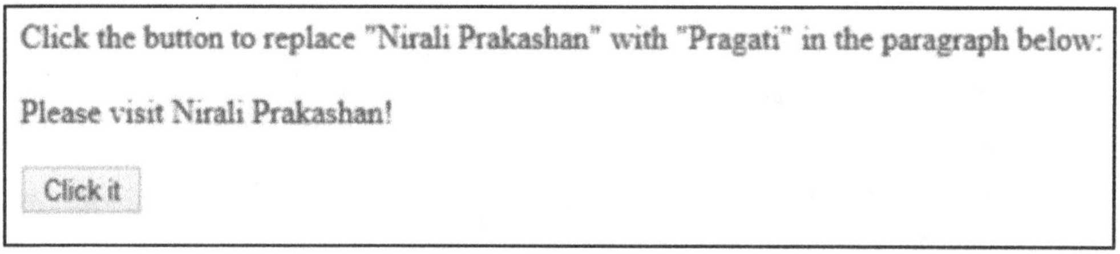
Click the button to replace "Nirali Prakashan" with "Pragati" in the paragraph below:
Please visit Nirali Prakashan!
Click it

After you click on the button you will get the following screen:

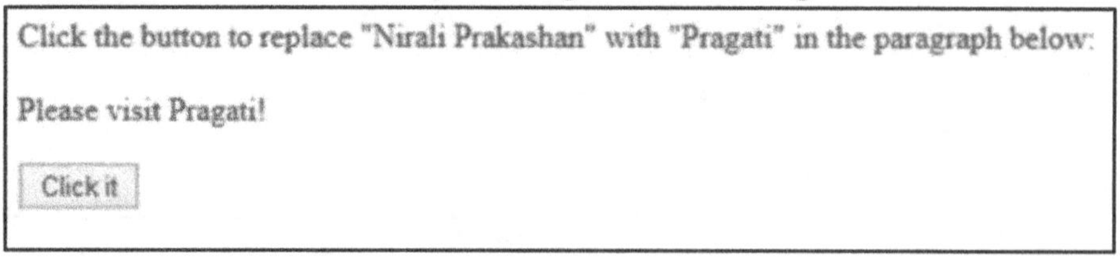
Click the button to replace "Nirali Prakashan" with "Pragati" in the paragraph below:
Please visit Pragati!
Click it

5. **A string is converted to upper/lower case with the methods toUpperCase() / toLowerCase().**

```
<!DOCTYPE html>
<body>
<script>
    var txt="Hello JavaScript World!";
    document.write("<p>" + txt.toUpperCase() + "</p>");
    document.write("<p>" + txt.toLowerCase() + "</p>");
    document.write("<p>" + txt + "</p>");
</script>
    <p>
        The methods returns a new string.
        The original string is not changed.
    </p>
</body>
</html>
```

Output:

```
HELLO JAVASCRIPT WORLD!
hello javascript world!
Hello JavaScript World!
The methods returns a new string. The original string is not changed.
```

6. **Example of concating string.**

```
<html>
<head>
<title>JavaScript String concat() Method</title>
</head>
<body>
  <script type="text/javascript">
    var str1 = new String( "Amar" );
    var str2 = new String( "Salunkhe" );
    var str3 = str1.concat( str2 );
    document.write("Concatenated String:" + str3);
</script>
</body>
</html>
```

Output:

```
Concatenated String:AmarSalunkhe
```

7. **Example of charat().**

```
<html>
<head>
<title>JavaScript String charAt() Method</title>
</head>
<body>
<script type="text/javascript">
 var str = new String( "This is string" );
 document.writeln("str.charAt(0) is:" + str.charAt(0));
 document.writeln("<br />str.charAt(1) is:" + str.charAt(1));
 document.writeln("<br />str.charAt(2) is:" + str.charAt(2));
 document.writeln("<br />str.charAt(3) is:" + str.charAt(3));
 document.writeln("<br />str.charAt(4) is:" + str.charAt(4));
 document.writeln("<br />str.charAt(5) is:" + str.charAt(5));
</script>
</body>
</html>
```

Output:

```
str.charAt(0) is:T
str.charAt(1) is:h
str.charAt(2) is:i
str.charAt(3) is:s
str.charAt(4) is:
str.charAt(5) is:i
```

5.11 JS POP-UP BOXES (ALERT, CONFIRM AND PROMPT)

(April 15)

- When you want something highlighted, prompted or any important thing to say to users, so you can use Popup Boxes.
- In JavaScript you can create three kinds of popup boxes i.e., Alert Box, Confirm Box, and Prompt Box.

1. **Alert Box:**

- An alert box is often used if you want to make sure information comes through to the user.
- When an alert box pops up, the user will have to click "OK" to proceed.

  Syntax: `alert("Alert Message")`

  Example:

```
<html>
<head>
<script language="javascript">
```

```
    function show_alert()
    {
        alert("Hi! This is AlertBox!!")
    }
</script>
</head>
<body>
    <input type="button" onclick="show alert()" value="Show alert box" >
</body>
</html>
```

- In above example when user click on button the function show_alert() will be called, which display an alert box with the message "Hi! This is AlertBox!!" and one Ok button.

2. **Confirm Box:**

- A confirm box is often used if you want the user to verify or accept something.
- When a confirm box pops up, the user will have to click either "OK" or "Cancel" to proceed.
- If the user clicks "OK", the box returns true. If the user clicks "Cancel", the box returns false.

Syntax: `confirm("Message")`

Example:

```
<html>
<head>
<script language="javascript">
function disp_confirm()
{
    var r=confirm("Press a button")
    if (r==true)
    {
        document.write("You pressed OK!")
    }
    else
    {
        document.write("You pressed Cancel!")
    }
}
</script>
</head>
<body>
<input type="button" onclick="disp_confirm()" value="Display a confirm
box" />
</body>
</html>
```

Output: The confirm box.

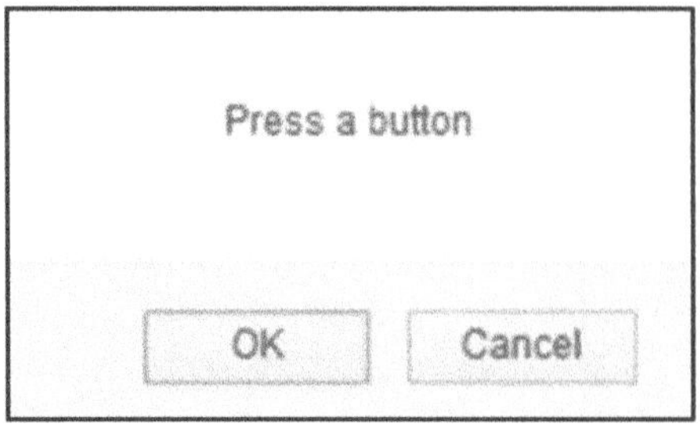

- In above example when user gets box with ok and cancel when user click on ok then text shown you pressed ok if cancel clicked then you pressed cancel.

3. **Prompt Box:**

- A prompt box is often used if you want the user to input a value before entering a page.
- When a prompt box pops up, the user will have to click either "OK" or "Cancel" to proceed after entering an input value.
- If the user clicks "OK" the box returns the input value. If the user clicks "Cancel" the box returns null.

Syntax: `prompt("sometext","defaultvalue")`

Example:

```
<html>
<head>
<script language="javascript">
function disp_prompt()
{
   var c=prompt("Please enter 1st Rank IT Company","Infosys")
   if (c!=null && c!="")
   {
      document.write("Hello, " + c + " is the best IT company.")
   }
}</script>
</head>
<body>
<input type="button" onclick="disp_prompt()" value="Display a prompt
box">
</body>
</html>
```

Output:

After clicking button this asked to enter value from user but also it's come with default value which is Visions Developer.

And after getting proper input from user print that value as given in function.

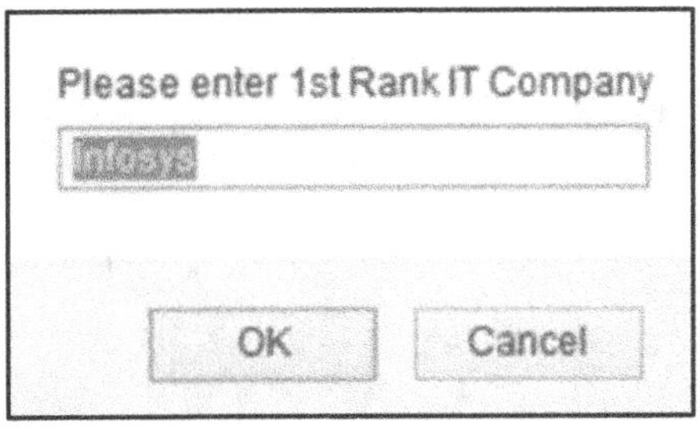

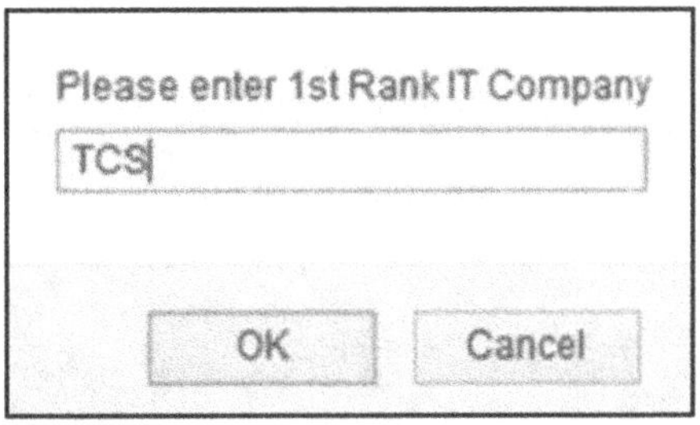

After you click OK you will get the following text:

```
Hello, TCS is the best IT company.
```

5.12 CHANGING PROPERTY VALUE OF DIFFERENT TAGS USING DHTML

- JavaScript allow for dynamic enhancement of pages, you can change styles of pages based on some user interaction. All of these come under DHTML, that is, CSS, JavaScript, and the DOM, all of these technologies will be used together to create DHTML.
- All HTML elements, attributes, and text become objects and the DOM provides methods and properties allowing not only access to all these objects, but the ability to use CSS to style them on the fly. With the W3C DOM, a Web page can be restructured by creating, adding, modifying, and deleting any item on the page.

1. **The document.getElementById() Method:**

- All browsers implement the id attribute for accessing the elements in a document. Id attribute uniquely identifies any HTML element in a Web document.
- For example, you have a paragraph tag defined with an id attribute:

```
<p id="para1">This is the paragraph.</p>
```

- Now in JavaScript you can get a reference to the p element with the getElementById() method as follows:

```
p_element = document.getElementById("para1");
```

- After getting reference to an element you can work on that element as explain in the next topic.

2. **The innerHTML Property and the Element's Content:**

- You can get or modify the content of an element by using the innerHTML property. The innerHTML property is useful for inserting or replacing the content of HTML elements; that is, the code and text between the element's opening and closing tag.
- By changing an element's innerHTML property, after some user interaction, you can change the text that occurs between that element's opening and closing tag.

Example: JavaScript to insert new text in the div container.

```
<html>
<head><title>Modify Text</title>
<script type="text/javascript">
```

```
function myFunction()
{
    document.getElementById("divtest").innerHTML = "Inserting new text in
                                                     the div container.";
}
</script>
</head>
<body>
    <button onclick="myFunction()">Click to change text </button>
    <div id="divtest">
        Original text in div container.
    </div>
</body>
</html>
```

Output: The two screens i.e. before you click and after you click on the button:

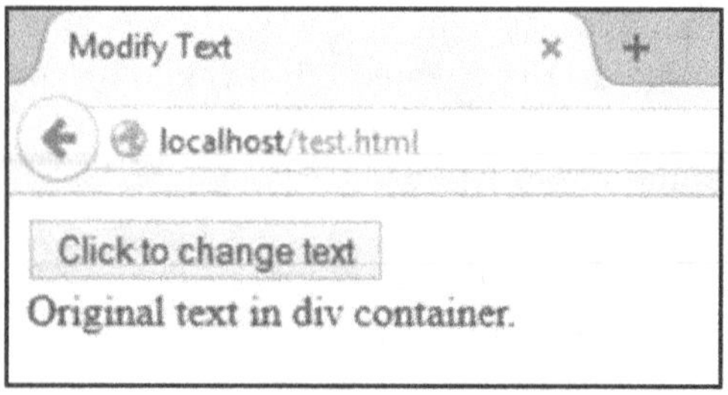

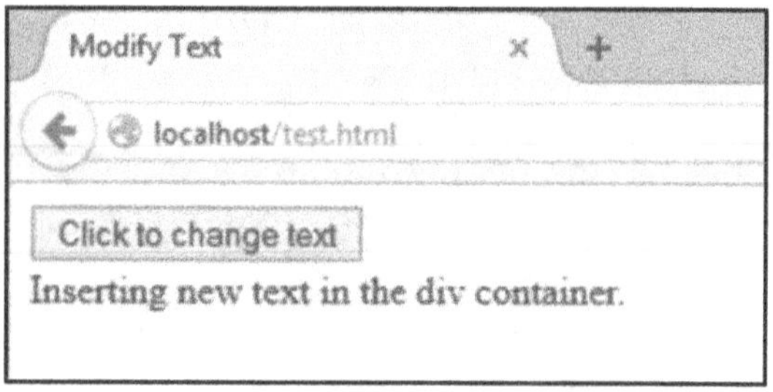

- When you click on the button the function myFunction() is executed.

  The new text will be replaced by the original div element identified by its id, divtest. So after you click on the button, the new text will be displayed. Hence, the innerHTML property is used to change the text within the <div></div> tags.

3. **Image src Property:**

- The src property sets or returns the value of the src attribute of an image. This property specifies the URL of an image.
- To return src property the following syntax is used:

```
imageObject.src
```

- To set the src property the following syntax is used:

```
imageObject.src=URL
```

For example: Change the URL of an image:

```
document.getElementById("myImg").src = "college.gif";
<html>
<html>
<head>
<script>
```

```
        function myFunction() {
            document.getElementById("myImg").src = "mail.png";
    }
    </script>
    </head>
    <body>
        <img id="myImg" src="login_icon.png" width="107" height="98">
        <p>Click the button to change the value of the src attribute of the
                                                                    image.</p>
        <button onclick="myFunction()">Try it</button>
    </body>
    </html>
```

Output: The two screens i.e. before you click and after you click on the button.

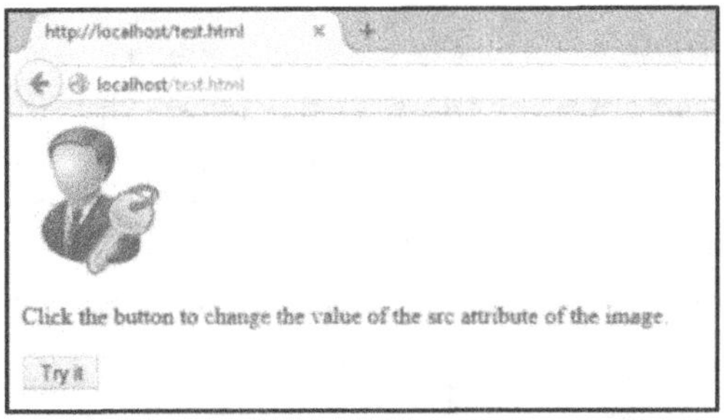

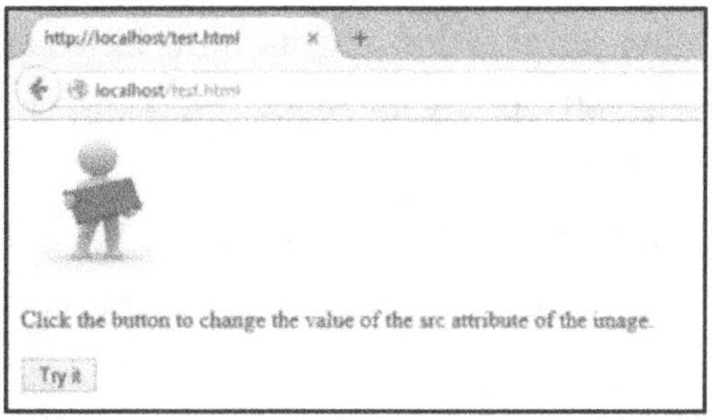

SUMMARY

- JavaScript is an object-based scripting language.
- DHTML uses collection of technologies together to create interactive and animated web sites. It uses combination of a static markup language (such as HTML), a client-side scripting language (such as JavaScript), a presentation definition language (such as CSS), and the Document Object Model.
- JavaScript supports conditional statements which are used to perform different actions based on different conditions.
- We can use the if statement to execute some code only if a specified condition is true.
- We can use the if....else statement to execute some code if a condition is true and another code if the condition is not true.
- The if ... elseif ... else statement is the one level advance form of control statement that allows JavaScript to make correct decision out of several conditions.
- Switch statement is used to execute one of the statements from many blocks of statements.
- Loops can execute a block of code a number of times.

- Function is a block of statements that performs certain task.
- The way that document content is accessed and modified is called the Document Object Model, or DOM.
- Events are signals generated when specific action occurs.
- The JavaScript string is an object that represents a sequence of characters.
- In JavaScript you can create three kinds of popup boxes i.e., Alert Box, Confirm Box, and Prompt Box.
- An alert box is often used if you want to make sure information comes through to the user.
- A confirm box is often used if you want the user to verify or accept something.
- A prompt box is often used if you want the user to input a value before entering a page.
- JavaScript is the programming language of HTML and the Web.
- DHTML stands for Dynamic HTML. DHTML is combination of HTML, JavaScript, DOM and CSS.
- JavaScript supports data types like numbers, strings, arrays, objects.
- Variables in JavaScript are named containers. Variable declaration starts with var keyword.
- JavaScript does NOT have any built-in print or display functions. It uses functions like window.alert(), document.write(), console.log() etc.
- A JavaScript function is a block of code designed to perform a particular task. It is invoked when some event occurs or it needs to be called explicitly.
- JavaScript allow executing functions when certain events occur. There are events like mouse is moved up or down, mouse is clicked etc.
- Strings in JavaScript are sequence of characters enclosed in single quotes. Special characters in strings are escaped with backslash.

PRACTICE QUESTIONS

1. What is JavaScript?
2. What are the data types used in JavaScript?
3. What is a function? How to create it?
4. Enlist various operators in JavaScript.
5. Explain number function with syntax.
6. Describe navigation object with example.

7. What is meant by array? How to define an array.
8. What is event? Explain event handling in JavaScript.
9. Create a personal home page named home.html with the following content:
   (i) Your name written in the <title> and an <h1> tag at the top.
   (ii) A picture of yourself after or next to the heading. If we do not have a digital picture of yourself, use clip art or a favourite landscape.
10. Create a home page named toy Store.html for a company that sells toys. Include images of balls, jacks, whistles, skateboards, dolls, and other items that the toy company sells. We should be able to find the images we need from an online clip art library.
11. Write a program to display even and odd number between 1 to 20.
12. Explain various control statement with example.
13. What is a loop? What are its types? Explain with example.
14. Write short notes on: (i) math object, (ii) string object.
15. What is function? How to create and call it? Explain with example.
16. Write a program for finding prime numbers using functions.
17. Explain DOM object in detail.
18. What is DHTML?
19. Alert box of Javascript.

Ans. Please refer to Section 5.11.

20. What is java-script object?

Ans. Please refer to Section 5.2.

21. How variables are declared in javascript?

Ans. Please refer to Section 5.3.3.

22. Explain any two windows object method in java script.

Ans. Please refer to Section 5.7.

UNIVERSITY QUESTIONS AND ANSWERS

1 Mark Questions:

1. Write syntax of script tag. **(April 2013)**

Ans. Please refer to Section 5.3.

5 Mark Questions:

2. Discuss three kinds of popup boxes in JavaScript. **(April 2015)**

Ans. Please refer to Section 5.11.

■■■

CHAPTER 6

Ajax

Contents ...

Objectives...

- To Understand Ajax
- To Learn Ajax-PHP Framework
- To Study Handling XML Data Using PHP and Ajax

6.1 INTRODUCTION TO AJAX (April 13, 15, 16; Oct. 14)

- Ajax stands for Asynchronous JavaScript and XML.
- Ajax is a new technique for creating better, faster, and more interactive web applications with the help of XML, HTML, CSS, and JavaScript.
- Ajax is not a technology but group of inter-related technologies as given below:
  1. **HTML/XHTML and CSS:** These technologies are used for displaying content and style. It is mainly used for presentation.
  2. **DOM:** It is used for dynamic display and interaction with data.
  3. **XML or JSON:** For carrying data to and from server. JSON (Javascript Object Notation) is like XML but short and faster than XML.

4. **XMLHttpRequest:** For asynchronous communication between client and server. For more visit next page.
5. **JavaScript:** It is used to bring above technologies together. Independently, it is used mainly for client-side validation.

- Ajax is a technique for creating fast and dynamic web pages.
- Ajax allows web pages to be updated asynchronously by exchanging small amounts of data with the server behind the scenes. This means that it is possible to update parts of a web page, without reloading the whole page.
- Classic web pages, (which do not use Ajax) must reload the entire page if the content should change.
- Examples of applications using Ajax like Google Maps, Gmail, Youtube, and Facebook etc.

6.1.1 Advantages and Disadvantages of Ajax

Advantages of Ajax:

1. **Better interactivity**: Ajax allows easier and quicker interaction between user and website as whole pages are not reloaded for content to be displayed.
2. **Easier navigation**: Ajax applications on websites can be built to allow easier navigation to users in comparison to using the traditional back and forward button on a browser.
3. **Compact**: With Ajax, several multipurpose applications and features can be handled using a single web page. It just require a few lines of code.
4. **Backed by reputed brands**: Several complex web applications are handled using Ajax, Google Maps is the most impressive and obvious example.

Disadvantages of Ajax:

1. **The back and refresh button are rendered useless:** With Ajax, as all functions are loaded on a dynamic page without the page being reloaded or more importantly a URL being changed (except for a hash symbol maybe), clicking the back or refresh button would take you to an entirely different web page or to the beginning of what your dynamic web page was processing. This is the main drawback behind Ajax but fortunately with good programming skills this issue can be fixed.
2. **It is built on JavaScript:** A percentage of website surfers prefer to turn JavaScript functionality off on their browser making the Ajax application useless.
3. **Browser support:** All browsers do not support JavaScript or XMLHttpRequest object.

4. **Security and User privacy:** Not all concerns are addressed. Issues surrounding security and user privacy need to be considered when developing an Ajax application.
5. **Accessibility:** Because not all browsers have JavaScript or XMLHttpRequest object support, you must ensure that you provide a way to make the web application accessible to all users.
6. **Bookmark and Navigation:** Since, Ajax is used to asynchronously load bits of content into an existing page, some of the page information may not correspond to a newly loaded page. Browser history and bookmarks may not have the correct behavior since the URL was unchanged despite parts of the page being changed.
7. **Search engine:** Ajax applications are not searchable; however, it is possible to use Ajax features and elements within an application that is searchable.

6.2 AJAX WEB APPLICATION MODEL (April 13)

- Before understanding Ajax, let's understand classic web application model and Ajax web application model first.

1. **Synchronous (Classic Web Application Model):**

- The nature of interaction between the client and the server is of start-stop-start-stop (i.e. click-wait)
- The browser response to the user action by discarding the current HTML page.
- The request is sent to the web server.
- When the server completes the processing of request, it returns the response page to the Web browser.
- Browser refreshes the screen and display the new HTML page.
- This is called as synchronous request response model.

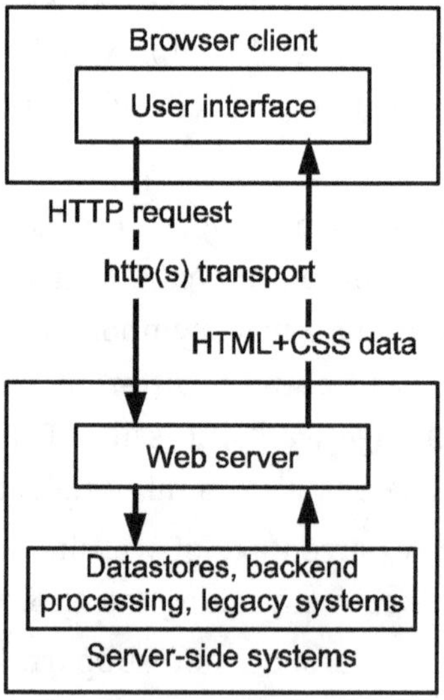

Fig. 6.1: Synchronous Web Application Model

- This approach makes a lot of technical sense, but it doesn't make for a great user experience. While the server is doing its thing, but user is waiting. And at every step in a task, the user waits some more. In fact, why should the user see the application go to the server at all?

2. **Asynchronous (Ajax Web-Application Model): (April 13)**

- The intermediary layer (i.e. Ajax Engine) is introduced between the user and the Web server.
- The Web page sends its requests using JavaScript.
- The request is done asynchronously, meaning that code execution does not wait for response.
- The server response comprises of data and not the presentation.
- The Ajax engine can understand and interpret the data.
- Most of the page does not change, only parts of the page that need to change are updated.
- The JavaScript dynamically updates the web page, without redrawing everything.
- For the Web server nothing has change; it still responds to each request.
- This way you never have to wait around.
- The Ajax engine, irrespective of the server, does asynchronous communication.

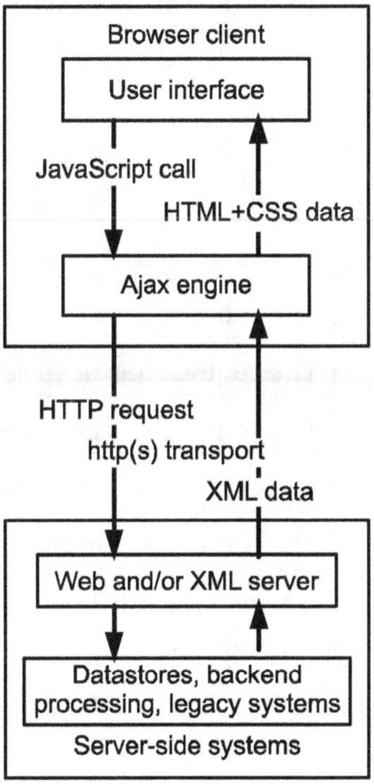

Fig. 6.2: Asynchronous Web Application Model

Understanding XMLHttpRequest:

- The XMLHttpRequest object is the key to Ajax.
- XMLHttpRequest is used for asynchronous communication between client and server.
- The XMLHttpRequest object can send HTTP request, and receive responses.
- The XMLHttpRequest object transfer the XML and other text data to and from the Web server by using HTTP.
- The XMLHttp Object can be used in calling the web page in either synchronous or asynchronous mode.
- It establishes an independent connection channel between a webpage's Client-Side and Server-Side.
- It performs following operations:
    1. Sends data from the client in the background,
    2. Receives the data from the server, and
    3. Updates the webpage without reloading it.

XMLHttpRequest Object's Properties:

1. **onreadystatechange:** An event handler for an event that fires at every state change. This property sets the method to be called on every state change.
2. **readyState:** The readyState property defines the current state of the XMLHttpRequest object.

   The following table provides a list of the possible values for the readyState property:

State	Description
0	The request is not initialized.
1	The request has been set up.
2	The request has been sent.
3	The request is in process.
4	The request is completed.

   (i) **readyState = 0** After you have created the XMLHttpRequest object, but before you have called the open() method.

   (ii) **readyState = 1** After you have called the open() method, but before you have called send().

   (iii) **readyState = 2** After you have called send().

(iv) **readyState = 3** After the browser has established a communication with the server, but before the server has completed the response.

(v) **readyState = 4** After the request has been completed, and the response data has been completely received from the server.

3. **responseText:** Returns the response as a string.
4. **responseXM:** Returns the response as XML. This property returns an XML document object, which can be examined and parsed using the W3C DOM node tree methods and properties.
5. **status:** Returns the status as a number (e.g., 404 for "Not Found" and 200 for "OK").
6. **statusText:** Returns the status as a string (e.g., "Not Found" or "OK").

XMLHttpRequest Methods:

1. **abort():** This method is used to cancel the current XMLHttpRequest and reset the object to be uninitialized state.
2. **getAllResponseHeaders():** Returns the complete set of HTTP headers as a string.
3. **getResponseHeader(headerName):** Returns the value of the specified HTTP header.
4. **open(method, URL)**

   open(method, URL, async)

   open(method, URL, async, userName)

   open(method, URL, async, userName, password)

   Specifies the method, URL, and other optional attributes of a request.

   The method parameter can have a value of "GET", "POST", or "HEAD". Other HTTP methods, such as "PUT" and "DELETE" (primarily used in REST applications) may be possible.

   The "async" parameter specifies whether the request should be handled asynchronously or not. "true" means that the script processing carries on after the send() method without waiting for a response, and "false" means that the script waits for a response before continuing script processing.
5. **send(content):** Sends the HTTP request to the server and receives the response when the readyState value is 1.
6. **setRequestHeader(label, value):** Adds a label/value pair to the HTTP header to be sent.

Creating the XMLHttpRequest Object:

- The XMLHttpRequest is implemented in different ways by the browsers. In Internet Explorer 6 and older, XMLHttpRequest is implemented as an ActiveX control and you instantiate it like this:

```
xmlhttp = new ActiveXObject("Microsoft.XMLHttp");
```

- For the other web browsers, XMLHttpRequest is a native object, so you create instances of it like this:

```
xmlhttp = new XMLHttpRequest();
```

- The following code is used to create XMLHttpRequest object:

```
function loadXMLDoc()
{
    // will store the reference to the XMLHttpRequest object
    var xmlhttp;
    if (window.XMLHttpRequest)
    {
        // code for IE7+, Firefox, Chrome, Opera, Safari
        xmlhttp=new XMLHttpRequest(); // try to create XMLHttpRequest object
    }
    else
    {
        // code for IE6, IE5
        // try to create XMLHttpRequest object
        xmlhttp=new ActiveXObject("Microsoft.XMLHTTP");
    }
}
```

How XMLHttpRequest Object Works in Synchronous Pages Pattern:

- The XMLHttpRequest object works in the following pattern:
    - Create the object.

      For example: `xmlHttp = new XMLHttpRequest();`
    - Create the request.

      For example: `xmlHttp.open ("GET",url,false);`
    - Send the request.

      For example: `xmlHttp.send (null);`
    - Hold the processing until you get the response i.e. get the response by responseText property,

      For example: `var xmlHttp = xmlHttp.responseText;`

How XMLHttpRequest Object Works in Asynchronous Pages Pattern:

- The XMLHttpRequest object works in the following pattern:
    - Create the object.
    - Set the readystatechange event to trigger the specific function.

- Check the readyState property, to see if data is ready. If it is not, then check it again after an interval.
- Open request.
- Send request.
- Continue the processing. Interruption is done only when the response is received.

- The above steps are performed by the following code:

```
xmlHttp = new XMLHttpRequest();
xmlHttp.onreadystatechange = stateChanged
xmlHttp.open ("GET", url, true);
xmlHttp.send (null);
var xmlHttp = xmlHttp.responseText;
function stateChanged()
{
  if (xmlHttp.readyState == 4)
  {
     var objXML = xmlHttp.responseXML;
  }
}
```

- **Example:** Ajax program to read a text file and print the contents of the file when the user clicks on the Print button.
- Create a text file named "a.txt" and write text "Ajax Example" into it.
- Create an HTML file with the following code:

```
<html>
<head>
<script>
    function loadXMLDoc()
    {
    var xmlhttp;
    if (window.XMLHttpRequest)
    {// code for IE7+, Firefox, Chrome, Opera, Safari
                                        xmlhttp=new XMLHttpRequest();
    }
    else
    {// code for IE6, IE5
    xmlhttp=new ActiveXObject("Microsoft.XMLHTTP");
    }
    xmlhttp.open("GET","a.txt",true);
    xmlhttp.send(null);
```

```
        xmlhttp.onreadystatechange=function()
        {
            if (xmlhttp.readyState==4 && xmlhttp.status==200)
            {
                document.getElementById("myDiv").innerHTML=
                xmlhttp.responseText;
            }
        }
    }
    </script>
    </head>
    <body>
        <button onclick="loadXMLDoc()">Print</button>
        <div id="myDiv"></div>
    </body>
    </html>
```

Output:

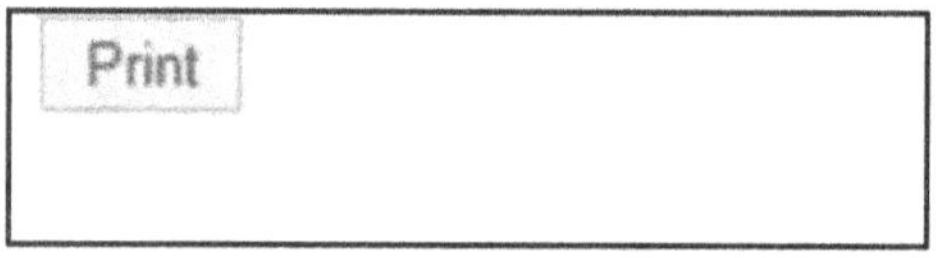

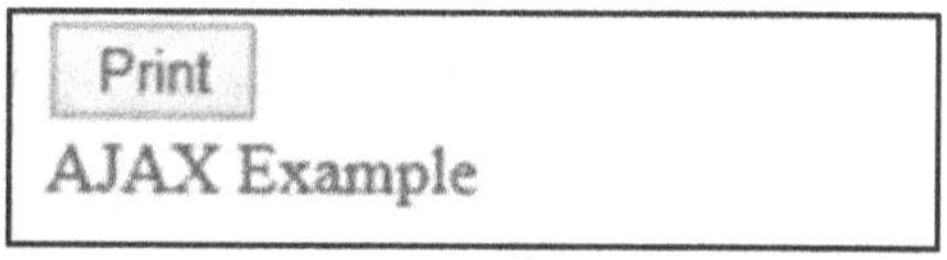

- The above program will start from HTML body tag which contain a button tag and a div tag, when user click on the 'Print' button, the JavaScript function loadXMLDoc() will be called. Inside the function the Ajax works and it send a GET request for the file 'a.txt', and if request is completed then the value of the readyState property is equals to 4 and status is 200, so it fetches text from the file using property responseText and display the text in place of div tag.

6.3 AJAX - PHP FRAMEWORK (Oct. 14)

- The PHP-frameworks gives different ways to affect the client view in both template based view (uses technologies like JSP, ASP and RHTML) and server-side technologies (like ASP.NET and JSP).
- This functionality becomes popular in the serverside Ajax packages, because it automatically create javascript code for us.

- There are various PHP frameworks available, like Ajax Core, CakePHP, Xajax, Sajax, XOAD, Zephyr, Feather Ajax 1.1 and Tigermouse to integrate Ajax with PHP. These frameworks supports Model, View and Controller (MVC) architecture. They reduces the writing of same code and common function repeatedly.
- The Sajax is an Ajax based framework which generate Ajax -enabled JavaScript from many server side languges like PHP, ASP, ColdFusion, Io, Lua, Perl, Python and Ruby. This Sajax bridge execute server side code and uses Object Remoting technique.
- The object brokers enable remote exchange and the client-side methods are tied to the server side object. There are network round trips involved and messages are sent via service oriented frameworks.

Sajax Framework Example:

- In this example, JavaScript function generates from PHP function on server side that manipulates data and returns result to other javascript function on client side.
- The Home page of mult.php has three text fields where user can enter two numbers in first two text field and in third text field, result is displayed. There is one submit button in home page. We have to include Sajax.php in mult.php.
- We need to setup Sajax using Sajax_init ( ) method. This file contains function mult for multiplication of two numbers. To access this function in JavaScript by another name, we need to export this method, like x_mult.

  The part of mult.php:

```
<?
    require ("Sajax.php");
    function mult ($no1, $no2)
    {
        return $no1 * $no2;
    }
    Sajax_init ();
    Sajax_export ("mult");
    Sajax_handle_client_request ();
    //it connect mult function with Sajax and generate JavaScript?>
```

- The generated javascript code can be embed in web page using PHP function Sajax_show_javascript ( );
- After Clicking on Submit button, it invokes x_mult function, which in turn calls mult function on server side.

The part of mult.php:

```
<script>
<?
Sajax_show_javascript ();
?>
function show_results (result)
{
    docment.getElementById("result").value=result;
}
function do_add ()
{
    var no1, no2;
    no1 = document.getElementById("No1").value;
    no2 = document.getElementById("No2").value;
    x_mult (no1, no2, show_results);
}
</script>
```

- The x_mult uses three argument, first is value, second is value and third is a function name which will display the result of multiplication.

6.4 PERFORMING AJAX VALIDATION

- The validation may done for checking integer, email id or phone number etc. The first page for application displays the text field to enter the username. It has JavaScript code to create the XMLHttpRequest object. The validate method sends request to validate the PHP page with parameter name.
- When status of response is OK, the <div> element having id res, is populated with the text response received from server. When new request comes in the abort, method exists from the previous request.
- **Example:** Ajax program to carry out validation for a username entered in textbox. If the textbox is blank, print 'Enter username'. If the number of characters is less than three, print 'Username is too short'. If value entered is appropriate the print 'Valid username'.

  a.html

```
<html>
<head>
<script type="text/javascript">
    var xmlHttp = false;
```

```
    function validate(name)
    {
        //alert(str);
        if(window.XMLHttpRequest)
        {
            xmlHttp = new XMLHttpRequest();
        }
        else if(window.ActiveXObject)
        {
            xmlHttp = new ActiveXObject("Microsoft.XMLHTTP");
        }
        //alert("c3");
        if(xmlHttp==null)
        {
            alert("Browser does not support HTTP request");
            return;
        }
        //xmlHttp.abort(); //alert(name);
        xmlHttp.open("GET", "validation.php?name=" + name, true);
        xmlHttp.onreadystatechange=stateChanged
        xmlHttp.send(null);
    }
    function stateChanged()
    {//alert(xmlHttp.readyState);
        if(xmlHttp.readyState==4)
        {
            document.getElementById("res").innerHTML=xmlHttp.responseText;
        }
    }
</script>
</head>
<body>
    <form>
        Username: <input type="text" name="name"
                                    onKeyUp="validate(this.value)" />
    <div id="res"></div>
    </form>
</body>
</html>
```

- The Ajax.html and validate.php files are stored into the server www directory and executed in browser.

```
http://localhost/a.html
```

- The a.html file calls validate.php where validation is done. If name is blank or name is less than 3 characters or if name is already exists, the corresponding messages are given.

validate.php

```
<?php
    function validate($name)
    {
        if($name == '')
            return 'Please enter any username';
        if(strlen($name) < 3)
            return 'Username is too short';
        if(strlen($name) > 10)
            return 'Username is too long';
        return 'User name is valid';
    }
    echo validate($_GET['name']);
?>
```

Output:

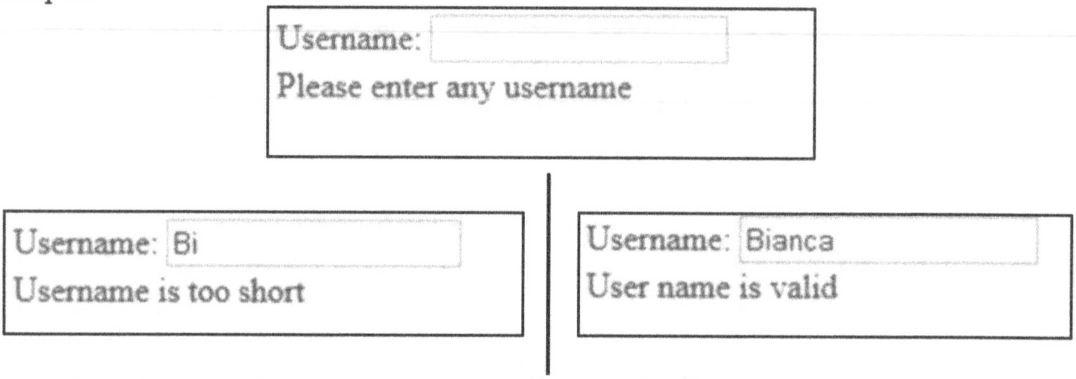
Username:
Please enter any username
Username: Bi
Username is too short
Username: Bianca
User name is valid

6.5 HANDLING XML DATA USING PHP AND AJAX

- XML files are used to store data using our own defined tags. The following example shows how to get the data from XML file using Ajax.
- The index.html file use choosebook.js JavaScript file. This form shows the Book title to the user and when user select the title from list box, the sendTitle method from choosebook.js is called.

index.html

```
<html>
<head>
<script type="text/javascript">
    var xmlHttp;
```

```
    function sendTitle(str)
    {
        if(window.XMLHttpRequest)
        {
            xmlHttp = new XMLHttpRequest();
        }
        else if(window.ActiveXObject)
        {
            xmlHttp = new ActiveXObject("Microsoft.XMLHTTP");
        }
        if(xmlHttp==null)
        {
            alert("Browser does not support HTTP request");
            return;
        }
        var url="getbook.php";
        url=url+"?q="+str;
        xmlHttp.onreadystatechange=stateChanged
        xmlHttp.open("GET",url,true);
        xmlHttp.send(null);
    }
    function stateChanged()
    {
        if(xmlHttp.readyState==4)
        {
            document.getElementById("res").innerHTML=xmlHttp.responseText;
        }
    }
</script>
</head>
<body>
    <form>
```

```
        List of book titles:
        <select name="titles" onChange="sendTitle(this.value)">
            <option value="AJAX ">AJAX </option>
            <option value="Java2">Java2</option>
            <option value="HTML5">HTML5</option>
            <option value="PHP6">PHP6</option>
        </select>
    </form>
    <div id="res">Book details will be given here</div>
</body>
</html>
```

- The booksdata.xml file stores the Book's details like Title, Author, Year and price sub elements.

bookstore.xml

```
<?xml version="1.0" encoding="iso-8859-1"?>
<bookstore>
    <book>
        <title>AJAX </title>
        <author>author1</author>
        <year>2000</year>
        <price>250</price>
    </book>
    <book>
        <title>Java2</title>
        <author>author2</author>
        <year>2005</year>
        <price>600</price>
    </book>
    <book>
        <title>HTML5</title>
        <author>author3</author>
        <year>2010</year>
        <price>300</price>
    </book>
```

```
    <book>
        <title>PHP6</title>
        <author>author4</author>
        <year>2013</year>
        <price>400</price>
    </book>
</bookstore>
```

- The XMLHttpRequest method create URL to request getbook.php file. This URL has parameter q which is used to initialize the value of list box, then sends the request to getbook.php page. After completion of response by the server, the stateChanged method is called.
- The server page getbook.php create XML DOMDocument object user select an Option. Then booksdata.xml file is loaded. The Title send from HTML form search in booksdata.xml file. This way the details of the selected book are displayed.

getbook.php

```
<?php
    $q=$_GET["q"];
$xmlDoc = new DOMDocument();
$xmlDoc->load("bookstore.xml");
$x=$xmlDoc->getElementsByTagName('title');
for($i=0; $i<=$x->length-1;$i++)
{
//Process only element nodes
if ($x->item($i)->nodeType==1)
    {
    if ($x->item($i)->childNodes->item(0)->nodeValue == $q)
        {
        $y=$x->item($i)->parentNode;
        }
    }
}
$book=$y->childNodes;
for($i=0;$i<$book->length;$i++)
{
//Process only element nodes
```

```
if ($book->item($i)->nodeType==1)
    {
    echo($book->item($i)->nodeName);
    echo(":");
    echo($book->item($i)->childNodes->item(0)->nodeValue);
    echo("<br/>");
    }
}
?>
```

Output:

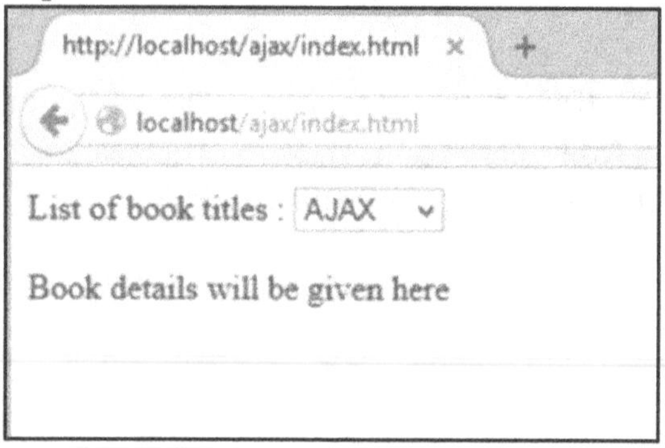

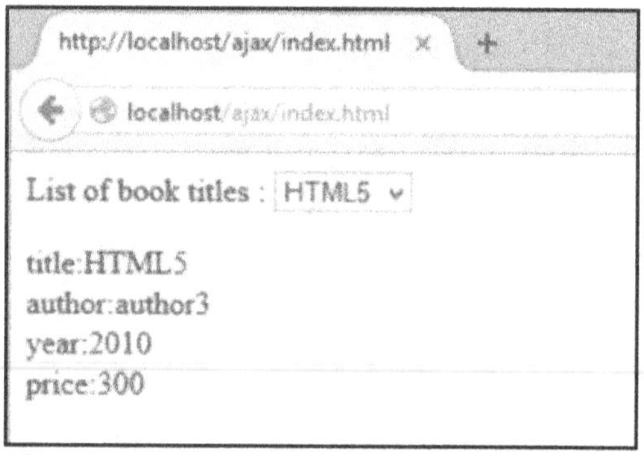

6.6 CONNECTING DATABASE USING PHP AND AJAX

- Storing the data into database and retrieving it from database, we can do this using PHP and PostgreSQL.
- Consider an example of employee database table. From index.html form, we can select the employee name using combo box and display its record details.
- Create 'Employees' table in PostgreSQL, with fields Name, Age, City, Designation. Insert the names as per db.html with all details.

db.html

```
<html>
<head>
<script type="text/javascript">
    var xmlHttp;
    function sendEmpID(str)
    {
        //alert(str);
```

```
        if(window.XMLHttpRequest)
        {
            xmlHttp = new XMLHttpRequest();
        }
        else if(window.ActiveXObject)
        {
            xmlHttp = new ActiveXObject("Microsoft.XMLHTTP");
        }
        //alert("c3");
        if(xmlHttp==null)
        {
            alert("Browser does not support HTTP request");
            return;
        }
        var url="getemployee.php";
        url=url+"?q="+str + "&sid=" + Math.random();
        xmlHttp.onreadystatechange=stateChanged
        //alert(url);
        xmlHttp.open("GET",url,true);
        xmlHttp.send(null);
    }
    function stateChanged()
    {//alert(xmlHttp.readyState);
        if(xmlHttp.readyState==4)
        {
    document.getElementById("emp").innerHTML=xmlHttp.responseText;
        }
    }
</script>
</head>
<body>
    <form>
```

```
        Employee List:
        <select name="names" onChange="sendEmpID(this.value)">
            <option value="1">Mahesh</option>
            <option value="2">Sachin</option>
            <option value="3">Tejas</option>
            <option value="4">Bhavesh</option>
        </select>
    </form>
    <div id="emp">Employee info will be listed here</div>
</body>
</html>
```

- The method sendEmpID() sends asynchronous request to getemployee.php file. The request URL has parameter q to store id. It sends the request to getemployee.php with parameter.
- After selecting the employee name, it sends the id as query parameter to getemployee.php page, this page establish the connection to PostgreSQL server. After successful connection, it will retrieve data and using HTML table, the fetched values are inserted into corresponding cell or row.

getemployee.php

```
<?php
$q=$_GET["q"];
$conn = pg_pconnect("dbname=test") or die("An error occurred.");
        $result = pg_query($conn, "SELECT * FROM employee WHERE id = ". $q) or
                                            die("An error occurred.");
echo "<table border='1'>
<tr>
<th>Name</th>
<th>Age</th>
<th>City</th>
<th>Designation</th>
</tr>";
```

```
while($row = pg_fetch_array($result, NULL, PGSQL_ASSOC))
    {
    echo "<tr>";
    echo "<td>". $row['name']. "</td>";
    echo "<td>". $row['age']. "</td>";
    echo "<td>". $row['city']. "</td>";
    echo "<td>". $row['designation']. "</td>";
    echo "</tr>";
    }
echo "</table>";
pd_close($conn);
?>
```

- We execute this using http://localhost index.html.

Output:

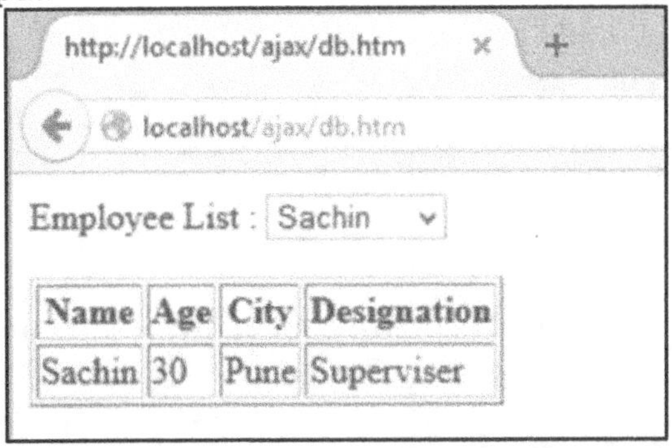

SUMMARY

- AJAX is asynchronous JavaScript and XML. AJAX is a technique for creating fast and dynamic web pages. AJAX allows user to update part of web page without reloading entire web page.
- Client and server communicate with asynchronous method. AJAX engine is placed between user and server. JavaScript engine sends request using JavaScript function as XML to server. Server response is also processed by engine to update relevant page elements.
- AJAX can be used for interactive communication with a XML and database.
- AJAX has two applications models i.e. synchronous and asynchronous.
- XMLHttpRequest is used for asynchronous communication between client and server.
- The XMLHttpRequest object can send HTTP request, and receive responses.

- There are various PHP frameworks available, like Ajax Core, CakePHP, Xajax, Sajax, XOAD, Zephyr, Feather Ajax 1.1 and Tigermouse to integrate Ajax with PHP.
- The Sajax is an Ajax based framework which generate Ajax -enabled JavaScript from many server side languges like PHP, ASP, ColdFusion, Io, Lua, Perl, Python and Ruby.

PRACTICE QUESTIONS

1. What is Ajax?
2. How we make web page interactive?
3. What is the use of XMLHttpRequest?
4. Write a code using JavaScript for implementation to Ajax.
5. Explain Ajax-PHP framework in detail.
6. Write a simple php program which implements Ajax for addition of two numbers.
7. Write a programs to access XML data using php and Ajax.
8. With the help of diagram describe Ajax Web Application model.
9. How to connect database with PHP and Ajax?
10. Enlist advantages and disadvantages of Ajax.
11. What is purpose of Ajax engine?

Ans. Refer to Section 6.2, Point (2).

12. Write note on AJAX PHP framework.

Ans. Refer to Section 6.3.

13. Write an ajax program to display list of book stored in an array on clicking ok button.

Ans. **Book_list.php**

```
<!DOCTYPE html>
<html>
<head>
<script>
function showMatch()
{
   //var str = document.getElementById("search_string");
/*if (str.length==0)
  {
   document.getElementById("txtHint").innerHTML="";
    return;
  }*/
if (window.XMLHttpRequest)
  {// code for IE7+, Firefox, Chrome, Opera, Safari
   xmlhttp=new XMLHttpRequest();
  }
```

```
else
  {// code for IE6, IE5
   xmlhttp=new ActiveXObject("Microsoft.XMLHTTP");
  }
xmlhttp.onreadystatechange=function()
  {
  if (xmlhttp.readyState==4 && xmlhttp.status==200)
    {
    document.getElementById("txtHint").innerHTML=xmlhttp.responseText;
    }
  }
xmlhttp.open("GET","getmatch.php",true);
xmlhttp.send();
}
function clear_suggetion()
{
   document.getElementById("txtHint").innerHTML="";
}
</script>
</head><body>
<p><b>Press Below button to check liast of books:</b></p>
<form >
<input name="submit" type="button" value="Show me book list"
                                              onclick="showMatch()" />
<input name="submit" type="button" value="Clear list"
                                         onclick="clear_suggetion()" />
</form ons>
<p>Suggestions: <span id="txtHint"></span></p>
</body>
</html>
Getmatch.php
<?php
//print_r($_GET);
// this is array to search
$arry_tosearch = array("statistic", "algebra", "java", "linux", "maths",
                                                           "chemistry");
// print above array
//echo count($arry_tosearch);
```

```
echo "<br><h4>Following are available books list</h4>";
for($i=0 ; $i<count($arry_tosearch); $i++)
{
    echo  "".$arry_tosearch[$i],'<br>';
}
?>
```

Output:

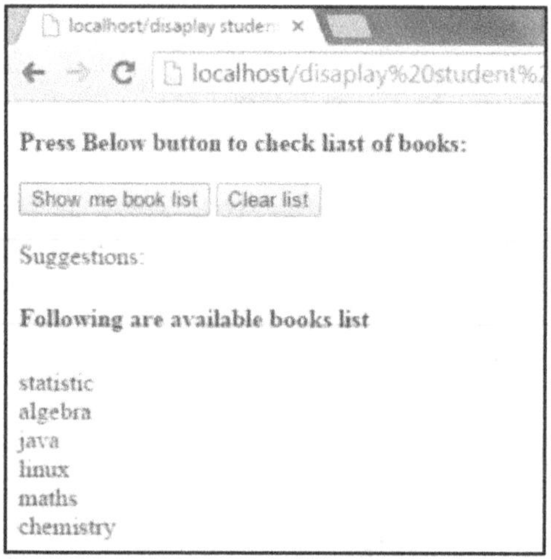

14. Write any two Ajax applications.

Ans. Refer to Section 6.1.

15. Write a note on Ajax web application model.

Ans. Refer to Section 6.2.

16. Write an Ajax program to search student name according the character typed and display list using array.

Ans. **New.php**

```
<html>
<head>
<script>
function showHint(str) {
    if (str.length == 0) {
        document.getElementById("txtHint").innerHTML = "";
        return;
```

```
    } else {
        var xmlhttp = new XMLHttpRequest();
        xmlhttp.onreadystatechange = function() {
        if (xmlhttp.readyState == 4 && xmlhttp.status == 200) {
      document.getElementById("txtHint").innerHTML = xmlhttp.responseText;
            }
        }
        xmlhttp.open("GET", "gethint.php?q=" + str, true);
        xmlhttp.send();
    }
}
</script>
</head>
<body>
<p><b>Start typing a name in the input field below:</b></p>
<form>
First name: <input type="text" onkeyup="showHint(this.value)">
</form>
<p>Suggestions: <span id="txtHint"></span></p>
</body>
</html>
```

Gethint.php

```
<?php
// Array with names
$a[] = "Amit";
$a[] = "Bob";
$a[] = "Chinmay";
$a[] = "Deepa";
$a[] = "Esha";
$a[] = "Faiz";
$a[] = "Gautam";
$a[] = "Harshal";
$a[] = "Ishant";
$a[] = "Jyotsana";
$a[] = "Kishor";
$a[] = "Lokesh";
$a[] = "Nina";
```

```
$a[] = "Omkar";
$a[] = "Pritam";
$a[] = "Amey";
$a[] = "Rahul";
$a[] = "Chaitali";
$a[] = "Dushyant";
$a[] = "Kavita";
$a[] = "Kavya";
$a[] = "Sunil";
// get the q parameter from URL
$q = $_REQUEST["q"];
$hint = "";
// lookup all hints from array if $q is different from ""
if ($q !== "") {
    $q = strtolower($q);
    $len=strlen($q);
    foreach($a as $name) {
        if (stristr($q, substr($name, 0, $len))) {
            if ($hint === "") {
                $hint = $name;
            } else {
                $hint .= ", $name";
            }
        }
    }
}
// Output "no suggestion" if no hint was found or output correct values
echo $hint === "" ? "no suggestion" : $hint;
?>
```

Output:

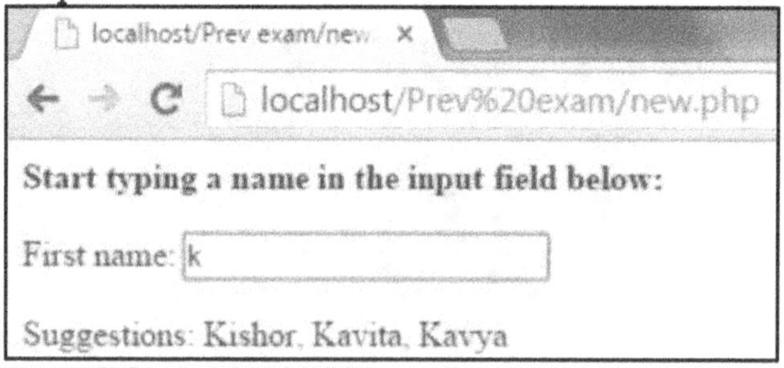

17. Write an AJAX program to search the book name according the character typed and display same list using array.

Ans. **New.php**

```
<html>
<head>
<script>
function showHint(str) {
    if (str.length == 0) {
        document.getElementById("txtHint").innerHTML = "";
        return;
    } else {
        var xmlhttp = new XMLHttpRequest();
        xmlhttp.onreadystatechange = function() {
            if (xmlhttp.readyState == 4 && xmlhttp.status == 200) {
                document.getElementById("txtHint").innerHTML
                                                = xmlhttp.responseText;
            }
        }
        xmlhttp.open("GET", "gethint.php?q=" + str, true);
        xmlhttp.send();
    }
}
</script>
</head>
<body>
<p><b>Start typing a name in the input field below:</b></p>
<form>
First name: <input type="text" onkeyup="showHint(this.value)">
</form>
<p>Suggestions: <span id="txtHint"></span></p>
</body>
</html>
```

Gethint.php

```
<?php
// Array with names
$a[] = "Advance Networking";
$a[] = "Business Application";
$a[] = "Brave new World";
```

```
$a[] = "Catch-22";
$a[] = "An American Tragedy";
$a[] = "Invisible Man";
$a[] = "Wings of fire";
$a[] = "The Amassadors";
$a[] = "The good soldier";
$a[] = "All the Kings Men";
// get the q parameter from URL
$q = $_REQUEST["q"];
$hint = "";
// lookup all hints from array if $q is different from ""
if ($q !== "") {
    $q = strtolower($q);
    $len=strlen($q);
    foreach($a as $name) {
        if (stristr($q, substr($name, 0, $len))) {
            if ($hint === "") {
                $hint = $name;
            } else {
                $hint .= ", $name";
            }
        }
    }
}
// Output "no suggestion" if no hint was found or output correct values
echo $hint === "" ? "no suggestion" : $hint;
?>
```

Output:

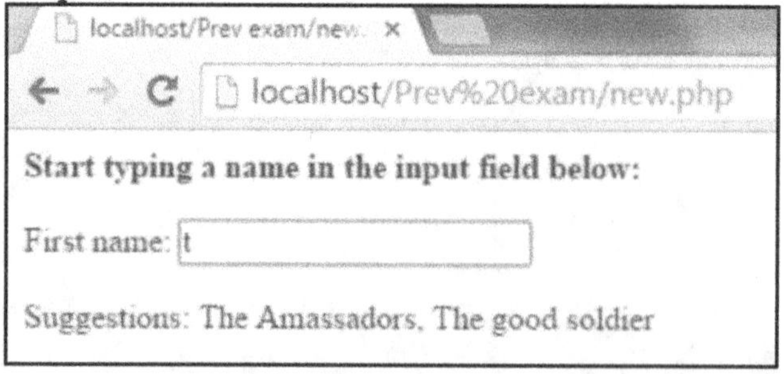

18. Explain advantages and disadvantages of Ajax.

Ans. Refer to Section 6.1.1.

UNIVERSITY QUESTIONS AND ANSWERS

1 Mark Questions:

1. Give any two applications of Ajax. **(April 2013, Oct. 2014)**

Ans. Refer to Section 6.1.

2. What is Ajax? **(April 2015)**

Ans. Refer to Section 6.1.

5 Mark Questions:

3. Write a short note on role of ajax engine in synchronization of Ajax programs. **(April 2013)**

Ans. Refer to Section 6.2 Point (2).

4. Write a note on Ajax php frame work. **(Oct. 2014)**

Ans. Refer to Section 6.3.

5. Write an Ajax program to display list of games stored in an array on clicking ok button. **(Oct. 2014)**

Ans. Disp_list.php

```
<!DOCTYPE html>
<html>
<head>
<script>
function showMatch()
{
   //var str = document.getElementById("search_string");
/*if (str.length==0)
  {
   document.getElementById("txtHint").innerHTML="";
    return;
  }*/
if (window.XMLHttpRequest)
  {// code for IE7+, Firefox, Chrome, Opera, Safari
   xmlhttp=new XMLHttpRequest();
  }
else
  {// code for IE6, IE5
   xmlhttp=new ActiveXObject("Microsoft.XMLHTTP");
  }
```

```
xmlhttp.onreadystatechange=function()
  {
  if (xmlhttp.readyState==4 && xmlhttp.status==200)
    {
    document.getElementById("txtHint").innerHTML=xmlhttp.responseText;
    }
  }
xmlhttp.open("GET","getmatch.php",true);
xmlhttp.send();
}
function clear_suggetion()
{
   document.getElementById("txtHint").innerHTML="";
}
</script>
</head><body>
<p><b>Press Below button to check list of games:</b></p>
<form >
<input name="submit" type="button" value="Show me game list"
                                         onclick="showMatch()" />
<input name="submit" type="button" value="Clear list"
                                    onclick="clear_suggetion()" />
</form ons>
<p>Suggestions: <span id="txtHint"></span></p>
</body>
</html>
```

Getmatch.php

```
<?php
//print_r($_GET);
// this is array to search
$arry_tosearch = array("hocky", "soccer", "cricket", "table tennis",
                                          "badminton", "chess");
// print above array
//echo count($arry_tosearch);
echo "<br><h4>Following are available game list</h4>";
for($i=0 ; $i<count($arry_tosearch); $i++)
{
   echo  "".$arry_tosearch[$i],'<br>';
}
?>
```

Output:

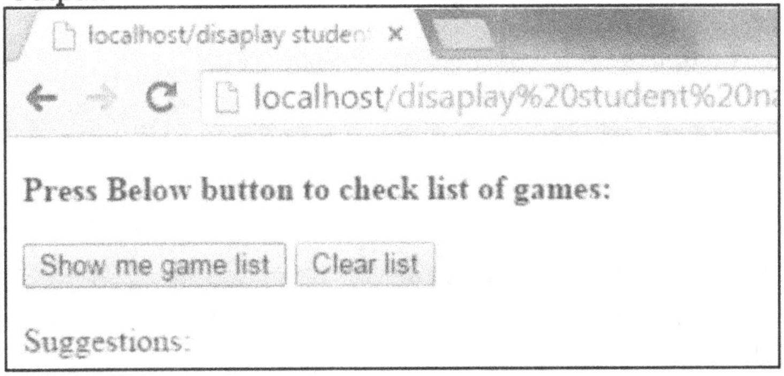
localhost/disaplay studen
localhost/disaplay%20student%20n
Press Below button to check list of games:
Show me game list
Clear list
Suggestions:

localhost/disaplay studen
localhost/disaplay%20studen
Press Below button to check list of games:
Show me game list
Clear list
Suggestions:
Following are available game list
hocky
soccer
cricket
table tennis
badminton
chess

April 2016

Time : Two Hours **Max. Marks : 40**

N.B.: *(i) All questions are compulsory.*
(ii) Figures to the right indicate full marks.
(iii) All questions carry equal marks.

1. Attempt all of the following: **[10 × 1 = 10]**

(a) Which function is used to determine whether file was uploaded?

Ans. is_uplodaed_file() is the function is used to determine whether file was uploaded or not.

Syntax: `bool is_uploaded_file ( string $filename )`

Function returns TRUE if the file named by filename was uploaded via HTTP POST otherwisae false.

(b) Write the protocols used to retrieve email from the server.

Ans. Post office protocol 3 (POP 3) and Internet Message Access Protocol (IMAP) are used to retrieve email from the server.

POP 3 provides simple, standardized way for users to access mailboxes and download their messages to their computers.

IMAP is standard protocol for accessing email form your local server.

(c) How we can send the data to server using Ajax?

Ans. To send a request to a server, we use the open() and send() methods of the XMLHttpRequest object:

```
xhttp.open("GET", "ajax_info.txt", true);
xhttp.send();
```

open(method, url, async) : Specifies the type of request, method: the type of request: GET or POST, url: the server (file) location, async: true (asynchronous) or false (synchronous)

send(): Sends the request to the server (used for GET)

send(string): Sends the request to the server (used for POST)

(d) State any two window objects in Javascript.

Ans. Refer 5.7, Page 5.32.

(e) List the applications of XML.

Ans. XML is used to store structured data: It allows to create documents that can hold data in structured way.

XML is used to transport data over the web. XML stores data in plain text format. This provides a software- and hardware-independent way of storing, transporting, and sharing data.

(f) Write the Javascript data types.

Ans. Refer 5.3.1, Page 5.8.

(g) XML is case sensitive. Justify true or false.

Ans. Yes, XML is case sensitive. Tags in XML are case sensitive. XML does not have any predefined tags, and it allows users to create tags. Therefore user defined tag <Root> and <root> looks different and they are not same.

(h) Which object is Ajax make web page interactive?

Ans.

(i) When IMAP4 protocol is used in email handling?

Ans. IMAP4 (Internet Mail Access Protocol V4) is an email protocol which is sometimes used instead of the POP3 protocol. With IMAP4 email is stored on the mail server and can be accessed from any IMAP4 email client on the network. With POP3 email is downloaded to the mail client where it is accessed. When using IMAP4 many of the functions of the email client are performed by the mail server instead. This includes things such as searching for messages, moving messages between folders etc.

(j) What is SSL?

Ans. Refer 1.6, Page 1.40-1.41.

Q.2 Attempt any two of following: [2 × 5 = 10]

(a) Explain alert dialog box in Javascript with the help of suitable example.

Ans. The alert() method displays an alert box with a specified message and an OK button. An alert box is often used if you want to make sure information comes through to the user.

Syntax: alert(message)

Example:

```
<html>
  <head>
      <script type="text/javascript">
      <!--
        function Warn() {
          alert ("This is a warning message!");
          document.write ("This is a warning message!");
        }
      //-->
    </script>
```

```
    </head>
    <body>
        <p>Click the following button to see the result: </p>
        <form>
            <input type="button" value="Click Me" onclick="Warn();" />
        </form>
    </body>
</html>
```

(b) State the difference between GET and POST method.

Ans. GET requests can be cached

POST requests are never cached

GET requests remain in the browser history

POST requests do not remain in the browser history

GET requests can be bookmarked

POST requests cannot be bookmarked

GET requests have length restrictions

POST requests have no restrictions on data length

GET requests data is visible in URL and thus it should never be used when dealing with sensitive data

POST requests encrypts data and thus safe to send sensitive data.

(c) Write short note on cookies.

Ans. Refer 1.5.1, Page 1.28-1.29.

Q.3 Attempt any two of following: [2 × 5 = 10]

(a) Write Javascript code to open new window which will have some content op it and then close this window.

Ans. My_function.html

```
<html>
<body>
<p>Click the button to open a new browser window.</p>
<button onclick="myFunction()">Try it</button>
<script>
function myFunction() {
    window.open("new_window.html");
}
```

```
</script>
</body>
</html>
New_window.html
<html>
<body>
    <h1>Welcome to new window</1>
</body>
</html>
```

(b) Write PHP script to accept string and check whether it is palindrome or not by using sticky forms.

Ans.

```
<html>
<head><title>String Comparison</title></head>
<body>
    <?php
        $s1 = @$_GET['str1'];
        $s2 = strrev($s1);
    ?>
    <form action="<?php echo $_SERVER['PHP_SELF'] ?>" method="GET">
        String 1:
        <input type="text" name="str1" value="<?php echo $s1 ?>" />
        <br />
        <input type="submit" name="Check Pallindrome" />
    </form>
    <?php
        if(strcmp($s1,$s2)==0)
        {
                echo" Strings are pallindrome";
        }
        else
        {
            echo "Strings are not pallindrome";
        }
    ?>
</body>
</html>
```

(c) Write an Ajax program to search the student name according the character typed and display list using array.

Ans.

```
<html>
<head>
<script type="text/javascript" >
    function m1(str)
    {
        var ob=false;
        ob=new XMLHttpRequest();
        ob.open("GET","slip20_2.php?q="+str);
        ob.send();
        ob.onreadystatechange=function()
        {
            if(ob.readyState==4 && ob.status==200)
            document.getElementById("a").innerHTML=ob.responseText;
        }
    }
    </script>
    </head>
    <body>
    <form>
    Enter Name Of Student :<input type=text name=search size="20"
    onkeyup="m1(form.search.value)">
    <input type=button value="submit" >
                                <!--onclick="m1(form.search.value)"-->
    <!-- onclick="matches(form.search.value)">-->
    </form>
    suggestions :<span id="a"></span><br>
    </body>
    </html>
```

PHP file:

```
<?php
$a=array("RAMESH","SURESH","RAJ","SEEMA","PUJA","SIYA","AJAY","SAMEER",
                                        "VIJAY","VINAY","VIRAJ");
    $q=$_GET['q'];
```

```
    if(strlen($q)>0)
    {
        $match="";
        for($i=0;$i<count($a);$i++)
        {
            if(strtolower($q)==strtolower(substr($a[$i],0,strlen($q))))
            {
                if($match=="")
                {
                    $match=$a[$i];
                }
                else
                {
                    $match=$match.",".$a[$i];
                }
            }
        }
        if($match=="")
        {
            echo "No Suggestios";
        }
        else
        {
            echo $match;
        }
    }
?>
```

Q.4 Attempt any one (A or B): **[2 × 5 = 10]**

(A) (1) Write PHP script bank.xml file contains bank name, MICR code, IFSC code, address etc. By using XML print bank data in tabular format.

Ans.

```
<?xml version="1.0" encoding="utf-8"?>
<bank>
  <account>
    <MICR>111</MICR>
```

```
      <IFSC>John</IFSC>
      <ADDRESS>10000</ADDRESS>
    </account>
    <account>
      <MICR>111</MICR>
      <IFSC>John</IFSC>
      <ADDRESS>10000</ADDRESS>
    </account>
     <account>
      <MICR>111</MICR>
      <IFSC>John</IFSC>
      <ADDRESS>10000</ADDRESS>
    </account>
     <account>
      <MICR>111</MICR>
      <IFSC>John</IFSC>
      <ADDRESS>10000</ADDRESS>
    </account>
</bank>
XML.html
<html>
    <head><title>XML</title></head>
    <body>
    <form action="xml.php" method="get">
        Select XML File:
        <input type="file" name="fname" />
        <br><br>
        <input type="submit" name="submit" value="Read and Display">
    </form>
    </body>
</html>
<?php
    $fname=$_GET['fname'];
```

```
    $xml=simplexml_load_file($fname)   or   die("Error:   Cannot   create
        object");
    echo "Contents of $fname in tabular format : <br><br>";
    echo"<table
        border=1><tr><th>MICR</th><th>IFSC</th><th>ADDRESS</th></tr>";
    foreach($xml->children() as $data) {
            echo "<tr><td>".$data->MICR . "</td> ";
            echo "<td>".$books->IFSC . "</td> ";
            echo "<td>".$books->ADDRESS . "</td>";
    }
    echo "</table>"
?>
```

2. **Write note on Ajax web application model.**

Ans. Refer 6.2, Page 6.3-6.8.

OR

(B) (1) Write a PHP script to accept username and password. If in first 3 chances username and password is correct then display second form, otherwise display error message.

Ans.

```
<?php
if($_SERVER['REQUEST_METHOD']=="GET")
{
?>
<form action="<?php echo $_SERVER['PHP_SELF'] ?>" method="POST">
<h3>Enter Username : <input type="text" name="uname"><br/>
<h3>Enter Password : <input type="password" name="paswd"><br/>
<input type="submit" name="submit" value="login">
</form>
<?php
}
elseif($_SERVER['REQUEST_METHOD']=='POST')
{
session_start();
session_register('nos');
```

```
if($_SESSION['nos']===3)
{
incorrect();
echo "<center><h2><B><U>No of Trials
                         finished!!!!!!</center></h2></b></u>";
}
else
{
if($_REQUEST['uname']=="ram" && $_REQUEST['paswd']=="ram")
{
echo "<center><h1><B><U>Welcome
                         ".$_REQUEST['uname']."</center></h1></b>";
}
else
{
incorrect();
++$_SESSION['nos'];
}
}
}
else
die("Unable to process form");
function incorrect()
{
echo "<center><h2>INCORRECT USERNAME/PASSWORD</center></h2>";
}
?>
```

2. Explain how email attachment is send with PHP.

Ans. Refer 2.4, page no. 2.7-2.10.

■■■

www.ingramcontent.com/pod-product-compliance
Lightning Source LLC
Chambersburg PA
CBHW080012040726
47505CB00016B/2226
* 9 7 8 9 3 5 1 6 4 9 1 2 0 *